C000255644

Don't Miss

David Baird (born in Shropshire, England) has worked around the world as a journalist and his articles have appeared in major international newspapers and magazines. Among his books is *Between Two Fires*, a highly praised account of the guerrilla movement which fought against the Franco regime in the years following the Spanish Civil War.

By the same author

Between Two Fires - Guerrilla war in the Spanish sierras

Sunny Side Up - The 20th century hits a Spanish village

Inside Andalusia

Back Roads of Southern Spain

East of Málaga

The Incredible Gulf

Don't Miss The Fiesta!

David Baird

Maroma Press

Copyright © David Baird 2009

Published in Spain by Maroma Press
Calle Real, 76
29788 Frigiliana (Málaga)
http://maromapress.wordpress.com/

First published October, 2009.

Printed by Gráficas San Pancracio S.L.,
Polígono Industrial San Luis, Málaga.

Depósito Legal: MA-2.883/2009
ISBN: 978-84-613-4417-8

All characters and places in this book are fictitious.

All rights reserved. No part of this book may be reproduced, stored in a retrieval system, or transmitted, in any form or by any means, without the prior written permission of the publishers.

La muerte viene sola. La vida hay que buscarla.
(Death comes on its own. Life you have to seek out.)
— Spanish proverb

AUGUST, 1936

The madness began at the noble residence of Don Ernesto. And then it engulfed the whole community. It had been so slow in coming that some had thought the village would not be touched. Many another conflict had passed it by, after all. But the hatred and fear blazing uncontrollably across the parched land that desperate summer stoked a funeral pyre that darkened the skies of all Spain. There was no escape for the pueblo. It too would fuel the flames.

When the madness finally unleashed itself, Don Ernesto Fernández Calixto, justice of the peace and landowner, was not at home. He had fled to his friends of the Falange in Granada, the provincial capital which few of the villagers had ever seen. The Nationalist rebellion had been successful in Granada and a purge was under way there. Leftwingers, effete liberals, misguided intellectuals, suspected Republican sympathisers, subversives of all stripes were being trucked at dawn to lonely cemeteries to face the crusaders' cleansing bullets.

In the pueblo, too small and too remote to rate highly on anybody's list of priorities, anarchy held sway. The 'Rojos', as the Right termed all those who opposed them, had worked themselves into a frenzy when the radio reported the advances of the fascist troops through Andalusia. Don Ernesto, the bullying overlord, was an obvious target. Who had not a tale to tell of his wealth and arrogance? They started by throwing rocks through his windows and invading the stables. There they found Don Ernesto's pride, the magnificent black stallion on which he used to ride around his estates, directing the workers. They released the animal and, alarmed by the uproar, it careered wildly away. Then they ripped down the coat of arms from above the house's main entrance and stormed inside.

As the terrified servants took to their heels, the rampaging villagers looted Don Ernesto's quarters. They slashed the tapestries and the Goya canvas over his desk. Gleefully, they who had never known what it was to have leather on their feet tried on the dozens of pairs of hunting and riding boots. The satin dresses of Don Ernesto's wife were added to the books and furniture tossed into the courtyard. Soon these were converted into a giant bonfire over which were roasted the landlord's best bull and a score of his sheep. Men, women and children joined in the banquet, eating until their stomachs groaned.

There had never been a feast like it. They gorged and drank and sang as the flames flew up from the wrecked house. Hot animal fat trickled in rivulets from their mouths and the wine they had pillaged from Don Ernesto's cellar stained their skin and clothing. Then, intoxicated with drink and their own daring, they marched on the church to pulverise with hammer, sickle and axe the faith and superstition that had held them in thrall for so long.

The church bell tolled a crazy accompaniment to the destruction that followed. Young children ran laughing to help their elders wrench the religious paintings from the walls and slice them to shreds. The saints' statues adorning the niches were toppled and their heads sent rolling along the floor. Jesus suffering on the Cross, the Virgin of the Snows in her frozen grief, San Sebastián pierced by a dozen arrows, all the images venerated and dutifully carried in procession for centuries were pulled down and smashed. Even the big Bible, bound in iron and leather, the one from which the priest always read, was destroyed. In the general insanity, one of the devoutest members of the congregation seized the book, tore out the pages with their illuminated lettering, and scattered them in the air.

It was as the pages flew about like confetti and the frenzy was at its height that Father Salvador burst into the church. He was beside himself, fear and anger battling for supremacy on his crimson features, his double chin wobbling ludicrously.

"You are profaning the House of the Lord!" he cried. "In the name of God, stop!"

Sanity might have prevailed at that point. But then somebody hurled a fragment broken off one of the holy images. No matter who was responsible, the incident changed the course of events. The missile struck Father Salvador square on the nose and spelled his ruin for his newly acquired dignity was shattered. The priest reeled back, clutching his bleeding nose, his grotesque belly quivering under the soiled cassock. Abruptly, he was reduced once more to a figure of ridicule. The mob surged forward with redoubled fury. Feeling they had nearly been cheated of their revenge, the people vented their blind rage on the defenceless form of Father Salvador. The bile harboured within them for centuries flooded out that day. Even Don Ernesto's horse seemed possessed by the same devilish rage. As Salvador fell before the mob, it plunged through the village, its eyes blazing like searchlights, its hoofs striking sparks from the cobbles...

Afterwards, when the Civil Guards rode in, they could find no witnesses. Don Ernesto demanded retribution, so they made random arrests and administered summary justice, but the ringleaders had fled. Shame and fear stilled the villagers' tongues. They did not talk about what had occurred at the church. Those who were not drafted into the army went back to ploughing the land. The war was fought far away, on other fronts. Peace came at last and the old rituals were resumed. The whole affair might never have happened.

CHAPTER ONE

October, 1980

As soon as he saw the village, Scully knew he would stay. Security and cosiness, an air of permanence, emanated from the flock of tiny dwellings nuzzling about the old church, warm in their togetherness amid the bleakness of the sierras. It was a womb. And far enough from the rest of the world. He knew he would stay.

The bus journey had contributed to the feeling of remoteness. It had begun in the limpid brightness of early morning. The highway had run through a surging ocean of sugar cane on the coastal plain before darting inland up a dry river-bed. Then it had climbed in dizzy curves past terrace after terrace of custard apple trees, slotted into the steep valley sides. Plump-armed women of astonishing girth gasped aboard, distributed dummy-sucking offspring and baskets over seats and floor, and machine-gunned gossip at one another in sharp bursts. Occasionally, the bus-driver fired off an obscene salvo and the women and their weathered menfolk rocked in paroxysms of laughter.

Only the withered twig of a man sitting next to Scully remained unmoved. He chewed on a tooth-pick and stared straight ahead, showing no interest in the bus's progress nor the other passengers. His skin was nearly black, stretched over high cheekbones and a narrow jaw. A sack tied with twine rested between his feet.

Everybody alighted at Cerrogordo, the end of the line. It was a small, straggling town with a domed church and a large market. Gypsies sat around the market square, guarding piles of cheap clothing, plastic kitchen utensils and handmade baskets. A ramshackle bus with worn tyres was parked at one side of the square. The old man, suddenly chirpy after reviving himself with black coffee and anise, materialised at Scully's side and jerked his thumb at the decrepit vehicle and a cluster of people heaving their purchases aboard.

"She's going now. You don't want to miss her."

Scully boarded the bus too. He had no idea where it was going, but that was of no consequence. Minutes later, with an impressive revving and a volley of missed gears, the bus set off. Soon the paved road ended and they were bumping over a succession of corrugations and potholes, chassis and coachwork complaining loudly.

They headed deeper into the mountains. As the valley narrowed and the scenery became wilder, Scully felt his spirits lift. Far below he could see water tumbling along, but there was scant room for cultivation except on ledges carved out from the hillside to create fields of beans and tomatoes. They soon gave way to bare rock and tussocky grass, dotted here and there with stunted oaks and olive trees that looked as though they were a thousand years old. Scully sniffed at the air. It was already perceptibly keener than the gentle, subtropical embrace of the coastal breezes.

With every curve, the road grew worse and Scully felt better. The road was only wide enough for one vehicle to pass. This did not deter the driver from careering around hairpin bends with cheerful abandon, often lurching to within inches of the unprotected edge, while he continued to chat gaily with the passengers. Scully prayed that the driver's faith was justified in the array of religious symbols dangling over his seat. These included a St. Christopher medal, a plaster Virgin and Child, and a sign indicating "In God we trust". Scully recalled that, before committing themselves to the journey, the driver and several passengers had crossed themselves.

"There's the pueblo."

The old man with the tooth-pick was nudging Scully in the ribs, awakening him from a doze brought on by the constant jogging motion.

"Your village?"

"Sí, sí. The village. Pretty, isn't it?"

So it was. A handful of whitewashed cubes spread over a

ridge in a snowy crescent that dazzled the eye. Most of the houses were flat-roofed, lending an African aspect to the village. Instead of a mosque, however, a stumpy church tower thrust up from amid the dwellings. As the bus bumped around the last bend, Scully examined the village and saw security and stability.

On one of the shelves of land that fell away below the houses a man was ploughing with oxen. The heavy beasts lumbered with infinite care over the desiccated soil. On the ridge behind the village, rows and rows of vines paraded amber leaves, yielding finally to fig, almond and olive trees. Desperate, eternal toil had tamed and regulated this land. It was a triumph of human stubbornness, made all the more impressive by the hostility of the mountain ranges that loomed on all sides.

"How many people live here?" asked Scully.

The man shrugged.

"Who knows? Maybe 500. Once there were many more, but they left in the hungry years, after the war. My uncle, two brothers, many. They all went to Argentina and never came back. Everybody went to America."

"You never got to visit them?" asked Scully, struggling to understand. He had once studied Castilian Spanish. But the old-timer spoke a rural Andalusian dialect. That was bad enough, but by the time he had chewed the words between his toothless gums they came out badly wounded.

"I?" The old man blinked at the very idea. "How could I pay the fare? There's only poverty here. We have no industry, no tourists, no money. The earth is poor and yet we're its slaves. It's all we've got, señor, our only wealth. But sometimes I think it's a curse. Yes, señor, no wonder they never came back."

"Well, maybe you are lucky in some ways. Your pueblo looks so beautiful and contented."

"Hombre, of course it's beautiful, the most beautiful place in the world." The old man laughed and spat. "But contented? I don't know. I never heard anybody say that, no, not about Benamargo."

The bus pulled up at the edge of the village, where what

passed for a highway ended. A gaggle of women draped in black stood watching the passengers descend. A goat nibbled at some tattered weeds sprouting next to a stone bench where three withered pensioners sat like statues. The first thing that Scully noticed, as he stretched his aching limbs, was the silence. Cries of greeting to the arrivals only emphasised the total calm. The air was scrubbed clean of distracting elements.

It was like learning to hear all over again, thought Scully, as he stood for a moment, drinking in the scene. He realised that years had passed since he had been in a place where traffic and urban clamour were so completely absent. From somewhere came the splash of water and the peal of cow or goat bells. How long had it been since he had heard anything so sharply? The village was in suspension, floating in a great emptiness.

Lightheadedness overcame Scully, until he became aware that the bus driver was addressing him. He noticed that the driver's eyes were bloodshot and there was an unmistakable smell on his breath, which no doubt explained his defiant style at the wheel.

"We leave at four. Don't miss it or you'll have to stay in Benamargo for ever."

Scully strolled down what he took to be the main street. It was empty, but for a barefoot child playing with a top and a woman shaking blankets. The child fled indoors at his approach, while the woman stared down curiously from her balcony.

"Buenos días," said Scully, attempting a smile.

"Go with God," she replied, her face impassive. She watched him as he walked on.

Every second house seemed to be abandoned for many were falling into decay, their whitewash flaking, doors and window-frames rotting. But the narrow street was clean. Indeed, every cobblestone looked as though it had been polished. At the end of the street, Scully came on a plaza. A row of gnarled carob trees offered shade on one side and a forlorn palm tree wilted in one corner. Towering over them was the church, solid, enduring, with a lofty brick tower, patterned like a Moorish minaret. Broad, well-worn stone steps led up to the doors, massive affairs studded with nails. The clock on the tower had stopped at 8.41.

Scully wondered why they made church doors so large, then recalled a visit long ago to Seville during Holy Week. The processions had wound right through the cathedral and its entrance had easily accommodated the great floats bearing tear-stained Virgins and blood-stained images of Christ. No doubt Benamargo had similar processions, when its own images were solemnly carried through the streets.

The opposite side of the square to the church was bordered by iron railings. Scully leaned on them and looked out over the valley. Irrigation channels laced green terraces with silver. On the banks of a stream he could see women busily scrubbing. Sheets and articles of clothing were spread over rocks to dry. He wandered on, along a side-street. Where the cobbles petered out, a path began a zigzag course up through the olive trees. Scully marched boldly along it, although not for long.

Soon he was forced to halt to regain his breath. When he resumed the climb, he maintained a slower pace, painfully aware of the slackness of his muscles. Too many expense account lunches, too much soft living. It had been a long time since he had done much more than pick up a telephone. He passed a man vigorously hoeing a small plot and envied him. Half an hour of that sort of exercise would exhaust him.

Beyond a vineyard and a grove of almond trees, the path levelled out before ascending steeply towards a bare slab of rock. It was scarred and deeply creviced. Near the summit, a lone, lightning-blasted pine leaned from a crag as though contemplating a jump into the void. Scully was not unduly sensitive to atmosphere. He had been criticised as thick-skinned often enough. Even so, there was something about the rock, a more impressionable person might have said an air of menace, which made him pause.

Breathing hard, he decided against continuing as far as the rock and turned off instead towards a hillock where thyme, fennel and rosemary flourished. He felt the strength of the sun and removed his denim jacket, made a pillow for his head and lay down. The blue sky stretched for ever. He gazed at the distant peaks. He had finished with what went on behind them. He had stayed for a while on the coast, too long, in the company of retired expatriates and back-packing teenagers. The expatriates had bored him profoundly, with their eternal rounds of golf and bridge, gossip and booze, and their depressing attempts to embroider humdrum life stories in order to keep up with the neighbours.

The teenagers, well, they had amused him, at first. They had also stirred familiar urges. Sheer perversity had carried him into that ridiculous liaison with a 17-year-old nymph on the run from Illinois. He had known it would end disastrously, but he had extracted some entertainment from observing how the relationship broke up. His clinical detachment had surprised even Scully.

It was high time to escape that never-never land of expatriates with invented pasts, wrinkled widows and bloated real estate developers. Perhaps he could find a bolt-hole in the interior, away from the Mediterranean whose sickly, tideless movement reminded him of decaying civilisations. Sheer impulse had led him that morning into the bus depot, ready for any journey as long as it would take him into a limbo free of memories. Scully gazed blankly at the unfathomable blue and listened to the murmur of crickets.

The flat chorus of goat bells roused him. He sat up quickly, not sure where he was. The goats were scattering over a slope several hundred yards away, leaping from boulder to boulder, jostling for the sparse fodder.

The sight of them reminded Scully that he was hungry, hungrier than he had been for some time. Eating had become a chore, bereft of any enjoyment, but the unaccustomed exercise had sharpened his appetite.

He had finished his ham sandwich and was biting into an apple when he realised that he was under scrutiny. A youth was sitting on a rocky outcrop, watching over the goats. Scully could not make out his features, but saw that he had a lean muscularity and appeared taller than the average Andalusian. The goat boy was staring with unashamed curiosity in Scully's direction. No doubt it was quite an event to see a stranger. Scully lifted a hand to wave, but there was no response.

Then a movement caught his eye. Around the ridge that obscured the view of the village the figure of a woman had appeared. Squinting against the sun, Scully could see that her hair was covered by a white scarf and that she wore a long-sleeved blouse and a voluminous skirt. Her movements were girlish and sprightly. Scully watched her negotiate the broken surface of the hillside no less surefootedly than the goats and set down a basket by the youth's side. He said something and she turned to look across to Scully, then quickly away. She tossed her head and he heard her laugh. She squatted down by the goatherd's side as he took what must have been his lunch from the basket.

When the girl set off back down the path, Scully watched her until she disappeared from sight. She moved without hurry and without care. No burden weighed down those slim shoulders. Her youthful image lingered in Scully's mind. There was something about her that made an indelible impression. Perhaps it was the mixture of spirit and innocence that withers so quickly with the passing years. She would learn fast enough, thought Scully. Fast enough. He felt a surge of melancholy.

CHAPTER TWO

By the time Scully had digested his lunch and trudged back to the village, he had made his decision. He sought out the village bar, an echo chamber of highly-coloured tiles, strip lighting and Formica-topped tables. In one corner a bunch of wrinkled, short-statured men were playing dominoes. They halted their game to examine the stranger.

"Buenas tardes," ventured Scully.

They returned the greeting, carried out a further lengthy perusal and went back to their game.

"What do you desire, sir?"

The bartender was an overweight individual with a wisp of precisely-razored moustache and close-set eyes. Not exactly the type from whom I would want to buy a second-hand mule, reflected Scully.

"Do you have whisky?"

"Whisky? Of course."

He picked up a bottle of Spanish-made whisky, but Scully forestalled him.

"No. I mean Scotch."

"Escot? Escot? Ah, whisky escocés. No, señor, that we don't have."

He appeared offended at the request, as though Scully had tried to catch him out.

"In that case, a glass of brandy, please."

The barman wiped a glass with his apron, which seemed due for a wash, and with an extravagant flourish filled it to the brim.

He eyed Scully closely as he drank.

"Better than Escot, eh?"

"Well, it's strong."

"What a man needs. Strength for the women," said the barman, winking ponderously. "Visiting?"

"Yes, just for the day."

"Ah. Not many come. Sometimes a few bigwigs at the weekends, to go hunting. There are wild goats in the sierras."

"Safer than hunting women," said Scully, getting into tune with the conversation as the brandy warmed him.

"Sí, sí. Safer than women."

The barman chuckled and thumped the counter, spilling some of the brandy.

"Here," he said. "Have some more. More strength to hunt the women."

"Have one yourself."

"No, not me. I've a bad stomach. Ulcers. I only drink at Christmas and during the annual fair."

He scrutinised Scully through eyes with a yellowish, unhealthy tinge.

"French?"

"English."

"Ah, football. Manchester United, yes? I saw them on the television once. Queen Isabel, right? And El Príncipe, Carlos. That is why you like the Escot. But, for an Englishman, you don't speak bad Castilian."

"I keep trying," said Scully. He looked around the bar. "It's quiet here."

"As the catacombs. Nothing ever happens in Benamargo. We don't even have a mayor, you know that? Nobody wants the job. It's just a load of trouble. The last one, well, there was a scandal and he quit."

Scully wondered what administrative headaches there could be in a place the size of Benamargo. He looked inquiringly at the barman.

"Is there anywhere I could stay here?"

"A hotel?" The barman appeared stunned by the suggestion. "No, not in Benamargo. You could find a lodging house in Cerrogordo, but for a hotel you have to go to the coast or to Granada."

"No, I'm not looking for a hotel, just a place where I can get a bed and meals."

"That's not so easy. When peddlers come, they stay at

Pedro's place. He calls it an inn, but phew!" The landlord held his nose. "You wouldn't want to sleep there, with the mules. Wait." He called over to the domino players. "This gentleman is looking for a bed. Does Doña Carmen have a spare room?"

Forgetting their game, the old-timers entered into a noisy argument. They dismissed Doña Carmen. Her son-in-law and family were staying with her so she had no room. Other names were suggested, discussed and dropped, so many that it appeared to Scully that they were running through the entire population. Finally, somebody put forward the name of "La Caída".

"Sí, sí, Dolores La Caída. She may have something."

"It's possible. She needs the money."

One of the clients offered to show Scully the way and he was led through a maze of streets to a house with an imposing double door. Dolores proved to be a thickset, middle-aged woman with well-developed forearms and a pale, severe face. Like most of the village women, she was dressed in black, which Scully took to be in memory of her husband. She regarded him doubtfully.

"I don't usually take guests."

Scully turned on the smile that had worked in so many other situations.

"I understand. The trouble is that I would like to stay in the village but there is no pension. I was hoping you might be able to help."

Dolores seemed unconvinced.

"Why would you want to stay here? Benamargo has nothing to offer."

"I am looking for somewhere to relax and it is so tranquil here."

"Tranquil? Yes, I suppose it is," said Dolores, as though this was the first time the idea had struck her. "Have you been sick, señor?"

"Not exactly, señora," said Scully. But it was true, he thought. He had been, still was very sick.

"Well, if you want to recuperate, you won't find any purer air than what we have here. That's what everybody says.

You are married? You have your family with you?"

"No, I have no family."

"But, if you have been sick, you need somebody to care for you."

"I just need a good rest, for a month or so.'

"A month or so. I see."

Dolores considered for a moment, then led Scully out into the street and to the house next door. It was a simple, barely furnished place, two rooms downstairs, two above, an ancient brass bedstead with sagging mattress, some rush-covered chairs, a worm-eaten table, and little else.

"I don't see the bathroom."

Dolores pointed to a tiny rear courtyard which contained a washstand and a cubicle.

"Water has to come from the fountain. But there's electricity. Sometimes it is cut off because the lines from Cerrogordo are always falling down, but not every house here has electric light. And you haven't seen the terrace. There's a splendid view from there."

She led the way upstairs again, unlocked a door, and Scully stepped out on to a small, flat roof. Afternoon sunlight bounced back from the whitewashed surroundings. Half-blinded, Scully felt the same light-headedness he had experienced when stepping off the bus. The terrace overlooked the whole village and he could see straight across the valley to an outcrop of dark-ribbed rocks and down to a sliver of water gushing past ploughed and planted fields. Late swifts flirted with the tumbling rooftops and swooped across the void. Scully felt that at any moment he too might take wing and glide away.

"You're right, señora. It is a beautiful view. And Benamargo is a beautiful village."

"That is what they say," said Dolores. "But you can't eat beautiful views. The young all go away."

Her words hung in the air like a reproach.

Scully nodded.

"The way of the world, I suppose. Youngsters always think the grass is greener somewhere else. But Benamargo seems fine to me. I like the house. How much is it?"

The woman debated with herself for a while.

"Would 15,000 pesetas be all right, for the month?" she asked, quickly adding: "That would include coffee in the morning and an evening meal too, and your laundry. We can't afford meat often, but you will eat well."

"That's fine. I have to go back to the coast to pick up my bag, but I'll be back in a week's time. Is that okay?"

Dolores nodded, and smiled for the first time.

"Good. Then, 15,000 for the month."

She paused expectantly and Scully burrowed into a pocket and peeled off the peseta bills. Dolores counted them very carefully, then tucked them into an apron pocket. They descended to the street and shook hands.

"You'll find it very boring here. I'm afraid, señor," she warned. "Nothing ever happens in Benamargo."

Scully smiled, and took his leave. As he walked down the narrow street, he was aware that he was being scrutinised from behind some of the shutters. No doubt by evening the whole village would know that a stranger had rented Dolores La Caída's house and would be guessing how much he had agreed to pay. That was all right. He felt only relief that he had made the decision. He could do without so-called civilisation for a while.

He paused outside the church, admiring the great doors a second time, and then, on an impulse, pushed his way in through a smaller entrance to one side. A cool gloom enveloped him as he paced towards the altar. Against one wall stood a pedestal on which rested the carved wooden image of some saint. Half a dozen candles guttered in a side chapel, revealing the waxen features of the Virgin Mary. A heavily embroidered cloth was draped over the altar and, eyes adjusted, Scully made out behind it a large cross. Dark stains marred the heavy woodwork, which towered over altar and pews. It was disturbing, that cross, a dominating presence in the dusty silence.

Scully felt the internal tremor he had experienced as a boy when he entered a place of worship. Years had passed since he had set foot in a church. He was an agnostic. Yet he could not help being impressed — or was it depressed?

— by the atmosphere of this place. He felt uncomfortable, uneasy. This was where man came to unburden his soul, to seek consolation or uplift. This building sold hope. Scully turned to go.

"We don't get many visitors. Are you looking for something in particular?"

Deep and vibrant, the voice came so suddenly that Scully was startled.

"Er, no, I was just strolling around."

"You may find these interesting." The speaker emerged from the shadows, his long black cassock rustling. He was almost as tall as Scully, but more heavily-built and considerably older, possibly in his 60s. His hair was grey and close-cropped, accentuating the square solidity of his head. "See. These are ex-votos, offerings from people the Lord has helped."

He indicated some crude paintings on the wall. In one, blood poured from the wounded chest of a figure lying on the ground. The inscription read: "In gratitude to the Virgin for saving me after a fight." Another depicted a child sinking under water. Below it, Scully could decipher: "José Rodríguez fell in a reservoir. He was almost drowned, but his parents prayed to Our Father and he was saved."

"Faith can work miracles, you see," declared the priest, fingering a large silver cross hung across his broad chest. "It is one commodity we have plenty of in Benamargo. We have few worldly goods, but yes, thanks be to God, we are rich in faith."

"Then you are wealthier than I am, Father."

The priest studied Scully's face, as though searching for something.

"There is nothing worse than poverty of the spirit. But it can be rectified, you know, if the will is there. If the will is there.

"But then, perhaps all this here..." He waved an arm about the church. "...perhaps all this for you is just empty ritual, just silly superstition. You're not a Catholic, are you? I observed you when you came in. You did not cross yourself. Where are you from, my friend?"

"From England. I've been staying on the coast."

"Ah, the coast," said the priest, nodding as though that explained everything.

"But I'm planning to stay here. It is such a pleasant spot."

"Here in the pueblo?" The priest raised dark, bushy brows. "You will find little diversion. No dancing, no cinemas, no fine restaurants, not even television. The sierras make it impossible to receive the signals."

Scully smiled.

"It sounds like paradise."

"And the people are very simple. Peasants. They know only how to raise goats and grow grapes."

"I could do with some simplicity, Father."

"Yes, that is what you say now. But you may change your opinion. A certain blessed naivity still exists here. Our remoteness has kept some of the contamination away, all those drugs of 20th-century man. But somebody who is accustomed to that world would find a lack of stimulation here, perhaps."

"One can have too much of that stimulation," noted Scully, vaguely irritated by the priest's words.

"Another foreigner came here once and tried to start a business exporting raisins. Naturally, it was a failure. He did not understand the character of the people and they rejected his ways. He soon left. You see, my friend, to the people here God really lives and that is why they turn their backs on temptation. They see His good works. They feel His wrath."

Power radiated from the man. There was an immense strength and assurance in the priest's firm, blunt features, in the stubbornly set chin and the broad sensual mouth. No wonder the Church was so influential, reflected Scully, offering such certainty. He almost wished he could believe.

"Look at the charred beam up there." The priest was pointing to the timber roof. "That is the only reminder we need. The Rojos, the Reds, did it, back in 1936. They sacked the church and destroyed everything. They did the same right across Spain. Lawless times. What happened in those terrible days is burned into the minds of the people. They used this holy place as a stable, did you know that? They kept pigs and donkeys here. And what they did to the Cristo, that was the worst." He gripped Scully's arm and gestured towards the altar. "From that cross they ripped down the beautiful carved figure of our Lord and smashed it to pieces. And then, they played football with the head, kicking it along the streets. What a barbarity!"

They stood gazing at the cross. The gloom and the stillness were oppressive in the little church. Scully shifted, wanting to get away.

"Why didn't they replace the image?" he asked.

There was a surprising fierceness in the priest's tone.

"They do not need to. That empty space serves better than any image to remind the people of their past sins and what they did to the Lord."

"But the Civil War ended so long ago. The new generation ..."

"The younger generation is being poisoned by worthless values," snapped the priest. "To save them, we can never drop our guard. We must keep our memories fresh so that we are always ready to do battle for our cause." He paused and uttered a short laugh. "But this is not your fight. Please, if you find peace here, come to the church whenever you wish. Judge us kindly, for all our superstitions."

Scully waited by the bus. The scrawny dogs and even the crickets slept. This was the end of the line, no doubt about it. The driver turned up only half an hour late, his eyes more bloodshot than ever. After loading several sacks of tomatoes and some boxes of figs, he eased off the brake and let the bus roll down the slope from the village until, at the third attempt, the gears meshed, the engine sputtered into life and the vehicle rocked thunderously off down the track. Scully looked back at the receding huddle of dwellings, gilded by the declining sun. They said nothing ever happened in Benamargo. Well, that suited him fine.

CHAPTER THREE

Scully dumped his bags and walked out on to the roof terrace. Thudding hooves attracted his attention. He leaned over the low wall to look into the street. An aged grey mule led by a young boy was plodding by. A shambling youth brought up the rear, clinging to the animal's tail with one hand and gesticulating wildly with the other. He caught sight of Scully and treated him to a wolfish grin, followed by an obscene gesture. Scully returned the gesture, without ill will. Walking back to the inner wall, he sat down and leaned back. Sheltered from the wind, the sun's rays reflected from the white walls, the rooftop was like a furnace. Scully removed his shirt but the sweat dripped from his pores. He paid no attention. Let it burn. Let it scour. Tension drained out of him as the heat built up and the sun seared his body, cleansing the flesh, cauterising the wounds in his head.

Maybe, for a while he could stop running. He had been running for months now, yet making no progress. He left no forwarding addresses but the past clung to his trail. It pursued him relentlessly, nagging him in careless waking moments, assaulting him in his dreams. It exasperated him because he had no more emotion to expend on his earlier life. He felt no pangs, even when he thought about his children. His children? They had never been his. They belonged to Stella. They were part of her game.

He recalled how she had demanded them. It must have been the fashion that moment, in her particular circle, motherhood for the career woman. It had not lasted long. Then she had utilised them, implanting her bitterness in them, casting him in the role which — he admitted — he fitted easily enough, that of the negligent father.

Affairs? Hell, of course there had been. Nobody who knew Stella would blame him for that, and she wasn't exactly the faithful little homebody. So now the kids were hers. The lawyers could sort it out. That battle had nothing to do with him any more and he doubted if winning it would make Stella a jot happier. The hell with the past. What mattered was the future. If only he could take an interest in that.

On his second journey to Benamargo, carrying his few belongings, Scully had smiled grimly at the realisation that he was running again. Good. It was better to run than to arrive. He had no plans to reconstruct his broken existence, no wish to achieve anything, no curiosity about what lay ahead. It was enough to float and forget. The forgetting was the only problem. But they were all dead for him, Stella, Klease, the company, the whole nasty mess, so he could detach himself and merely float. He would read the dozen or so books he had brought. He would walk over the mountains. He would sit on his rooftop. And nobody would find him. When he decided to leave, he would pack his bags and go, anywhere. But perhaps it would be so pleasant that he would stay for ever. It didn't matter really.

Adrift above Benamargo's rooftops, Scully dozed, then awoke abruptly to find himself drenched in sweat. He rose and pushed back through the bedroom door, sensed the blood pounding threateningly in his head and blacked out. He came to, sprawled face down on the elaborately embroidered bedspread, the scent of rosemary in his nostrils from the worn sheets. Rolling over, he studied the beams overhead, painted a disturbing shade of green to cover up the wormholes. He had eaten no lunch after the lengthy bus trip and the intense heat followed by sudden movement had knocked him out. He remembered seeing a jugful of water in the patio at the rear of the house. He stumbled down stone steps and poured cool water over his head, then towelled himself vigorously.

After pouring himself a hefty shot of whisky, he flopped back on the bed. In his absence, Dolores had scrubbed out the house and whitewashed a wall where the damp had entered. The perfume of fresh-cut flowers almost banished the mustiness about the place. Occasional street noises came to Scully's ears. A trill of pipes, which usually signalled the arrival of a knife-grinder, a woman calling to her child, a female voice raised in song. It could have been Dolores, except that it sounded too clear and youthful. Scully realised that he had been hooked on noise and when it was removed he felt like an addict suffering withdrawal symptoms. It reminded him of a newspaper report that some householders enjoyed overlooking a four-lane highway because the endless stream of traffic added excitement to their lives. Even as it slowly killed them, the din and the fumes must have reminded them that they were alive. It was different here. There was no clamorous movement to provide such a distasteful reminder. Scully felt grateful.

"Señor, señor!"

The call came from below.

"Yes. I'm here."

"Excuse me, señor. I did not want to disturb you. It is only that, if you want to eat, I am serving the meal."

Next door, a dim entrance hall led to a small living-room, which was almost filled by a circular table laid for dinner. In one corner an oil lamp burned before a plaster replica of the Virgin and Child. Around the walls were arrayed a series of pictures, hand-painted in unnatural colours and framed in baroque frames. The subjects of the photographs were posed with military stiffness.

"Wine, señor?"

Dolores poured out a tumblerful of thick, amber-coloured liquid. It was sweet and heavy and Scully let it linger on his tongue.

"It's very good. I can taste the grapes."

"Of course. This is pure wine, not like you get in the bars, no chemicals, no watering down. This is some of the best, from last year."

Already Scully could feel the liquid taking effect on his empty stomach.

"This is strong stuff."

Dolores smiled.

"Don't worry, you won't get a hangover, because it's pure. Be careful if you go to the bar though. That Sebastián, he does things to the wine. A real good-for-nothing he is." She shot a sharp glance at Scully. "And the house? Everything is all right?"

"Fine, thank you. Just what I want."

Dolores nodded approvingly and disappeared into the kitchen. When she returned, holding a large tureen of soup, she was followed by a young girl.

"My daughter, Marisa."

"Hello, Marisa."

The girl looked quickly at Scully, then lowered her eyes. She plucked at the table-cloth as her mother dished out the soup, a thick liquid in which floated some chick peas and cabbage. Dark, shoulder-length hair obscured the girl's features from Scully but, as she tossed the hair back out of her eyes and picked up a spoon, he realised he had seen her before. That afternoon, a week previously, when he had lain on the mountainside. She had been the girl in the long dress, bringing lunch to the goatherd.

"Are you still at school, Marisa?" he asked, hoping more for a better view of her face than for an answer. But Marisa merely shook her head and went on eating.

"There is no school here for her," Dolores told him. "The children can go to classes until they are 11 or 12, then they have to go to the school at Cerrogordo. But there's no daily bus, so that's difficult. Anyway, the boys have to work on the land, to help their fathers. And with girls, well, it doesn't matter. They don't need so much education. Cooking and sewing, that's what a girl needs to know. Marisa is a fine seamstress. She makes all her own clothes. True, Marisa?"

"Yes. But I wish I could go to the school at Cerrogordo, like Lola does," Marisa put in spiritedly.

She had looked up, revealing a neatly-formed nose, a firm chin and a pouting mouth. Dolores had obviously heard this before. She sighed and the lines on her face multiplied into an expression of greater severity.

"We'll have no more of that nonsense. Where would you stay in Cerrogordo? In any case, it's for your own good to stay here. Ask the priest. All those girls learn in Cerrogordo are bad habits. As for Lola, she's a sinverguenza, a shame-less one, anybody will tell you that. Did you see her last time she came home, her hair done up like one of those film stars, a dress all the colours of the rainbow?"

Marisa shrugged, and Dolores went off for the second course. It proved to be a plateful of rather soggy rice dotted with chunks of dried cod. Scully drained his second glass of wine and, a little light-headedly, tried to imagine what Dolores would have made of Stella. A new hair-do every week, a wardrobe that would have done justice to a model, nail varnish in every shade from black to scarlet. Stella had spared nothing to keep up her morale, so badly battered by his alleged neglect. For a while he had gone along with it, amused by her attempt to project herself simultaneously as a trendy feminist and The Perfect Mother.

He had been married to a poor imitation of a cover girl, massaged, painted and deodorised. She was pressed out of cocktail party plastic. Feed her dry Martinis and she spouted brittle laughter. She came with with canapés and poisoned gossip and whispered adulteries, and him. Sure, he had played along. He had been as much a part of the charade as she.

Rolling the word "sinverguenza" around in his head, Scully found more to relish in it than in the meal before him. It was a struggle to finish. The rice was unspeakable and the cod too salty. The saltiness increased his thirst and he gladly allowed his glass to be filled again. Neither Dolores nor her daughter touched the wine. Women did not drink, said Dolores primly. He wondered then whom the wine was for? Had it been acquired in his honour or were male visitors that frequent? He asked about children.

"I have three, a son in Barcelona and Marisa and Ramón," declared Dolores, pointing out their portraits on the walls. "There were two more, but they died." She crossed herself. "The priest said it was a judgment. But it was hard."

"And your husband?"

Dolores set her lips in a thin line.

"I have no husband." She rattled the plates, gathering them up. "Do you have family, señor?"

"Two boys, 12 and 15. They're in England."

"Ah, you're lucky. Boys can always earn a living."

Scully guessed that one of the faded pictures was a wedding-day portrait of Dolores and her husband. He appeared a serious young man, with thick eyebrows over wide-set eyes and a rebellious curve to his lips.

"Difficult, isn't it?"suggested Scully, trying to wash away the fishy taste in his mouth with more wine. "I mean, not having a breadwinner."

"Ramón is the man of the house." Pride rang in Marisa's voice as she suddenly took an interest in the conversation. "He's only 18, but he's stronger than almost anybody. Isn't it true, mother?"

"If he's anything like you and your mother, I'm sure he's a handsome fellow too," said Scully.

The girl smiled and for the first time looked directly at him. Her prettiness was revealed, dark wide eyes, high cheekbones, a laughing mouth, with none of those sour lines that life had knifed into Dolores's features. And, maybe it was the tilt of her head, there was a wilful air about her. She had been corralled, but she had not been tamed.

Dolores frowned.

"My daughter needs no compliments from strangers. They'll only turn her head. Not I mean, of course, that you are exactly a stranger now, señor. But you understand what I'm saying. Marisa is very young and like all girls her age she's impressionable. It's different with boys. They can look after themselves. They aren't weak and stupid like we women. Yes, weak and stupid, that we are." She compressed her lips into a thin, bitter line. "It's just as well we have Ramón. I don't know how we would manage without him."

"It's a pity Marisa can't finish her schooling," said Scully. "Maybe if you sold the spare house that would help with the expenses."

Dolores stiffened.

"It's not a question of money. We may seem poor but we can manage very well." She sniffed derisively. "In any case, who would buy a house here? Half the village is empty. And when Ramón decides to marry, he will want that house."

"Or possibly your son in Barcelona?"

"No, he will never come back. He has made his life there.

It's 10 years since we saw him. He brought his wife. A city girl. She would never fit in here. Just as I could never survive in the city. Once, years ago, I went to Granada, to see the doctor. Well, it was like a trip into the inferno. Full of thieves and gypsies and women dressed like hussies. I couldn't get away fast enough. No, Benamargo is my home, thanks be to God."

Marisa concentrated on peeling an apple while Scully could think of no response. A righteous certainty flowed from Dolores that brooked no argument. Scully decided to retire in good order.

'Thank you for the meal, señora. I'm most grateful. It was beyond my expectations."

"You haven't eaten much."

"I don't have much of an appetite these days."

"Ah well, you don't work on the land. That's real work and it gives a man a hunger that would kill." She eyed him, a little as though inspecting a rather unappetising piece of meat. "You said you had been sick, señor? You don't look very strong."

"Sick? Yes, I suppose you could call it that. But I'm sure Benamargo will be good for me."

"If God wishes. The good prosper here."

"And the bad?"

Dolores fixed him with a flinty glance.

"They receive their reward too, señor."

There was silence for a moment, finally broken by the sound of Marisa biting deeply into her apple.

CHAPTER FOUR

Blackness intense as the golden light of day had invaded
the streets of Benamargo when Scully set off for a stroll.
Although it was late autumn, the air was still warm and
heavy. Something flickered past his head as he moved halt-
ingly forward, as though struggling through a vat of pitch.
In the light of a solitary street lamp he saw that bats were
swooping about the street. A mule was being stripped of its
esparto baskets and harness by a toothless old man who
dived into a stable and emerged like a mole coming up for
breath.

"Adios," said Scully.

The man carried on unstrapping a girth. In the dimly-lit
church square three children were skipping over a rope,
chanting in unison. But generally the village appeared to
be already asleep. From the bar, however, the noise volume issuing forth suggested a riot had broken out. Scully
approached warily and peered around the door. The harsh
strip lighting revealed that there were only three customers and only two were talking. They appeared to be on the
point of coming to blows as they yelled and gesticulated.
Competing with them was a battered radio firing a barrage
of flamenco anguish. The other customer sat by himself in
a corner, a dog at his feet. Oblivious to the racket around
him, he was studying a newspaper.

Sebastián the bar-owner treated Scully to something
close to a smile.

"Ah, your grace." Scully could not determine whether he
was exercising his sarcasm or merely being courteous by
using this antiquated form of address. "You have returned.
This calls for a celebration."

Sebastián looked, if anything, in a worse state than the
first time Scully had seen him. A button had popped off

the grimy white shirt stretched taut over his dangerously bulging belly. His bloodshot eyes blazed out above stubble-covered cheeks.

"Brandy, right? You see, I never forget a client's tastes."

One of the customers had begun smashing his fist on the counter while his companion glared at him, red-faced. Scully raised his eyebrows, to the landlord's amusement.

"Don't worry. They're discussing a mule. He says the price is too high. It's like this every time they come in. They drink and argue, drink and argue. They've been going on about that cursed mule for months.'

"What will they talk about if one of them actually buys the beast?"

"Please, that would be bad for business. I pray every night to the Virgin that it never happens."

Sebastián winked, an exercise that gave him such a ghoulish aspect that Scully sincerely hoped he would not repeat it.

"So Dolores fixed you up?"

"Yes. She rented me her second house."

"Better not tell her you were in here. She might throw you out." Sebastián snorted scornfully. "She's what we call a beata. Know what that is? Somebody who's always running to the church. She goes to Mass so often I'll swear she must spend half her life on her knees. They say that's what drove her husband to drink. Man, it's come to something when you have to tell your wife to choose between you and the Pope, hasn't it?"

Sebastián grinned wickedly at Scully.

"Are you a bachelor?"

"In a manner of speaking."

Sebastián cranked up his features for another heavy-duty wink.

"Careful, man, careful. I always reckon these old biddies who spend so much time praying must be asking the Lord to send along the right man. Dolores isn't a bad prospect, you know. She's got a bit of land, some property, maybe some cash under tne mattress. Only one thing she lacks, so far. And that's a man."

Scully grinned.

"Don't worry. I've been stung once. That's enough."

"You Frenchmen can divorce, can't you? Very convenient. It will be legal in Spain soon, but you won't find folk around these parts divorcing, no way. It's not the custom, you see. And the wagging tongues, well, you'd either end up jumping into the chasm or you'd have to move away. In my case," He leaned over confidingly. "there's no need. You can have plenty of fun on the side. I know some good addresses in Granada and Almería, so if ever you go there...lovely girls, and clean too. I mean, nothing that a gentleman like you would turn your nose up at."

He enunciated "caballero", the Castilian word for gentleman, in such a leering manner that visions of unheard-of perversions floated across Scully's slightly fuddled mind.

"Thanks," he said. "I'll bear that in mind."

"A man has to let go sometimes, right? I mean, we can't all be like the cura, can we? Married to the church. It wouldn't suit me."

"The priest? He's pretty well respected here?"

"Who? Father Saturnino? More than that, hombre. Feared, I would say. Ask the fellow over in the corner what he's like." Scully glanced at the seated customer, a stocky man with an intelligent face and a sweeping black moustache. His dog, a black and white mongrel, sat patiently by him. "That's Bruno, he used to be mayor until he fell foul of the priest. Well, only one could win in that battle. Saturnino just gulped him up and spat him out. His sermons are something to hear, I tell you. Not like the last one they had in Cerrogordo. He didn't even wear a cassock. I saw him once, in jeans and a check shirt, no collar. Can you believe it? He was always in hot water, preaching politics and going on about hunger and revolution."

"What happened to him?"

"Just what you'd expect from a Rojo. The archbishop wanted to throw him out but he couldn't find a reason. Then it came out that he'd had it away with half the village. Three girls, three mind you, all pregnant! Phew! The son of a whore was lucky to escape with his life. Mind you, you had to admit he had more balls than most of them down there, for sure. But Benamargo —" The innkeeper sighed. "This is a different sort of place. Our women wouldn't dare step out of line."

"Not much fun for you."

"I told you." Sebastián rubbed a forefinger down the side of his nose. "I've got some good addresses."

The two hagglers had ceased arguing and were swapping songs with one another when Scully left the bar. Their hoarse voices followed him down the street. Two brandies on top of the potent local wine had succeeded in diluting a little of his pessimism and he found himself even taking a benevolent view of the landlord's nudges and winks. On his doorstep he stopped to listen. A slight breeze had come up the valley, flapping the washing on somebody's line. But there was no other sound, except for an odd muffled noise. He listened intently. It came from one of the neighbouring houses. It was laughter, with a crazy edge to it. It went on and on.

Scully shook himself and opened his door. He wished he had something to laugh about. Climbing his stairs, he wandered about the women of Benamargo, those black-clad wraiths that peered from windows and doorways. What went through their minds? Did they all meekly accept their lot? Surely they could not all be as smug and strait-laced as Dolores? Even in as tightly-ordered a society as this one, there must be rebels. And his mind was filled with an image of an unruly-haired girl skipping boldly down a hillside.

CHAPTER FIVE

Iron smacking on rough cobbles roused Scully. It was the sound that was to become his daily alarm clock, as the villagers and their beasts of burden began moving out to the fields. He was to see many mornings in Benamargo, more than he had planned but he never forgot the first one. Perhaps because no other ever approached the freshness, and the innocence, of that first one.

Hoofbeats vibrated through the thick walls of the house, as though the animals were passing through his bedroom. He dressed and stepped out on to the terrace. Village and valley were still in shadow, but a woman was already scattering water and sweeping the street with a large broom. Above the whisper of broom-strokes, he could hear a stream cascading over rocks. Then the sun flamed over the ridge opposite, spilling gold over terraced fields and tiled roofs, flushing the church tower. The sierras glowed magenta against washed-out blue. A tangle of twisted steeples, scarred buttresses, tumbling fortresses, they loomed over the tiny houses as in a bad painting which lacked proper perspective. Everything here was overdrawn, mused Scully, offering a framework for grand opera.

Not an olive leaf stirred. Exhilarated by the clarity of the air, Scully filled his lungs. The trees were as immobile as the rest of the painting. Even the column of smoke that curled up from the valley floor seemed frozen. The whole of Benamargo and its valley was frozen in space and time, and Scully, visually swamped, felt overwhelmed. It was too beautiful, too pure, reminding him that he was an intruder. What the devil was he doing here anyway, among these peasants? They must think him rather strange, unless they dismissed him as one of the idle rich from whom one could only expect eccentricities. He could imagine Stella curling her lip. Slumming it, Charlie? Getting back to nature, to the stink of manure and raw garlic? Trying to wash away your sins with cold water and rotgut? The bitch!

A clear, youthful voice raised in song intruded on his thoughts. This time he recognised it as that of Marisa. Her notes dropped into the silent valley like pebbles into a pond. Scully could not understand what she was singing, but it hardly seemed to matter. He fixed his eyes on the sierras, ebbing rust colour as the sun rose, and drank in every-thing, almost fiercely as though he could somehow purge his whole body. He lit a cigarette and watched the sun climb and reflected that this was how mornings should be.

It was the beginning of a routine he was ready to fall into. Around 8.30 there was a knock on the front door and Dolores deposited on his living-room table a large mug and a plate of churros. The first morning he took a large gulp from the mug and then realised that the liquid was not cof-fee. He discovered later it was concocted from roast barley. Worse, it was diluted with goat's milk. The strong goat taste lingered in his mouth for hours afterwards. Remembering previous experiences in Spain, he knew how to handle the churros, greasy sticks of deep-fried dough, dipping them in the ersatz coffee before transferring them to his mouth. They were palatable enough, although for the first few days his stomach emitted warning rumbles after every breakfast.

Scully accepted the diet as though it was part of his pen-ance. He felt no longing for bacon and eggs or more soph-isticated fare. Once he had considered himself a gourmet, frequenting the best expense-account restaurants, but now he barely had any interest in food. If it were necessary to eat to sustain life, he would do so. To stop eating or to stop breathing required a decision and that was an effort he was not prepared to make. In fact, Scully had reached what some mortals would regard as a sublime state. He was con-tent merely to exist.

Taking a walk around his new home, Scully came across a battered van parked in the plaza. A swarthy, sideburned man was laying out clothing and cheap jewellery on a stall, while village women picked at the merchandise, admiring or criticising in sharp, birdlike voices. Scully perched on the church steps and watched for a while.

The way in which the black-clad women swooped and pounced around the stall reminded him of a covey of jackdaws squabbling over some find. Occasionally the man put on a show of losing his temper, ordering them to put the wares down or make a purchase, scoffing at their attempts to bargain. His wife, a balloon of a woman with pomaded, jetblack hair and golden earrings, sat nearby, breastfeeding an equally plump infant and ignoring the fuss.

"Children are easily led astray, are they not?"

Scully recognised the deep, assured tones without looking around. The priest was standing behind him.

"A few baubles and they forget everything. The devil is always looking over their shoulders."

Scully shrugged.

"You don't agree?"

Scully betrayed puzzlement.

"I must confess, Father, that I see no devil here."

The priest smiled.

"Perhaps that is because you know his face too well. It is often the case. Some cannot see the devil when he is right before them because his face is so familiar. They think he is a friend."

"I think you have more experience of such matters than I do, Father."

"My son, if you mean that fighting evil, rooting it out, is my vocation, you are correct. Some of us blind ourselves, refusing to admit the evil before them. That is why I can never rest, for the devil is here, among us, offering temptation and reaping his harvest among the weak."

The priest had raised his voice so that his final words boomed out across the square. Abruptly the housewives quietened, as though they had been caught in an unclean act, and began whispering together. The priest turned to study Scully.

"So you decided to stay. Well, perhaps you will learn something from us simple folk of Benamargo."

"Perhaps indeed."

Piercing grey eyes scrutinised Scully.

"You don't appear the happiest of men, señor. And, forgive me for mentioning it, but you seem a little agitated. Your hands are shaking. What has brought you to our village? Are you looking for something in particular?"

"No, Father, I seek nothing, nothing," replied Scully, biting his lip and wishing the man would leave him in peace.

The priest regarded him gravely.

"In that case," he pronounced, "you are in much greater trouble than I imagined. When a man ceases to have either interest or hope in this life, he is a danger to himself. But what is worse is that he is a danger to others, señor, a danger to others."

With that, the priest strode off across the plaza, cassock flapping, a square resolute figure in the morning sunshine. As he drew level with the stall, several women approached him and bowed to kiss his right hand on which he wore a heavy signet ring. He extended the hand with an almost imperious gesture, murmuring a blessing as each woman made her obeisance. Then he uttered some sharp words to the stallholder and continued on his way. Only one or two of the now-subdued women stayed to haggle over the goods. Defiantly, the gypsy picked up a battery-powered megaphone and began proclaiming his wares.

Pursued by the tinny garble, Scully wandered towards the edge of the village where he came across the only modern building he had seen. It was a squat block with large windows, in marked contrast to those of the village houses which mostly resembled slits in a fortress wall. From the building came the steady chant of young voices but, just as Scully stopped to listen, a bell rang and out came the children, jostling and chattering. He was about to walk on when somebody called to him.

"Good day. I don't think we have met."

A tall, stooping man, clearly the teacher, was standing in the school entrance.

"You will be the one staying with Señora García. La Caída, as they call her around here. Everybody has a nickname in this place."

The teacher spoke in educated Castilian, which Scully found a welcome relief after straining to understand the local dialect.

"How did you end up in Benamargo of all places?"

Scully shrugged.

"I took a bus and here I am. This is where it stopped."

"The end of the line, eh? So you're an escapist?"

"I don't feel any pressure here. That appeals to me."

The teacher chuckled, brushing back his thinning grey hair. He looked like a predatory bird, with his bony, beak-like nose, sharp eyes and thin lips from which the words escaped like projectiles.

"No pressure? Well, of course, you're a newcomer. But forgive me. My name is Baldomero Suárez Conde, not one of the Suárez family of Ávila, you understand, although there was some connection on my mother's side. No, my origins are more humble. I come from Segovia. Perhaps you know it?"

Scully admitted he had been there once.

"A noble city and rich in history. And the Castilians, of course, so different from your Andalusians. I'm afraid there is little culture here, and no respect for learning. May I ask where you are from?"

"From England. Scully is the name, Charles Scully."

They shook hands. The teacher's face had brightened. Stooping a little more, he peered inquiringly at Scully.

"London?"

"I lived there, once."

"I was there once too, as a young man. Magnificent. I went to the Houses of Parliament and to a cricket match. It was all so gentlemanly. Polite conversation, applause for the loser, wonderful. What sophistication! All Spaniards should be made to watch one of your cricket matches for a week. It would be an education."

"It would be very boring," suggested Scully. "But not as boring as watching those politicians in Parliament."

"Ah, but we could learn so much. You know, we Spaniards are slaves to the most paltry emotions, to sentiment, wounded pride, outrageous nationalism. We prefer to spout easy tears or to toss bombs rather than engage in civilised debate. We breed anarchists and barbarians. Whereas you English, even when you're stabbing somebody in the back, you do it so politely, over cucumber sandwiches and tea. That's style. That is the secret of civilised society.'

"Civilised?" queried Scully. "It seems to me that there is more civilised behaviour in a little place like Benamargo than in the big cities, more respect for a man's dignity at any rate."

"Ha! There's precious little dignity around here, Señor Scully. No, in comparison we are in the Dark Ages. This is no place for a scholar. I'm surrounded by Philistines."

"That must represent a challenge for you. I mean as a teacher?"

The schoolmaster shrugged his bony shoulders scornfully.

"Yes, I saw it in that light once. But without allies it is a hopeless fight. Progress is so slow. You gain a centimetre and lose a metre." He looked around at the shrieking pupils. "The brightest run away. The others follow their fathers. If I can persuade one to read a comic, it is a triumph. But you must excuse me. I have to attend to these young devils. We shall talk again. Come to my house for dinner one evening. I promise something better than cucumber sandwiches."

He hurried indoors and a bell crashed out, summoning the children back to class. Scully walked on, wondering with whom the teacher communicated in this tiny village. There could surely be few others of equivalent education or intellect. There was no doctor. Possibly he and the priest exchanged scholarly barbs over sherry. The teacher was a strange mixture of nostalgia and bitterness. He seemed to have no respect for the villagers, yet he had chosen to bury himself here.

Scully manoeuvred around a blank-eyed teenager who was picking up stray bits of rubbish in the street while muttering to himself in obscene fashion. In the warm sunshine a tiger cat preened itself on a doorstep but, when Scully reached out a hand to stroke it, the animal arched its back and hissed alarmingly. He wandered on, looking for one of the grocery shops which he had been told existed in the village but there were no shop signs or any indications of commerce. Finally, he halted before an old-timer sitting on a bench.

"The shop?"

The old man bared his gums and cackled. His clothes were so worn as to be almost transparent but an almost new trilby hat perched on his head.

"Don't know where the shop is?"

He shook his head in disbelief and raised a knobbly stick carved from an olive branch.

"There. Behind you."

Scully hesitated before a whitewashed dwelling that looked no different from its fellows. The old man cackled again and shook his stick vigorously.

"That's it," he said, and began muttering to himself. "These strangers, they know nothing."

Scully ducked through a low doorway and found he had stepped into what at first glance appeared to be a witches' coven. The only light filtered from a tiny barred window. In the gloom Scully was dimly aware of little old women scuttling about his feet or gaping at him from behind heaps of canned food, piles of detergent and sacks of beans and flour. They reminded him of wild creatures, shy, beady-eyed, hiding from the light and intruders. At the counter overhung with dangling bunches of spicy sausages, a group stopped their conversation to turn and scrutinise him. As his vision adjusted, Scully saw that half a dozen hams were suspended from blackened roof-beams. The air bore the rich aroma of cured ham and decaying foodstuffs.

"Can I help you, your grace?"

The words came from a face thrusting through the sausages, an extremely fat face specked with moles. "Yes, but I'll wait until the others have finished." The woman stared at Scully, then turned to her customers. "I don't understand him. What does he say?" "He says he'll wait," said somebody. "Wait? For what?" "Perhaps he expects a message from the hereafter," suggested a voice, and the witches cackled among themselves. "Excuse me, your grace," said the proprietor with what to Scully seemed exaggerated concern, "Do you want to buy something?"

It took him quite a time to purchase a chunk of spicy sausage, a bread roll and a dusty bottle of Valdepeñas wine. Carmencita, or Little Carmen, moved ponderously due to her many rolls of fat. Her breath came in laboured gasps as she cut off a few samples of the sausage for him and searched the shelves for wine, to an accompaniment of cackled advice from the other clients.

"You're staying here, your grace?"

"With Doña Dolores."

"Ah, La Caída."

The rest of the shop exchanged views on this piece of information.

"She's a cousin of mine, a fine woman," declared Carmencita, as though challenging Scully to say different.

"She appears a very honourable person," he agreed.

"Honourable is not the half of it, señor. And after all she has suffered. Especially that of her husband."

"I didn't know."

"Well, of course not. It's a family matter."

Carmencita leaned over the counter until he could clearly see the black hair on her upper lip. A confidence was on its way, but Scully forestalled her with a 500-peseta bill.

"How much will that be?"

Carmencita sniffed. The money had distracted her. She did some complicated work on her fingers and a piece of wrapping paper before coming up with the figure of 150 pesetas. She waved away the cash.

"I have no change for big notes. Pay tomorrow."

Immediately he was outside the shop, Scully heard the murmur of conversation rise to a crescendo.

"Escaped, did you?" It was the old man across the street, with a grin on his face. "It takes a brave one to go into Carmencita's."

He shook his stick at Scully in a paroxysm of glee that turned into a coughing bout. The coughing lasted so long that Scully thought at first the fellow was about to expire and, rather than risk any blame being attached to him, he set off down the street. He took his lunch by the tumbling stream in the valley below. Only when he had settled in a shady spot did he realise that he had no corkscrew. But, with some thumb pressure, he was able to force the cork into the bottle, losing only a few drops of wine. It was light and dry enough and went well with the sausage spiked with hot peppers and garlic.

After finishing the bottle, he watched a hawk lazily riding the air currents, occasionally tilting a wing to slip into a dive. Then he leaned over a rock to gaze into one of the succession of pools in the stream. Something flickered in the shadows and he stared harder. It was a trout, at least a foot long. No, there were two, lying in the lee of the bank, flicking their tails to keep position. From time to time they made a quick surge to snap up some morsel floating down to them.

Scully watched, fascinated. His ears were full of the whirr of crickets and the rush of water over rocks. His thoughts drifted with the stream. Normally, at this time... He stopped himself. What had been normal about it? He would have been leaning back at Langan's or Le Gavroche, sniffing at a globe of Hennessy's, rolling a cigar between his fingers, surrounded by others like him, growing fat on padded expense accounts and company-provided perks.

He thought of Plimpton, rubicund, plummy Plimpton, chuckling over the latest piece of gossip, nudging him with off-colour jokes, complaining at the state of the country, ordering another bottle, calling for control over the unions, debating whether it would be Saint Tropez again this year. And Charteris, like a needle, or rather a stiletto. Rimless spectacles and stoat's eyes, a gargantuan appetite (when the company was paying) and an obsession for detail. As efficient, and as humourless, as an adding machine. He could pick out a loophole, spot a weakness as deftly as he could impale an oyster.

That was Charteris, the sharp instrument. And he, Scully, had been the blunt one. Charteris, the legal magician. Plimpton, the master of accounting. And Scully, with the drive, the ideas, the contacts, the killer instinct. They had been quite a team, playing with millions. When it came to stripping a company of its assets, of feinting take-over bids, of persuading unwilling tenants to quit a valuable piece of real estate, of shifting assets to the Seychelles, they had been a formidable trio. And by god! They had soared high. It had been good living. A Porsche, a Jaguar and a Mercedes, the yacht at Hamble, the penthouse off Marble Arch, Berkshire manor house, holidays in the Caribbean and the Rockies. Stella had enjoyed every bit of it. And so had he.

But he had worked for it, taken the chances, sweated days and nights. It was living on a knife-edge, dangerous, exhilarating. The weak dropped out, consumed by the flames. But the game went on. Always raising the ante, calling others' bluff, going right to the edge. You did not need cash, just nerve. On paper you could be worth more than Getty. It was all Monopoly money. Put down a pittance, take an option, slice it, dice it, peddle it, form an empire around it, and then — before the stack of cards collapsed — make your exit. But you had to move fast. And, in the end, somebody dragged their feet. The blow had fallen at the end of one of those long luncheons. Amid the cigar smoke, Plimpton had appeared, his face an odd colour, even for Plimpton. There was talk of a public inquiry. Then came questions in Parliament, reporters clamouring at the door around the clock. The world falling about one's ears. And then, on top of everything, that bitch Stella.

Even Mark had refused to speak to him. He would be 15 by now. Mark loved fishing. If he could see these trout... But he never would. Nor Paul. It was in the past and there was no sense even thinking about it. Better to drift with those flickering shapes and with the bubbles on the water. Scully followed the bubbles, until they tipped over the next cascade in an eruption of foam. One world demolished. And a new one? Well, for that one needed foundations, something to drive the first pile into. He no longer had the energy, the will, to clear this bomb-site, covered with twisted emotions. Perhaps the old dynamism would come back, as the scars healed. Or was he past repair?

Scully lay on a rock overlooking the stream and did

not care. He needed this rural peace, this tranquillity, a breathing space that perhaps would allow him eventually to pick up the pieces and start again. The effects of the wine weighed heavily on his eye-lids and he was not aware of a rustling in the dried grass near him.

A small animal was moving through the stalks, approaching the water. It moved slowly, tentatively, constantly sniffing the air and darting looks left and right. Abruptly a thunderbolt fell from the heavens. Flash of talons and hooked beak, and then the hawk was spiralling aloft, the small field-mouse crushed in its claws. Its life was already extinguished as it was borne up into the perfect blue.

The creature's last piercing cry of terror and pain aroused Scully. He opened his eyes, but the sky was still blue, the stream still burbled away. Nothing disturbed the rustic peace. Scully closed his eyes and dreamed.

CHAPTER SIX

Within a few days Scully grew to dread the moment when Dolores removed the dishes from the main course of the evening meal and placed on the table a round, pungent disc. He had made the mistake of saying he liked goat cheese and, as a result, he seemed doomed to eat the abominable stuff every evening. He grew to know every variation in taste, every shade of flavour, but he never overcame his repugnance for the slippery texture nor the strong odour that pursued him everywhere.

"Better cheese than you get in England, isn't it?" said Marisa one evening. She had spoken few words to him since the first meeting, keeping a demure silence. But now he saw that she was eyeing him mischievously. He had finished a reasonable plate of fried chicken and had been brooding over the goat cheese in front of him, wishing it were a slice of crumbly Cheshire or a slab of honest Stilton.

"It's fine," he said, suppressing a scowl. "But we have fine cheeses too. You'll have to try them some day."

"Benamargo cheese is good enough for her," put in Dolores severely. She was on her usual track. "I've brought up my children with simple tastes. They know right from wrong. There are temptations enough here, without any from outside."

Marisa grimaced.

"Nothing ever happens here. One day I'd like to go to England, and Paris, and Madrid. Just to see."

Dolores sniffed contemptuously, but Marisa looked at Scully. "What's London like?"

"Phew! That's hard to explain. It's so big, so different."

"Is it much bigger than Granada?" "Twenty times bigger, at least."

"And do all the girls wear mini-skirts?"

"Mini-skirts? No, they wear whatever they want, whatever the fashion says. It changes so fast. But lots wear jeans. Just like Spanish girls."

"Trousers are for men and skirts are for women," interjected Dolores. "Why on earth should anybody want to change that? It's the natural way of things. Men do the ploughing. Women look after the children and the home."

"Not all women," put in Marisa defensively. "Some are actresses, or lawyers, or even taxi-drivers. Anyway, I don't see anything wrong in wearing jeans. Next time we're in Cerrogordo can't I buy some?"

"Listen to the girl! Do you want everybody calling you shameless? And what about Don Saturnino? He would have something to say if a daughter of mine danced around the village like a...excuse me, señor...like a whore."

"Most girls wear jeans these days," murmured Scully. "Nobody sees anything wrong in it. Some girls look most attractive in them."

Dolores treated him to one of her most withering looks.

"I dare say. But it will never happen in Benamargo!"

Scully's eyes met those of Marisa who bit her lip as though biting back a reply.

"What? What will never happen in Benamargo?"

A young man stood in the doorway, hands on hips, grinning at the room in general. Scully recognised him immediately as the goatherd he had seen from a distance on his first visit to the village.

At close quarters there was no doubt that Ramón was a handsome youth. Though barely out of his teens, his labours and responsibilities had already given him the physique and bearing of a man. His dark hair was thick and curly, even on his sunburnt chest which seemed about to burst from his frayed work shirt. He was tall and wiry, with the alert, bouncy air of an athlete. His facial features betrayed a certain wildness, an untamed, gypsy streak that could not have come from his mother. It showed most in the lips, full and wilful, shaped for laughter but quick, it was possible to imagine, to curl in anger. Behind it all was a haughtiness. A Roman face, decided Scully.

The two women began fluttering about to serve dinner for their man. It was the first time Scully had met Ramón since he left early every morning to attend to his goats and returned late after feeding and milking them in a tumble-down barn on the edge of the village.

Scully was grateful for his arrival as it reduced the pressure on him to consume more of the cheese that came from his goats. Ramón examined him curiously.

"You have been up near Piedra Negra, correct?"

"Piedra Negra? I'm not sure."

"I saw you there, a week or so ago."

"Ah, yes, near that big crag. You were there with your goats."

"Yes, the big black rock. It has a bad name, that rock. Never stay near it during a storm. The lightning always hits it. But a stranger would not know that."

Scully smiled.

"It's worth knowing."

"Right. The people who know most here are the old fellows. They can't read or write and you might think they were simple, but they're not. They know every inch of these mountains. They've got a story to tell about every bush. Put them in a city and they would be dead within minutes, but here they can live off the land, off air. They have seen a lot, those old fellows."

He considered Scully with open interest.

"On holiday?"

"In a manner of speaking."

"Lucky you. We don't take holidays around here. There's always too much to do, with the animals, the olives, the vines, the almonds. Always something. It's all work. What is your work, señor?"

"Well, once I ran a property company."

"Then you are one of the rich. You are an executive, a capitalist?"

"No, I have quit. I've finished with all that."

Ramón nodded, as though he did not really believe this.

"A lot of foreigners go to the coast to retire. But nobody comes here to the pueblo. Are you a hunter?"

"A hunter?" Scully considered the question while Ramón attacked a steaming bowl of soup. "Yes, you could say that."

"There are wild goats up in the sierras, but you'd need a good guide to get anywhere near them. We don't see many foreigners here. Once one stayed six months. But then he went out of his mind. To tell you the truth. I think he had a screw missing from the start. He used to talk to himself. That did not worry anybody, but then he began talking to the mules, just as though they were human. Can you imagine? Then one day he had a fit in the church, yes, a real fit. He jumped on a seat and began blaspheming and yelling insults at Father Saturnino and they had to throw him out. It was big scandal. Every night he used to drink two litres of wine and fall down in the street. One morning — " Ramón chuckled. "One morning he woke up in the street and found he had no trousers left. True. Some pigs had found him and chewed his pants up, I swear it, chewed them all up."

"What happened to him?"

"Who knows? One day he was here, the next he had gone. Maybe one night he got so drunk he fell in the river, or he just got on the bus and went away. We never saw him again. I tell you, he was crazy."

Ramón grinned at Scully. It was a frank, ingenuous grin and his teeth were white and strong, unlike those of most of the villagers.

"But you don't look crazy, señor. I think you'll be okay."

"I hope so. I've only got two pairs of trousers with me, so I can't afford to feed one to the pigs."

"Be careful then. The pigs here are special. They eat anything. Last year El Colorín lost a hoe and he didn't find it until he killed his old sow. And there it was, inside the beast. And some years back there was a case of a family sleeping in the same room as the pig. They were very poor, of course, they only had one room, and not too bright. Well, one morning the mother went to feed the baby and guess what? Eaten, yes, eaten up. All right, not all of it, but enough.

"Our pigs are famous, you see. In Cerrogordo they make jokes about about us and the pigs, because they all think they are so smart down there. But our hams are nothing to joke about. They are the best. People come from other parts of the province just to taste our ham."

"Are you going to talk all night?" demanded Dolores, thrusting a plate of fried chicken in front of Ramón. "Remember, you've got a meeting tonight. You don't want to miss it."

"What's the meeting?" inquired Scully.

"Just the Cofradía," said Ramón, between mouthfuls.

"Cofradía? That's a religious fraternity, isn't it?"

Ramón shrugged.

"That's it."

Marisa nodded.

"It's called the Cofradía de Las Animas, the Brotherhood of the Spirits," she said. A mischievous smile twitched at her lips. "Very important they are. Or so they think."

"Shut up!" snapped Ramón, suddenly angry. "Some day your tongue will get you into trouble. Always blabbing away."

"Phooey! Just because you're one of Las Animas you think you're above everybody. Well, don't think I'm impressed. You and Las Animas!

Ramón concentrated on finishing his supper, but twin red spots showed on his cheeks.

"If you weren't such a silly little female, I'd give you a clout right now," he snapped.

"Go right ahead. It's not fair anyway. You don't even allow girls to join."

"It's lucky you are my sister, because some of the other brothers would be less lenient than me, I'll tell you. Blasphemy, that's what you're talking."

"Enough!"

Their mother was glowering at them from the kitchen.

"Marisa! Come in here and do the washing up. I never want to hear you talking about the brotherhood that way again. Your brother is right. And in front of a visitor too."

"Please, don't mind me," said Scully, shifting uncomfortably. "I only asked because I'm interested in the life of the village."

"Ramón is lucky to be a member," explained Dolores. "Not everybody is invited. It's an honour for the family. You should see the float they carry in the Easter procession. And how finely they dress the Virgin. It's as impressive as anything they have in Granada. Will you be here at Easter? That is something to see."

"We raise funds for the church and for the poor." Ramón's eyes glowed. "Why, there's hardly anything that goes on here that Las Animas don't have a hand in. In a way, well, we stand guard over the village. You could say we're the, the..."

"The conscience of the pueblo, that's what the Cofradía is," finished his mother.

Marisa was on the point of saying something, but Ramón got in first.

"To the kitchen, sister. And remember 'En boca cerrada no entran moscas'." He turned to Scully, grinning. "Know what that means? Keep your mouth shut and you won't get any flies in it."

"I shall remember that," said Scully. "So who organises the Cofradía? Do you elect officials?"

"The elders. They're in charge," replied Ramón.

"And the cura. Don't forget him," Dolores shook her head in wonder. "He's an example to us all. He is so strong and knows so much. You should see the books he has in his study. Just looking at them makes my head burst."

"I met him. He is indeed an —" Scully looked for the appropriate word "— impressive person."

"More than that. He is a real crusader," declared Ramón. "He'll stand up to anybody when he's defending the faith. Remember that time when the Communists tried to hold a meeting on the church steps. They brought in some fellow from the capital to speak. There he was, spouting all sorts of pretty words, when out comes Don Saturnino. 'What's this?' he says, in that tremendous voice of his. 'What's this? Begone, godless Reds!' And when the fellow took no notice and went on ranting against the church, the cura picked him up, like a sack of straw, and tossed him straight off the steps. You should have seen it. The cura said 'When the godless are at the door, it's time to use fire against fire'. Those were his words. I was there. And I'll tell you, the Reds never came back."

"There are a few around here, but they don't say much these days," said Dolores. "Gonzalo El Correo for one. He's a bad one, for sure. And Bruno, of course."

"No, the Reds don't reap any harvests around here, not since the war," said Ramón.

Dolores crossed herself.

"The war! Let's not talk about that. It's enough to start the tears running just to hear the word. Better to forget about those times."

"But there are some things that should not be forgotten, you know that, mother. We should remember so they can never be repeated," said Ramón, rising to his feet and tearing off a last piece of bread.

"That's what you may say. But I lived through those times. I know how it was. I don't want to hear any more talk of it."

Dolores went into the kitchen, muttering to herself. Scully said good night and strolled through the streets, lit by only a few feeble lights. Pausing outside Sebastián's bar, he observed the same couple were still debating the merits of a mule and walked on. Back at the house, he picked out a book from the pile he brought with him and climbed into bed. On his first few nights in the village he had slept just as badly as during the previous months. The sagging springs and deafening silence had not helped. But regular exercise, the invigorating air and the deliberate laundering of his thoughts about the past were taking their effect. Now pleasantly relaxed, he opened the bottle of whisky he had had the foresight to bring with him and filled a tumbler.

By the dim light of the bare 25-watt bulb hanging over the bed, he began reading. It was a paperback blockbuster he had picked up from a second-hand bookshop on the coast. Scully waded painfully through the first 50 pages of rape, flood and tempest, lust, blackmail and hate, clearly an authentic insight into everyday Californian family life. Then he checked how many pages there were to go and yawned. Six hundred. But anything was better than the risk of his own thoughts intruding. He reached for the whisky bottle, but at that moment the light flickered and went out. A power failure. It occurred frequently enough due to the village's antiquated electricity system. He waited for the light to flicker back on, but before that happened he was asleep.

Nightmares had become part of Scully's existence after the company crashed. The press had gone to town on the scandal and reporters had camped out on his doorstep. Then had come the phone calls filled with anger and hate, writs in the mail, physical threats. And Stella supporting him all the way, with a knife in the back. Insomnia and a whisky bottle had become his only companions. This night in Benamargo, however, he drifted into a deep sleep.

And then he dreamed that he was awakened by somebody or something, some force that attracted him irresistibly to the terrace. And it seemed that he had stepped outside his own body and was watching himself gaze down into the narrow street yawning below. Blackness enveloped the whole village, muffling all sound. Scully was alone in the overpowering darkness and silence, staring down into the chasm with a strange obsessiveness. He dreamed that he could hear his heartbeats, pounding loud enough to split his chest open, pounding, pounding. What drew him there? What was he looking for below his window?

Then the demons in Scully's mind betrayed themselves. A wraith moved down there in the blackness, another, and another. There were countless numbers of them, moving in a dark torrent, eddying and flowing, invading the imagination. And they were not silent after all. They were voicing obscene twisted words, mouthing unintelligible curses, flooding the night with their cries. And from this tormented army emanated a fearful power that ripped at the senses...

Scully found himself sitting on the step leading to the terrace. He was bathed in sweat and trembling uncontrollably. He shook his head and rubbed a forearm across his eyes. A dog howled mournfully from the other end of the village, but there was no other sound.

A cluster of stars blinked down. The night was peaceful. Shivering, he went inside and noticed that the light had gone on again. He went downstairs and splashed his face with water. For a moment he gazed at himself in the mirror. It was something he had avoided doing for some time and he regretted doing it now. He hardly recognised this haggard mask as that of a man who so recently had been dubbed Mr Dynamo by one alcoholic business editor and had charmed so many executives' wives. The once-clear grey eyes had a bloodshot, hunted aspect and the tan he had recently acquired could not conceal the fast march of wrinkles across his lean features. There had been no grey in that curly brown hair a year ago.

Scully cursed and went to look for the whisky.

CHAPTER SEVEN

"It's like tossing grain on to those sierras, my dear friend. Something may spring up, but it would be a miracle. No, culture is a lost cause here, believe me. Strange, isn't it? Centuries ago Andalusia had its poets, philosophers, thinkers, yet none of their thoughts touched this village and others like it. Even now hardly any of the older generation can read or write. The place is steeped in ignorance."

Baldomero was away on what appeared to be one of his favourite hobby horses.

"Last week for instance — this will illustrate what I mean — one of my pupils took a book home. He is one of the brighter ones. The next day he returned in tears and with the book in pieces. Do you know that his father had beaten him and told him it was wicked to read such nonsense and threatened to stop him coming to class?"

The teacher strode about his living room, gesticulating dramatically.

"Barbarians, sir! Barbarians!"

Books overflowed from floor-to-ceiling shelves and swamped a large desk, mingling with unmarked school exercise books. Baldomero paused to refill Scully's glass with dry sherry.

"What on earth was the book?" inquired Scully, although the teacher's monologue had already begun to weary him.

"Hah! You won't credit it. One of the classics. Earth, La Terre, Zola's masterpiece."

"Stony ground, in this case."

Baldomero chuckled and Scully laughed to keep him company. He had been in the village several weeks and the teacher had finally pressed him to come to dinner in his house, which adjoined the school.

"Excuse me for asking, but if you find people here so

unresponsive, then why do you stay? Surely a man of your abilities...."

A shadow flitted over the teacher's face.

"You say that. But one's capacities are not always recognised. Once, I worked in Salamanca, the university city, where culture counts for something. But I fell out with my superiors. Pure professional envy, nothing less. And here I am." He sighed. "At least here I have time to study. Come over to the desk. You see all these papers. And those reference books. Look, look." The teacher used the same declamatory manner of speaking in and out of the classroom and Scully felt himself assuming the role of the obedient, slightly awe-inspired pupil.

"What am I studying? I don't bother to discuss it with these buffoons around here, but you, señor, I shall tell. The life of Felipe II, yes, Philip the Second. You English know about him because he sent the Armada, but be assured we Spaniards know a good deal more because we had to suffer his rule."

"But wasn't he a great king?"

"Great?" Baldomero's voice rose to a squeak. "No, señor, he was a monster. A tyrant and a religious fanatic. And yet, at the same time, it's fascinating, he loved literature and printing. But that's no contradiction. He was simply a dedicated man. Unfortunately, both for Spain and for Europe, he really believed God had sent him to wage a crusade. Remember what he said once: 'I do not propose nor desire to be the ruler of heretics'. So, in the end, he was a disaster. As I shall demonstrate quite clearly." He rummaged among a pile of documents. "See, here, I have just received some important new data. These are actual letters of Cabrera de Córdoba, written in his own hand. You, of course, know of him. As Philip's court historian, he knew everything. And these particular letters have never been published. You may ask how I came across them. Research, sir, years of research."

He thrust some yellowed documents into Scully's hands.

"Evidence, more evidence. Spain has never had any luck

with its rulers, you know, and those damned clerics have crushed all critical thought in this country since they kicked out the Moors and the Jews. That is why we are so damned backward."

Scully smiled. "I trust you don't tell that to your parish priest."

Baldomero made a gesture of disgust. "Saturnino and I stopped speaking to one another 10 years ago. It is difficult to relate to somebody who believes the year is still 1500."

"He has a strong personality."

"So did Franco and Mussolini. The truth is that he would like to cut the road to Cerrogordo and pretend the rest of the world doesn't exist. Basically, the man's a peasant. He was born here, you know. He was a wild one in his youth, so I'm told, a real hell-raiser. Then he suddenly got religion and went off to study for the priesthood. From one extreme to the other. By the time he came back his ideas were set in stone. They say the reason he has never been posted elsewhere is that they couldn't find anybody else willing to be priest in this godforsaken spot. Christ stopped at Cerrogordo, I'll tell you. So Saturnino rules the village. It's amazing what he gets away with. Once the bishop called him to Granada and gave him a dressing down, but it didn't make the slightest difference."

"Even so, many of the people do seem to have a great respect for him," suggested Scully.

The teacher wagged a finger at him.

"Don't confuse respect with fear. He threatens them with hellfire and damnation and literally puts the fear of God in them. No wonder they daren't raise their heads. Once I tried to run classes for the old folk who cannot read or write. A useful service, you might think. Well, what happened? By the third lesson virtually nobody came. The priest frightened them off."

"But why? How?"

"Why? Because he sees me as competition, somebody challenging his authority. How? Very simple. He told them that I was one of those terrible Rojos and that my ideas were anti-Christian. That was enough. Most people here are

very ignorant so he can control them. Anybody who has the
nerve to challenge him, he cuts them down. That is why we
have no mayor. The last one was Bruno, a good fellow with
some brains in his head, but sure enough he fell out with
the priest and he was forced out. Nobody else dares take
the job."

Baldomero produced a dry, sardonic smile.

"That's the way it is here. You have stepped back into
the Middle Ages, my friend. Here, have some more sherry."
He topped up Scully's glass. "You don't know how pleased I
am to meet somebody I can talk to. And your Spanish, you
speak very good Castilian, you know that?"

Scully shrugged.

"I'm very rusty, I'm afraid. But I studied it at university
and spent a year in Madrid when I was a student."

"So you must know our classics." The teacher indicated
his shelves. "I have them all here, Calderón, Quevedo, Cer-
vantes, Lope de Vega...whenever you want to borrow one.
Oh, dinner must be ready."

Almost soundlessly, a woman had entered. Baldomero
introduced his sister to Scully with some formality. Her
hand was ice-cold, her grip lighter than a sparrow's tread.
She smiled quickly at Scully and looked nervously away.

"Amelia is the best, no, the only cook in Benamargo. I'm
sure you will enjoy the meal," said Baldomero.

And, considering his limited appetite, Scully did. The
schoolmaster produced a bottle of mellow Rioja wine to go
with the garlic soup, followed by grilled quail served with a
rich sauce.

"One thing you can say about this region, it has excellent
game," remarked Baldomero. "Goat, partridge, pheasant...
and superb trout too. Next time we shall have trout, with a
fine white wine. We may live amid barbarians, but we don't
have to live like them."

"Trout Navarre-style, with almonds and ham, that would
be good, wouldn't it, dear?" said Amelia, looking to her
brother for approval.

"Magnificent. We don't have English salmon, but we do
have some palatable things in this miserable corner."

"Señor," Amelia fixed her gaze on Scully. She had high cheekbones and deepset eyes. Once she could have been pretty, but now, in a plain grey dress, almost as thin as her brother and just as pallid, hair pulled severely back, she was merely mousy. "Señor, you have not told us why you have come to stay here. Surely not for the cuisine?"

Scully gave a gallant smile.

"Had I known meals like this were available, that would have been reason enough. But the truth is that the doctor ordered me to take a complete rest, to get away from things."

She returned the smile.

"Away from things? And have you succeeded?"

"Don't interrogate the fellow," interrupted Baldomero. "Of course he's found tranquillity. You know there's no quieter pueblo than this one. Nothing ever happens. Everybody enjoying the simple life."

The teacher's mouth twisted with bitterness.

"At least you don't have television here. That's a relief. I'm glad to get away from ringing telephones and television, although maybe I am being selfish."

"We did have it."

"You did?"

"Certainly," said the teacher. "They built a repeater station so we could receive all the programmes. Cost a bundle of money. And then a funny thing happened."

He paused and poured himself and Scully more wine.

"One night somebody blew the damn thing up. Sabotage. They repaired it, and it was blown up again, smashed to pieces. Hardly a fragment left. And we've never had television since. The authorities refuse to pay for a new one and we have no cash."

"But who would do that?"

"At the time the suggestion was that it was the work of terrorists. Anyway that was supposed to be the police theory. Didn't make much sense. Here, man — " Baldomero pushed a plate towards Scully. "Please finish it off. My mother's side of the family was famous for its cooking, you know, and for their wines. They owned a vineyard."

Amelia's pale sad face brightened for a moment.

"Those were happy times, when we used to go to the harvest. They had such a big house and everybody used to visit."

"Don't you miss your life up there?" asked Scully.

"One accepts what life brings. We had relations in Segovia and Madrid, but now we've lost touch."

"Amelia has plenty to do looking after me," noted Baldomero, with a touch of smugness. "And she gives some of the girls classes in painting and weaving. She has plenty to occupy herself."

"Even so," murmured Scully. "After the city? For a woman, I mean."

"Yes?" said Amelia, studying Scully.

"Well, the women here are not exactly liberated, are they?"

The schoolteacher guffawed.

"Liberated? Our dear priest does not accept the existence of the word. He is always blathering on about sin and woman's weakness. A woman's duty is to suffer. That's what he tells these ignoramuses."

"He says what he believes," retorted Amelia defensively. "He's a sincere man."

She turned to Scully.

"We all must do penance for our errors, I suppose. And Benamargo is as good a place as any for that."

She was suddenly shrouded in melancholy.

"Por Dios, woman, don't talk about sinning and penance. You're becoming as bad as Saturnino," said Baldomero, draining his glass. "All we need is another miracle and you'll be asking me to go with you to Mass."

"Another? You mean you've had one miracle already?" asked Scully, smiling.

"Ach, some nonsense. A woman was supposed to be dying and what should happen but she saw the Virgin in person. Cured her, just like that. Of course, she's one of the priest's favourites. Runs after him like a saviour, and he says she should be made a saint. Typical village mumbo jumbo."

Scully turned his attention back to Amelia.

"But you were talking about penance. Do you really think it serves any purpose? What's gone is gone, surely? You cannot change the past by suffering now."

"Don't you believe in the hereafter?"

"Angels and heavenly gates and all that? No more than I believe that there's fire and brimstone waiting for us down below. No, at the end, there'll be nothing waiting for us."

"That sounds terribly final, hopeless."

"Hopeless? No, realistic. Man just fools himself. He knows what I'm saying must be true but it makes him uneasy. So, just to be on the safe side, he takes out an insurance policy. It's called religion. So he does penance and says prayers. They're like insurance premiums."

"But they make a difference. They must do."

"But why should they? Every day is a new one. The good or the bad you did yesterday makes no difference to today or to what happens beyond the grave."

"Then you don't believe in God?"

Scully paused at the earnestness of her tone.

"I have no reason to. To tell the truth, I haven't much reason to believe in anything."

"You cannot be a very happy man."

The word itself had an alien ring to Scully's ears.

"Happy? I suppose not. And you, are you happy?"

The discussion had excited her, but now she looked down at the table.

"I accept that you have to pay for your transgressions, that in this life everything has to be paid for. I accept that."

"And you are paying...for something?"

She flushed uncomfortably and her brother broke in.

"There must be some reason she goes to Mass twice a day. Can you believe it? You would need all the horses of the Apocalypse to drag me anywhere near that church. But Amelia actually swallows that double talk. The truth is it's an embarrassment to me. I see my school as a bulwark of reason breasting the tide of ignorance and here is my own sister openly subscribing to that medieval claptrap."

Amelia shook her head despairingly.

"You know, Señor Scully, in Spain we say half the people follow the priest with a candle and the other half with a stick. Well, my brother is one of those with the stick."

Baldomero chuckled, spreading his hands in appeal to Scully.

"What can you do when your own family undermines you? To the devil with all this religious talk. How about another bottle? I'll go and find one in the cellar."

After her brother disappeared, Amelia began gathering up the plates.

"He appears a dedicated man, your brother," said Scully.

She shrugged.

"He is a brilliant teacher, intelligent, cultured. He's wasted here. He could have been principal of one of the biggest colleges in Madrid, but instead he chose to come to this tiny village to spread, as he put it, light in the darkness."

"He could still move."

"If he wanted to. Thirty years is a long time and, even though he complains so much about the people, he has become attached to Benamargo. There is a slow ritual to life here that does not exist in the cities. You become accustomed to the pace, to the ways, to the change of seasons. They plough, they scatter the seed, it sprouts up and it is harvested. And every season is marked by its festivals. Everybody takes part, like a true community. The rituals bind them together more closely."

"I can understand that," said Scully. "There's not much sense of community in some places I've lived. Wastelands, arid, empty, inhuman. I can understand that to be part of Benamargo would be, well, comforting."

Amelia smiled, a shallow smile.

"It makes one's burdens easier to bear. If you stay, you will find out. You will see what a warm feeling there is when there's a festival. Will you be here for El Día de los Difuntos, in November?"

Scully grimaced.

"The Day of the Dead? That sounds a little macabre."

"Not at all. It is when everyone renews acquaintance with

those of their family who have passed on. They all go to the cemetery. It is a big family occasion."

"Another bit of mumbo jumbo and my sister loves it all," interjected Baldomero, returning with a dusty bottle. "This obsession with death. Why don't we have a Day of Life, tell me? Tell me that, Señor Scully."

"Please call me Charles, or Carlos."

"Ah, Carlos. Well, this obsession with death, Felipe II loved it too. There's an interesting passage in a book I was reading last night, about his last days when he retired to the Escorial."

It was after midnight when Scully left Baldomero's house. The schoolteacher was buried in a book and his sister showed their visitor to the door.

"Thank you for coming. My brother loves to have somebody to talk to," said Amelia.

She touched Scully's hand and, as he walked a little unsteadily back to his house, he tried to decide whether the touch had lingered longer than was strictly necessary. Pausing in the church square, lit by a shred of new moon, he took a gulp of refreshing water from one of the spouts of a fountain.

"Good evening, señor. You are enjoying some of our pure water?"

Scully recognised the sonorous tones of the priest. He turned and saw him standing a few yards away.

"A cleansing draught? There is nothing like it sometimes," declared Father Saturnino. "I was thinking just now what a great responsibility is borne by those who guide the young. A young mind is so easily harmed, lured off the track, don't you agree?"

Scully was wary.

"The young are impressionable."

"Exactly." The priest moved closer, his face in shadow. "I could not help noticing you leave the teacher's house. How does he strike you, our schoolmaster?"

"Well, he appears a cultured man. He seems to have the interests of his pupils at heart."

"Possibly." The priest's tone indicated his true feelings.

"But we are all weak, are we not? And sometimes we cannot help our weaknesses ruling our heads. Even the most educated, a man who can quote Virgil and Plato, can yield to temptation. Yes, yes." He paused, only the noise of the gushing fountain breaking the stillness.

"May I give you some advice? Don't put too much store in what the teacher tells you. He is an embittered man. No doubt he has his reasons. But bitterness is like a poison. It can spread and gnaw at the hearts of the innocent. That is surely not healthy in a small community like ours. We have few secrets from one another here, but the teacher tends to keep his own counsel. That can be somewhat divisive."

"Well, I suppose he is entitled to his opinion," said Scully, trying to keep the edge out of his voice.

"Of course, of course!"

Alone with this ox of a man on the plaza, deserted but for fragments of paper spinning over the paving stones, Scully felt his physical power and his magnetism. The priest was very close to Scully. He spoke quietly but intensely.

"You are a man of the world, are you not? A businessman, perhaps? I can see that you would never do anything without first measuring the consequences." The priest sighed. "But even the most worldly can be out of their depth in a place like Benamargo. Not knowing local customs, I mean, possibly jumping to the wrong conclusions, even hurting feelings unknowingly. In this little pool the tiniest actions can create such great ripples."

"Don't worry. I'm aware of that, Father," said Scully. He sensed rather than saw the dark, deepset eyes burning into him.

"Of course you are. Well, goodnight. And go with God."

Watching his bulky shadow disappear around the corner of the church, Scully felt irritated with himself. Why had he felt so much on the defensive? It was no damn business of Saturnino where he ate or whom he talked to. Village Napoleon! Let these people fight out their own parochial battles. He was not touched by their gossip. Even so, the brooding presence of the priest stayed with him as he strode homewards.

CHAPTER EIGHT

"Are you going to the wedding, Don Carlos?"

Scully looked up in surprise from his breakfast.

"I didn't know there was a wedding. In any case, I am not invited."

Dolores twitched her mouth.

"That makes no difference. When there's a wedding here, the whole village goes. That's the custom."

"But I don't even know the couple."

"Better still. Old Carmela from across the street hasn't spoken to the groom's family in 20 years, but you can be sure she will be there. And she'll be the first to get her face into the refreshments. She's a shameless one."

Dolores was right. The whole village was at the wedding. Half the population appeared to have squeezed into the bride's house and the other half was waiting outside. Through the open door Scully could see that the living room was tight-wedged with people, all competing to make themselves heard. Now and again somebody emerged for air and answered bystanders' questions about the state of affairs within.

Finally, amid great commotion, the bride appeared, on the arm of her father, a diminutive man with one eye. She was plump and placid with complacent eyes. Cries of admiration went up at the sight of her flowing white dress and pink, blushing face. She smiled and blushed a deeper shade. She was pretty at that moment. The prettiest moment of her life, thought Scully, immediately feeling a stab of depression. Then he cursed himself for his cynicism.

Some way behind the bride walked two young men, both in ill-fitting suits. Scully guessed that the one who looked most embarrassed and nervous must be the future husband. He had an honest, sunburnt, country face and plastered-down hair. He moved awkwardly as though in a skin that did not belong to him, occasionally running a finger around his shirt collar.

The villagers trailed the couple and their families as they set off around the village, following a circuitous route until they ended up before the church. Having nothing better to do, Scully followed the crowd as it pushed into the building. Every pew was filled and he squashed in with the group standing at the back. Children ran excitedly up and down the aisle until Father Saturnino, an august presence in a white cassock, appeared and sternly rebuked them. They stole back to their mothers in subdued fashion, but even his booming tones could not still the whispering among the congregation. They commented on the couple's appearance, on the ceremony, on the priest's new cassock, on the altar flowers, and other points of engrossing interest.

Tittering rippled about the church when the bride, in a quavering voice, stuttered over her responses. As the bridegroom struggled desperately to fit the ring on her finger, his complexion growing redder by the second, the women nudged one another amid stifled laughter. The priest adopted his most chillingly authoritative expression to frown down upon the restless congregation, but it calmed the gossip and giggles only briefly.

Father Saturnino's sermon proved more effective, however. At first he waxed lyrical over the state of virginity, dwelling at such length on this subject that Scully wondered whether he had got his ceremonies mixed up. It seemed that those who put aside worldly pleasure had taken a significant step closer to Heaven, worldly pleasure in this context meaning only one thing. The congregation halted its whispering to gaze at the priest with rapt attention and Scully reflected sourly that Saturnino's full-blooded attack on lust might just be having the reverse effect to what he intended.

Saturnino roamed over a wide field, from the Immaculate Conception to the purity of those who chose to pass their lives sealed off from sin, praying for others. Then he turned to those who had not felt the call to make such a sacrifice. His gaze bored down on the happy couple much, thought

Scully, as one would regard a pair of distasteful insects. The newly-weds gaped at the priest as though hypnotised, while he explained to them that they had a sacred duty too, to procreate. Saturnino eyed the groom who was rocking slightly, sweat staining the collar of his spotless white shirt.

"Guillermo, you know why you are here today. To pledge yourself to this sacred bond of holy matrimony and to seek our Lord's benediction. And you know your duties. God gave you this bride. It is for you to protect her and cherish her all your days."

He turned to the bride.

"And you, Inmaculada, you have duties also, do you not?" Visibly trembling, the girl groped for an answer. "Of course, you have," continued the priest. "To honour, respect and obey this man. To care for him and bear him the children that the Lord determines, and to be faithful to him all your days. A simple requirement for those that walk in God's ways, and yet, and yet... Be on your guard, for Satan is always watching and waiting his chance."

Abruptly, the priest raised his voice, quelling the slightest murmur amid the congregation.

"Satan, I say, is always lurking in the shadows."

He had their full attention.

"Yes, he never sleeps. A creeping, grasping, crawling, slimy creature, sneaking through the darkness and the mud, waiting, prowling, scheming, sucking at the weak, dragging them down. And how do we recognize him? I shall tell you. Whenever you see temptation, you see the Devil. Be on your guard, Guillermo. Be on your guard, Inmaculada. Sweet words and sly flattery, these are his bait. They are the masks of evil, of slippery nastiness, and bottomless perversion."

The priest's face glowed.

"When you see Satan, Guillermo, what must you do?"

For a moment it seemed that Guillermo was about to answer, but Saturnino forestalled him.

"Smite him. Guillermo, smite him with all your strength. Smite the serpent, lest he gnaws his way into your soul.

You must be doubly on your guard, for who was it that first succumbed to the blandishments of Evil in the Garden of Eden? Who made that first breach in the walls of the citadel of virtue?"

The priest's lip curled.

"Yes, indeed, woman is weak. That is why man must be ever watchful, sword in hand to protect her from temptation and the ways of shame. He must build a fortress a thousand metres high about her and his family. That is his duty, his sacred trust. And woman? She has her burden too, willed to her down the ages, condemned to do eternal penance. She it is who must suffer the pain and joy of child-bearing, suffer..."

Scully had had quite enough. He edged out of the church. Most of the male members of the community were outside, chatting idly in groups. A lean individual with a scarred lip and darting eyes spoke to him.

"What's he saying, the priest?"

"He's talking a lot about virginity and suffering."

"Ah!" The man grinned. "Virginity! There's a subject he knows something about. It's his crusade."

"You're on a crusade too, aren't you, Juanito?" said another man, winking.

"That's true," agreed Juanito. "But I have a feeling the cura and I are on different sides."

Scully realised that this was the village Don Juan, Juanito the truck-driver with — or so the gossips claimed — a girl in every town.

Finally the service was over and the people spilled out into the plaza. Although the priest had warned against any such frivolity as confetti-throwing, when the dazed couple emerged they were battered by a hail of rice. The last shower, hurled from close quarters, caught Inmaculada full on her left cheek, raising an instant weal. She burst into tears as her mother, a fearsome figure in black, belaboured the guilty youth with her handbag and a far sharper weapon, her voice.

When peace was restored, the couple and their relatives paraded along the street to the school. Most of the villagers were already waiting expectantly outside the classroom which had been hired for the reception. Inmaculada's mother, holding the classroom key aloft, elbowed her way to the front of the good-humoured crowd. Scully was told that she had laboured half the night preparing the feast and was not prepared to let anybody else enter before her.

Once the door was opened, Scully could understand her concern. Men, women and children made a noisy, jostling rush for the trestle tables which had been set up. Within seconds, platefuls of sliced sausage, cured ham and cheese had been snatched up and cleared. Before the bride and groom could sit themselves behind the main table, sagging under a wedding cake with a disturbing resemblance to the Leaning Tower of Pisa, most of the food had already disappeared down the throats of Benamargo and glasses were already being refilled. A group of children was fighting over some packets of potato crisps, while two youngsters hardly into their teens were struggling for possession of a bottle of gin.

"Some party, eh?"

A middle-aged man was grinning lopsidedly at Scully. In one hand he held a half-finished bread roll, in the other a nearly empty bottle. He took a swig of liquor.

"Isn't the bride beautiful?"

Scully agreed that indeed she was, and was quickly pleased with his good sense when he noticed that the man was winking at him with his one good eye. It was Inmaculada's father.

"Beautiful as a spring flower! Thanks be to God she has married. It's never easy with daughters. And a good marriage too. Guillermo is a fine chap and he stands to inherit a few fanegas."

Scully was not sure what a "fanega" was, but he guessed it was a term for a piece of land.

Over at the main table, Guillermo had torn off his tie and his hair was standing on end as he gesticulated to those around him. Fingering her bruised cheek, a sulky Inmaculada appeared to have aged 10 years in the past hour, while her mother commanded proceedings with a trumphant air.

"My wife is some woman," confessed Inmaculada's father, raising his voice above the uproar. He tried to focus his single bloodshot eye on Scully. "You're the Frenchman staying with Dolores, aren't you? Now she was a beauty once, I'll tell you. We were all after her. But she only had eyes for Francisco."

He brooded for a moment.

"He was a handsome fellow, I'll grant you that. The girls liked him, for sure." He extracted a brandy bottle from the hand of a passing youngster. "They were a fine couple, until Francisco went off. It happened just like that. One day he was here, then he vanished. There was lots of talk but we never got to the bottom of it. Some said he'd been cuckolded." He sniffed. "But Francisco wouldn't run away. Not Francisco. He had a gypsy wildness in him, hot-blooded. He'd want vengeance." He rocked on his heels. "Here, have a drink. D'you like Benamargo?"

Since the hard liquor had swiftly run out, the guests were consoling themselves with the local wine. Laughing uproariously, shouting across the room to one another, belts and buttons slackened, buttons opened, faces glowing, eyes shining, they were hardly recognisable as the sober, submissive congregation of an hour previously. Steaming plates were being passed around. Somebody handed one to Scully. He tasted the chunks of meat swimming in a rich, saffron-hued liquid. They were tender, infused with olive oil and garlic.

"Goat, baby goat. Good, eh?"

It was Alejandro, the dark, volatile young man who had thrown the rice. He was smiling through chipped teeth, indicating that Scully should eat up.

"You don't get a feast like this every day, hombre. Eat, eat!"

Children chased about between the tables and in a corner Dolores La Caída was deep in conversation with two neighbours, oblivious to the cacophony around them. Marisa, face flushed, giggled with a posse of girls, occasionally launching cheeky retorts in response to the teasing of a group of youths. One of these started clapping his hands and the others joined in. It was a flamenco rhythm, hard and driving, and soon the whole room had entered into the mood. A short man, swarthier than most, with a red neckerchief knotted at his throat and a swaggering manner, jumped to his feet and began stamping out a fast tempo with his heels.

"Pepe!" whooped the guests. "Sing, Pepe, sing."

Pepe gladly obliged.

"Viva la novia, y el novio,
y el cura que los casó,
el padrino y la madrina,
y los convidaos, y yo..."
(Long live the bride and the groom,
and the priest who married them,
and the godfather and the godmother,
and the guests, and myself...)

The crowd cheered and demanded more. This time Pepe directed his song at the bride, launching into the true flamenco style, dragging the notes out of his innards as though his whole heart and soul were involved, lingering agonisingly on some notes until his audience burst into cries of "Olé! Olé!"

"El día que tu naciste
nacieron todas las flores,
y en la pila del bautismo
cantaron los ruiseñores."
(All the flowers were born
on the same day as you,
and in the baptismal font
the nightingales sang too.)

It pulled the bride out of her sulk. Forgetting even about her bruised cheek, she blushed and smiled as the guests applauded lustily. Guillermo, in shirt sleeves by now, laughed and cried for more. The singer was into his stride. He sang of love, how it was like a bunch of grapes, the freshness coming first, the drunkenness afterwards.

"Pepe el Gitano may not have much voice, but he does have what we call 'duende'."

Amelia was standing by Scully's side, a wry smile on her

lips. She looked less matronly than when he had last seen her, her hair brushed so that it framed her pale, delicate features and softened their lines, a discreetly cut, blue silk dress hinting at the woman within.

"What is 'duende'?"

"It's the word we use when we mean somebody has a certain magic. You can't really describe it. You can only feel it. When you hear somebody with 'duende' singing flamenco, you recognise it."

The gypsy was flicking his fingers and clicking his heels as he sidled towards a stout woman with laughing eyes. To giggles and jeers, he hoarsely detailed her charms. Her face resembled the sierras and her eyes bandits that roamed over it. Everybody laughed, including the woman.

"Only Pepe would dare," said Amelia. She glanced around. "Thank goodness Father Saturnino has gone."

Lured to her feet by the singer, the woman began to follow him in the exuberant movements of a sevillana dance, swaying her bulky hips with surprising grace. The guests clapped out a rhythm, while Pepe, arching his body and closing his eyes, appeared to be in ecstasy. One of the youths pulled a girl out into the ring formed by the guests and they joined the dance, with more energy but little of the grace of the older couple.

Scully looked towards Dolores and saw her gazing at the spectacle with disapproval. He imagined he could see the word "sinverguenza" forming on her lips. A glass smashed to the floor and the guests cheered and laughed, flushed with alcohol and excitement. The bride was tugging at her husband to make him stand up, but Guillermo, forehead shiny with sweat, eyes glazing, appeared in no condition to move. His mother, a tiny, frightened woman, fanned him with a palm-leaf fan.

"It must be time to leave," suggested Amelia, examining the scene with distaste. Scully nodded. But at that moment a great cry went up.

"The cake! The cake!"

They were forced to stay while glasses were filled once more and Guillermo was propelled to his feet to perform the ritual cutting of the many-tiered monstrosity which had assumed a perilous angle during the party. At first it seemed the impossible was being asked, for the groom was leaning one way and the cake another. Eventually, however, by a supreme effort they were brought together and Guillermo and Inmaculada managed to make the necessary initial slices.

Scully and Amelia consumed their share and made their escape. Outside, Alejandro was engaged in argument with two youths Amelia identified as the bride's brothers. His shirt was ripped and he was sucking his knuckles. Gradually, the clamour from the reception faded, as Scully and Amelia crossed the school playground and strolled along a path that led to the teacher's house. The building was perched at the cliff edge and Amelia paused to take several deep breaths. They looked out over the chasm.

"Sometimes I think my brother is right," said Amelia. Scully looked at her quizzically.

"They really are so...I don't know, so coarse here, so..."

Scully managed a twisted smile.

"Earthy? Is that the word you want? But is that so bad? At bottom we're all pretty earthy, no matter what they say about us being civilised human beings. They are having a fantastic time. I see no harm in that."

She seized on his words.

"You think so? But the way the gypsy acts, the way he leers. And the way those women react. It's too much, it's disgusting.

"Disgusting?" Scully's smiled. "Everybody was having fun, that's all, just innocent fun."

She reacted hotly.

"It didn't seem innocent to me."

Then hopelessness seemed to envelop her. Her shoulders drooped and she gripped the railing before them, the whites of her knuckles showing. When she spoke again, it was almost in a whisper. There was a trace, almost, of envy in her voice.

"You're right. They were having fun, weren't they? There's so little of that in this life."

He saw that there were tears in her eyes.

"Amelia, what is it?"

"Nothing, nothing, nothing."

He touched her shoulder.

"What is it?"

He spoke more softly this time.

"It's just that, sometimes, I feel so...empty. Nothing to look forward to, nobody even to talk to. Nothing. Just emptiness."

"It can't be that bad."

"You have no idea. I have no friends here, none. I'm shipwrecked, and Benamargo is my island."

He patted her shoulder mechanically and she leaned against him. It was almost dark and the house stood between them and the rest of the village. Scully wanted to get away. He could still taste the cardboard texture and oversweet icing of the wedding cake. He wanted to wash his mouth out. He scraped around for something to say.

"You're young enough. You can leave, go where you please, make new friends somewhere else."

She shrugged.

"You think so? Perhaps for you it is that simple, but not for me. You are free."

"And you are not?"

"My life is here. Someone must look after Baldomero."

"I'm sure that your brother could look after himself well enough if he had to. But then —" he looked keenly at her "— you believe in doing penance. That's what you said, isn't it, although you did not tell me what terrible sin you had committed."

She looked sharply at him.

"Is it really all a joke to you? Don't you have any beliefs, any commitments? You must care about something, about somebody."

"Why?"

She frowned, puzzled yet intrigued.

"Everybody must care about something. I have the feeling you are just playing with me, laughing at my naiveness, but never giving anything away." Amelia studied him, as though she might find some clue to what was behind the facade. "You are so cynical. And burying yourself here. Why? You must have a secret. You are a mystery, the village mystery man."

Scully laughed.

"You laugh, but I see no emotion. Your eyes say nothing. Yet you have the face of somebody who could be very fierce, yes, very intense."

She reached out and touched Scully's cheek.

"A mixture of so many things, a mystery."

Her fingers, smooth and cool, ran over Scully's mouth and he kissed them unthinkingly, then wished he had not. Her arms came around him and, as though detached from his body, he saw himself caressing her hair and pressing his lips to hers. Amelia pulled him closer, prolonging the kiss.

Scully could see the rim of the mountains fading in the darkness and glimpse the first stars. He could hear water rushing far below and distant sounds of revelry. He noted a faint trace of perfume. He reflected that he could do everything, except feel.

Baldomero's sister was squeezing herself against him with an alarming desperation. Sweat broke out on his forehead, even as ice lodged in his stomach. He stifled a bitter laugh. This was the meeting of a drowning man with a woman dying of thirst.

"What are you thinking, Carlos?"

"I was thinking," Scully paused. "that you are a very passionate woman."

Amelia was sobbing.

"Oh, Carlos, Carlos, if you only knew."

CHAPTER NINE

At least, thought Scully, as he worked his way up a rocky, zigzag path, I am in better physical shape than I was a month ago. Then I had to rest every 20 paces when I tackled any gradient. During those frenetic years in London, he had virtually given up sport, except for an occasional game of squash, but that only because it had been helpful in making business contacts. Stella's friends and the kids had monopolised the tennis court at the country house.

Years of doing no more exercise than signing contracts and raising whisky glasses had fleshed out the rawboned youth who had drawn blood in many a Saturday night brawl in his younger days. Hard to guess that he had been born in the shadow of a Yorkshire steel mill where once a youth had put a fist in his face for being "a bloody snob" when he said he was going to university. The scholarship had delivered him, and he had soon jettisoned his broad regional accent. That got you nowhere in class-conscious Britain. Contacts were what got you places and Scully had worked hard to cultivate the right ones.

Once out of university, he never went back to those mean streets which had spawned him, where the talk was only of football and unemployment. Instead, he had polished himself for another, smoother world, where hatchet jobs were performed not outside backstreet pubs but in civilised style, in boardrooms and executive suites, where the knife went in smoothly, guided by gentlemen who arrived in chauffeur-driven cars.

Scully had thrived in this heady atmosphere, guided by lessons that he had learned amid the blast furnaces. The old-timers never tired of repeating "If tha' ever does owt for nowt, do it for thissen!" It sounded quaint in their thick accents, but the advice proved just as valid when translated into plummy, upper-class English. Climbing nothing more demanding than the social ladder, Scully had become a soft city-dweller, belly burgeoning, a candidate for an early cardiac arrest.

In that condition he was as out of place in Benamargo as he would have been in his native streets. His lax muscles and pallid appearance contrasted with the lean, weathered aspect of the locals. Some walked a dozen miles a day just to reach their small plots of land, keeping pace effortlessly with their plodding mules. Their spare frames, sparse diet and resilience made Scully feel guiltily decadent. He began walking regularly. Every day he forced himself to go further. He took out on his body his sense of despair and disillusion, punishing himself with blisters and aching muscles, scourging himself sometimes to the point of exhaustion. Father Saturnino would surely have approved this mortifying of the flesh, he reflected ironically.

Now, however, he was finding that what had been a punishment had become a pleasure. His leg muscles had hardened, his breathing had improved. After a couple of weeks in the pueblo, in what he realised was a symbolic act, he had stopped smoking. His favourite brand of cigarettes was unavailable and the villagers mostly smoked Celtas, a cheap cigarette packed with pungent black tobacco. At first, the abrupt switch from 50 a day to none at all produced desperate cravings for food. He had taken to chewing the local grapes that were being brought in after being dried in the sun. But the craving for tobacco passed surprisingly quickly, as though it belonged to his previous existence.

He was breathing deeply but without strain as he crested a rise and saw ahead of him the blasted grimness of Piedra Negra. Although there were a few bushes around its base, the rock itself was too steep to allow any plant to flourish there. He noticed that its shape resembled a man's head, a Neanderthal head. The path snaked downwards through an olive grove and curved around the base of the crag.

"Hola!"

Scully halted and gazed about him.

"Don Carlos! Here!"

Then he saw a man gesticulating in the shade of an olive tree. He turned off the track and tramped along the hillside. He recognised the man. He had seen him in Sebastián's bar. This was Bruno, the former mayor of the village. He had been pruning the rows of vines that clung to the steep, stony hill-side and had paused to eat a snack of bread and tuna fish. His dog squatted beside, placidly watching his master.

"Have you a thirst? Try this."

Gingerly, Scully took the wineskin and directed the nozzle at his mouth. He had been caught out before, but this time most of the wine trickled down his throat, only a few drops splashing on to his shirt. It tasted like honey, warmed by sunshine.

"This is last year's," said Bruno, short of stature but with a dignified bearing and an intelligent face. He wiped his bushy moustache. "You'll never get better. Over there, in the cortijo, I've got this year's. It's still a bit cloudy, but it's about ready. Come on, I'll show you."

Without waiting for Scully's response, Bruno headed off down the hill towards a whitewashed farmhouse, the mongrel chasing at his heels. Geraniums glowed scarlet against one wall and a mule was grazing at the rear. The steel blade of a plough, hoes and other tools lay on the cortijo floor next to an open fireplace. A rickety table and two rush-covered chairs were the only furnishings.

"You sleep here?" asked Scully.

"No, no. My home is in the village. It's more comfortable in the pueblo. There's more life, and electricity. In the old days, yes, the family lived here. We used to have good times too, especially during the grape harvest, singing and dancing in the evenings, visiting the neighbours. But now, puf! nobody dances any more and the old songs are being forgotten. It's a pity."

He led the way into a second room where two large barrels stood. Picking up a length of bamboo cane, hollowed at one end to form a cup, he dipped it into a barrel. Expertly, he directed a stream of amber liquid into a glass.

"Try that," he said, with an air of pride.

Scully sipped. The same taste of sunshine and luscious grape and a heady aroma.

"Excellent!" said Scully.

Bruno nodded complacently.

"As I said, it's the best. Pure, nothing added. You can see it's not quite clear yet but I think this year's is even better than the last vintage. You don't get wine like this in your country, do you?"

Scully smiled.

"Not likely. Where I come from, they don't grow grapes. It's the wrong climate."

"Is that why you have come here, for the climate?"

"Yes, and to have a rest."

"And how did you come? From your country you have to cross the sea, don't you? Ah, by plane. I don't fancy stepping aboard one of those machines."

"Quite right," said Scully. "I don't like them myself."

"But you like Benamargo?"

"It's a pretty village."

"Yes, visitors always say that. A German came once and told me 'Señor, you are lucky, this is paradise'. That could be. I don't know. But we are very poor, and backward. And the people will not change their ideas. Look, I'll show you something."

He produced a battered card and held it out.

"See. I'm a member of the Socialist party. Now that Franco's gone we can organise and campaign, but it's difficult to get the people interested. They say politics only bring trouble. They don't realise it's the only way to get our rights, by uniting. We should form a cooperative to sell our wine and olives. We should have a library. We should have a better road. You've seen what we have now. A drop of rain and we're cut off. There's no way out, unless you walk over the sierras and the paths are hard to follow."

Bruno's enthusiasm shone through as he talked of what the pueblo should have.

"You were the mayor once, weren't you?"

Bruno shrugged.

"For a few months, yes. I had lots of plans. But there was

no money. I went to Granada to ask for money. I even went to Madrid. They promised help, but maybe that was just to get rid of me. In the end, I realised it was hopeless. A man can struggle so much."

"But it was worth trying."

"No," said Bruno harshly. "It was not worth it. A man can fight when he knows the people are behind him but not when they give him no support. Think of it! They voted for me in the first free elections in 40 years, but then they sat back and expected me to work miracles. I did work, 20 hours a day, but it was no use. By the end they turned against me, every last one of them."

Scully felt his attention drifting as the wine took effect.

"But why? What did you do wrong?"

Bruno shook his head and grimaced.

"What didn't I do wrong? I made stupid mistakes. I fooled myself that it was enough to tell the people the truth and that they would have enough sense to see through old wives' tales. Stupid, stupid. Divorce, for example. Why shouldn't a couple divorce if they throw pots at one another's heads? And abortion, why not in certain circumstances? And land reform. Why should a handful of dukes own all our sierras? So I spoke my mind and next thing the priest was attacking me from the pulpit, saying I was immoral and I don't know what. You know the cura?"

Scully nodded.

"He does seem a little, er, conservative."

Bruno chuckled without humour.

"He's more traditionalist than the Pope himself. We could never see eye to eye. After he started preaching against me, I stopped going to church. The man went beyond all limits."

The dog nuzzled up to Bruno and he stroked it absent-mindedly.

"He even said I was a Rojo. Me, a Rojo! That hurt. Wasn't it the Communists who killed my own father? I have always been against them. Anybody around here would tell you that. But the priest is a more powerful man than I am. I mean, God's on his side. The people believed him and soon they were spitting at me in the street, calling me a baby-murderer. So you see how things are. Now we've no mayor at all. Nobody wants the job, and I don't blame them."

He looked out of the farmhouse door.

"Here comes your neighbour. You're staying in the house of Dolores La Caída, aren't you?"

Marisa was approaching, walking along the path in a carefree manner. As usual, she was wearing a long-sleeved blouse and a skirt of heavy cotton which all but reached to her ankles.

"Pretty, isn't she?" said Bruno, winking at Scully.

He went outside to call to Marisa. She halted in surprise when she saw Scully, biting her lip in a vain attempt to check the blush that rose to her cheeks. She was pretty, thought Scully.

"I was going to Ramón," she said breathlessly, tossing back her glossy black mane. "Have you seen him?"

Bruno gestured towards the crag.

"His goats were over there, below Piedra Negra."

"Do you mind if I come too?" asked Scully. "I'm going that way."

Marisa masked another blush with an air of indifference.

"Why not? I'm sure Ramón would be glad to see you."

They walked on along the path, as Bruno went back to his vines.

"It must be lonely for Ramón, out here by himself all day," said Scully.

"Ramón doesn't mind being alone." She was tripping along at such a pace that Scully had difficulty keeping up. "He says that he just looks at the inside of his head and sees so many interesting things that it keeps him entertained all day."

"It sounds as though he's on LSD," said Scully, trying to joke.

Marisa glanced at him, wide-eyed.

"LSD? What's that?"

"Why, it's a drug that's supposed to expand your mind. You've never heard of it? Well, don't worry, you are probably better off knowing nothing about it."

"That sounds like my mother. She doesn't want me to know anything, except how to sew and clean the house."

"She probably believes that's important, for when you get married."

"Hmph! Who would I marry in Benamargo?"

"There must be some boys you like?"

"The boys here say such silly things. I don't think I'll ever get married."

"Don't you have a boyfriend then?"

"Of course not! And I don't want one. Caridad — she's my best friend — she has a fiancé and she's impossible. Now all she talks of is what she'll wear on her wedding day and what José said last night. She's always with José these days. I hardly see her. It's very boring."

They skirted a cavity bounded by a circular wall of rough-hewn rocks.

"That's where they make whitewash," Marisa informed him. "They light a fire inside and the rocks crack and they become blocks of whitewash."

"Do Caridad and her fellow ever go out alone, to a film say?"

"They went to Cerrogordo once, but Caridad's mother was with them."

"Then they're never alone?"

"No, no. In Cerrogordo the girls go out with their boy friends. They go to the disco. They even kiss in the street. But not in Benamargo. That would cause a real scandal. And Father Saturnino would be furious."

"Perhaps you would prefer to live in Cerrogordo?"

"It would be nice to be somewhere where nobody knew you and there was nobody to criticise. Here everybody criticises, all the time."

"Aren't you bothered that you'll be criticised for this? You could get into trouble."

"Into trouble?" Marisa stopped and looked at Scully in surprise. The sun burned hot. Only the whir of cicadas disturbed the silence.

"What do you mean?"

"Well, here we are, walking in the mountains, alone."

Marisa giggled.

"You're right. It's a scandal. But this is different. It's daytime and we're going to see Ramón and anyway..."

She paused, suddenly embarrassed.

"Yes?"

"Well, it's just that...you are old. You could be my father."

Despite himself Scully felt irritated at this ingenuous girl's remark.

"I'm not that old. I'm 38."

"Oh! I thought you were more than that."

She thinks I'm prehistoric, thought Scully, and I suppose I must seem that way to her.

"Some days I feel at least a hundred, but I didn't think it showed," he said, smiling.

Marisa scrutinised him carefully.

"Are you really an English lord?"

Scully burst out laughing.

"Who told you that?"

Once again the colour rose to Marisa's cheeks.

"It's just that everybody says you must come from an important family. They say that the only reason you came here was because the family cut off all your money and you can't afford to live anywhere else. Actually, you even have a nickname. Did you know?"

"A nickname? Tell me."

"You may be angry."

"Don't worry. I've been called plenty of names in my time."

She bit her lip. She feared that she had gone too far with this strange foreigner and gazed uncertainly at him through lowered black eyelashes.

"I'm sure they don't mean any harm but they call you 'El Desheredado'."

"The Disinherited One. That's good."

Dammit, it was true, mused Scully. He was cut off without a penny. The villagers weren't far wrong. What a depressing specimen he must appear.

As though in answer to his thoughts, Marisa said:"You

always look so sad. You must have suffered a lot."

"Yes, I've suffered, but it was probably my own fault."

"I don't want to suffer. I want to be happy always," said Marisa earnestly. "How can I be happy?"

"Just stay the way you are."

"That's easy."

"Not as easy as you think. You are young, innocent, sincere. It will change soon enough."

"Pooh! I'm going!"

Picking up her bag of woven esparto grass, she sped off, hopping as nimbly as a goat over rocks that had tumbled on to the path. More wary, Scully followed cautiously along the uneven track that wound downwards beneath the frowning buttress of Piedra Negra. Beyond, the terrain flattened out into a grassy plateau. Scattered over it were 100 or so goats, placidly grazing. They raised their heads, then scampered aside as Marisa skipped through the middle of them.

Ramón sat in the shade of a mighty carob tree, his stick hooked over one of the branches. He greeted Scully warmly. Days passed without their meeting, since Ramón had usually taken his herd off to the sierras before Scully was up and in the evenings he rarely returned home until after Scully had eaten.

"Looking after my sister, Don Carlos? That one needs a chaperon, believe me. She's too cheeky. Some fellow will take her down a peg one of these days."

Marisa responded by banging something wrapped in a cloth on Ramón's head.

"If I need a chaperon, what do you need, brother? You can't even remember your bread roll."

"So what?" scoffed Ramón. "I can manage on a bit of cheese and I had some raisins in my pocket anyway. And there's always the carobs." He picked up some brown dessicated pods which had fallen from the tree. "Ever tried these, Don Carlos? No, not the beans, the pod. Try it, it's sweet."

Scully chewed the carob pod and, indeed, it had a sweet, not disagreeable taste. Ramón chuckled.

"Don't let the neighbours see you eating them. They'll make fun. Only the mules eat them."

"That's why you're always gnawing away at them, is it?" said Marisa, and Ramón obliged her with a scowl.

"I had a message for you," she told her brother. "Guillermo called to say there was a meeting tonight of the Cofradía. He seemed to think it was important."

"All our meetings are important," retorted Ramón. "He didn't say any more? Never mind, I can guess what it's about."

Marisa was about to comment, then it seemed to Scully that Ramón flicked a warning glance in her direction and she bowed her head and said nothing.

"Why do they call it Las Animas?" asked Scully.

"Who knows? I suppose it must be something to do with souls of the departed," replied Ramón. "It dates back centuries. It's in the parish records, if you want to look."

"Are there many members?"

"Oh, about 50. Once you're in, you're in for life. So it's not often that we take a new member. And we're very strict about whom we choose. You have to take a solemn oath of loyalty and obedience to the Cofradía. It's a sacred duty and the brothers can be very severe if you break the rules."

"It's true," nodded Marisa. "Nobody disobeys Las Animas." She pulled a crust off the loaf she had brought. "It's time to eat. Give me a bit of your cheese, Ramón. I brought some green peppers, and oranges as well."

Scully shared his slices of ham and a can of paté and they sprawled in the shade, half-dozing to the hum of insects and the occasional bleating of the goats.

"There's a spring up there," said Ramón, jumping up. "Come on, I've got a cup."

They climbed the hillside to a clump of bushes where Ramón pushed through to the foot of a large boulder. Fresh water bubbled from a crack in the rock. It was cool, with a slight mineral flavor. Ramón poured the last cup of water over his forehead, then gestured to a path running around the boulder.

"That's the way to La Bruja."

"The witch? Who's she?"

"She's a crazy old hag who lives up the mountain, all by

herself. Completely nuts. But she's clever too. She knows all about herbs and how to cure diseases. Our uncle had terrible stomach pains once and the doctor could do nothing, so he went to see La Bruja. She made a potion of all sorts of stuff, garlic, fennels, ferns, or whatever. And do you know something? In 24 hours he was cured. Truly."

"I've got a cold. Maybe she can do something for me," said Scully in jest.

"She'll cure a cold in 10 seconds. But not many people want to go near her. She's so ugly, and she smells. Want to go and see?"

"Ugh!" Marisa shuddered. "I'm not sure I want to come. She's so creepy."

"If you're so scared, stay here, little sister," said Ramón impatiently. "It only takes 20 minutes. Let's go."

"But what about the goats?" queried Scully.

"They can look after themselves. They're on a good spot so they won't stray far."

Scully could barely distinguish the path as it wriggled upwards over stony ground dotted with gorse bushes and thyme and rosemary. A brown grass snake that had been sunning itself on a rock slid away at their approach and a brace of quail fluttered up in their faces before taking curving flight down the valley. Ramón moved almost at a trot, treading surely in his worn esparto sandals, Marisa determinedly keeping pace.

"Over there," said Ramón, pausing to point northwards and allow Scully to catch up. "Over there, a pass leads to Granada, the capital. You see, there's a sharp ridge that ends in a precipice. That's the Sierra de las Aguilas. And then, to the left, there's a rounded peak. That's La Corona. They call the gap between the two the Puerto de los Lobos. I suppose once there were wolves roaming around there. A path runs through the pass, but you'd never find a way. Not now. Trees and stones fell across it in a forest fire and anyway it's all overgrown since nobody uses it."

Scully shaded his eyes, gazing across the rough, broken country, an unending series of crags, chasms and scoured upthrusts of rock. Virtually nothing grew on the barren, fortress-like summits, but below, pines wedged roots into the crannies, spreading a thin mantle of green over the unforgiving landscape.

"Does anybody live up there?"

Ramón shook his head.

"Once there was an inn up near the pass, for travellers. Trains of mules used to cross all the time, bringing wheat from Granada and taking our olive oil and raisins. And there were one or two farmhouses. But they are all abandoned now. Everybody left after the Civil War when the bandoleros were in the sierras. Life was just too difficult."

"The bandoleros? Bandits? Outlaws?"

"Sure, the Reds tried to organise a rebellion and some fellows ran off to join them. You never heard of that? They wanted to overthrow Franco and bring back the Republic, but they never had a chance. They used to attack the Civil Guards, then hide in the mountains. At night they would come down to the pueblo looking for food. My father, Francisco, joined them. He was just a teenager. He told me how they were hunted down like dogs, always running, sleeping in caves, never knowing if they had been betrayed. But my father would still have escaped, because he knew every inch of these mountains, if somebody hadn't informed on him. Bastards! Some people would sell their own mothers for a piece of bread. Everybody was hungry then. Half the village went off to America, half the village!"

They topped a ridge and began traversing the other side. The path looped around until they were scaling part of Piedra Negra itself. They threaded their way past fallen rocks on the lip of a ravine. A wind, springing up from nowhere, soughed desolately about them as they edged through a narrow cleft. Ramón stopped, pointing ahead.

"It's up there. If she has seen us, she may have hidden. Keep your eyes open."

Marisa shivered and made a face.

"Where are you taking us, Ramón? This is an awful place."

Her brother laughed and pressed on. And then they saw La Bruja, watching them. Scully had been prepared for anything, but even he was impressed. She was undoubtedly one of the most bizarre creatures he had ever clapped eyes on. She was standing by a crude shelter under the rock, peering down at them fixedly. Her clothes were an assortment of cast-offs, patched and bleached. Her calloused feet and one gray shoulder were bare. Her forehead and lips appeared strangely bloated, while the facial skin was burned so dark as to be almost black, except where it had flaked into white blotches. Only the eyes were alive in this mottled wilderness. Bright and unblinking, they peered through a thicket of stringy, unwashed hair.

"Hola, Celestina!" shouted Ramón.

Two hounds, as unprepossessing as their mistress, slavered about her feet, baring their fangs at the visitors, but she remained unmoved. Odd fragments of timber and metal sheeting had been nailed haphazardly together to wall off an alcove in the rock. To one side, where water trickled from a crevice, La Bruja had created a vegetable patch. Two hens and an emaciated goat picked at a garbage pile of rotting food and old cans.

"Celestina, I've brought you a patient," cried Ramón. He grinned at the others. "She's a bit deaf. But be careful what you say. She's very proud."

The witch did not look over-enthusiastic at Ramón's news.

"Who is he? What does he want?" she demanded in a querulous tone, chewing her gums and eyeing Scully with great suspicion.

"He's sick," said Ramón. "A foreigner who needs your help."

"Everybody needs Celestina's help, but they put their faith in those idiots with their needles and their knives. Let him go to them. Why does a Frenchman bother me with his problems?"

"Your fame has spread across the seas, Celestina," said Ramón. "He has come all this way just to consult you."

"More fool he!" snapped the old woman. Then, suddenly cunning, she stole a look at Scully. "He hasn't brought any cigarettes, has he?"

Scully produced the pack of black tobacco cigarettes he carried to offer to the locals and held it out. She seized it and crouched over the embers of a fire to light one of the cigarettes. The rest of the pack disappeared inside her garments, which gave off a strong odour. She sucked greedily at the cigarette and proceeded to inspect Scully.

"Well, what is it?" she finally demanded.

"A sore throat. And I don't sleep well."

"What does the Frenchman say?" shrilled La Bruja, although Scully had spoken in Spanish.

Ramón repeated his words while Marisa stood by, wide-eyed. Muttering to herself, the woman motioned Scully closer. Shooting out a claw, she gripped his wrist with surprising strength. After holding it for about 30 seconds while staring intently into his face, she dropped it just as abruptly. Scully, Ramón and Marisa waited patiently as the woman sucked on her cigarette and grumbled to herself. At last, she spoke.

"You are troubled by something?"

Scully was willing to go along with the charade. Yes, he had been troubled.

"I don't understand this foreign stuff," said the woman irritably. "What is he saying?"

She puffed again at the cigarette, wreathing herself in smoke.

"You are strong. I see no disease in your heart or lungs. The only sickness is inside your head. Your eyes show me that. But those devils with their needles can do nothing for you."

"Come on, old one," rebuked Ramón. "Can't you give him something? He came all the way from France to see you."

"Better that he should have stayed at home." La Bruja sniffed contemptuously. "All I can do is cool his brain. Nothing more."

She shuffled off into the recesses of her ramshackle home and they could hear her rummaging around. She emerged with a bunch of leaves and withered roots.

"Here. Take these. Make an infusion and take it twice a day. That will cool your head, you'll see."

Scully eyed the unappetising bundle and asked what herbs they were.

"You don't need to know," snapped La Bruja. She picked up a stick and hurled it at the goat browsing amid the rubbish, following it up with a stream of curses. "It's Celestina's secret. Just do what I say. Have you any more cigarettes?"

When Scully admitted that he had no more, she lost interest and started poking the fire.

Scully turned to Ramón.

"Ask her why she lives here instead of in the village."

La Bruja jerked her head up sharply.

"Because they're afraid of me in the pueblo. I know too much." She leered at Scully. "They say I'm a witch, but they are the ones who are possessed, not Celestina. They are the wicked ones, not Celestina. On the day of judgment, they are the ones who will be consumed and Celestina will be safe on her mountain-top. Only Celestina La Bruja will be saved when they burn in hell."

CHAPTER TEN

"I shall have nightmares."

Marisa hunched her shoulders as though to ward off the memory. She and Scully were walking back towards the village, leaving Ramón to tend his goats.

"Uf! That woman! She really is a witch. Living like that, and saying such strange things. I thought she would change us all into frogs. Weren't you afraid, Don Carlos?"

"Afraid? No. But the smell did no good to my stomach. She needs a good wash and some proper attention. If she is loco, it's not surprising, stuck up there with only a goat to talk to. You saw how her skin was? If I'm not mistaken, she's a leper. I studied medicine for two years and I'll swear she's a leprosy case."

Marisa was aghast.

"But she touched you. That's dangerous."

Scully shook his head.

"Don't worry. Leprosy is not contagious. It can't be passed on just by a single skin contact."

Jagged storm clouds had been riding up over the sierras and, abruptly, the sun was obscured. Immediately, the tortured bulk of Piedra Negra, its summit shrouded in mist, took on a more sinister aspect.

"Marisa, why did she keep calling me 'the Frenchman'?"

"All foreigners are French to people in Benamargo. Most of the old folk don't know about other countries and all foreigners are the same to them." She quickened her pace as a wind sprang up. "Don Carlos, why did you stop studying? Didn't you want to be a doctor?"

"I did, until I discovered that I was better at other things." Yes, mused Scully, like padding expense accounts and pulling the wool over investors' eyes. "Actually, I would never have made a doctor. Everybody agreed on that. They kicked me out in the end. Ridiculous, really. All over a stupid skeleton."

"What!"

Marisa stared at him, wide-eyed.

"It was a demonstration model. They kept it in the lab. One night I got plastered and smuggled it out. It was for a dare. I disguised it by putting an overcoat and a trilby hat on it. So that passersby would think it was just somebody suffering a severe case of malnutrition."

Marisa had stopped and was examining Scully, uncertain whether he was joking or not.

"All would have been okay, if it hadn't been for the dean's wife, silly bitch. Trust her to have a breakdown."

"But what did you do to her?"

"Nothing, nothing at all. She was just a rather nervous type, neurotic in fact. When she came home late and discovered this bag of bones in the marital bed, well, she flipped. The dean blew his top. And that was the end of my medical career, luckily for all."

Marisa let out peals of laughter.

"Oh, por Dios, the poor thing! A skeleton in her bed. That is too much. I never thought you would do things like that, Don Carlos. I mean, you always seem so serious."

Scully laughed shortly.

"Believe it or not, I used to be quite a jokey fellow. But that was a long time ago." He dodged a lizard as it scurried off the track. "Marisa, do you mind doing me a very big favour?"

She glanced at him doubtfully.

"Well, yes, if I can."

"Please stop calling me Don Carlos. I am not a duke or an earl, or anything like that. Just call me Carlos, all right?"

"But you're a grown-up. And you're a guest."

"I'm plain old Carlos, okay? And if you go on calling me Don Carlos, I shall have to call you Doña María."

Marisa giggled.

"Oh yes, that sounds marvellous. Doña María, duchess of Benamargo. And everybody will have to kiss my hand and bow to me."

A large drop of rain splashed on Scully's forehead and, looking up, he saw that the storm had arrived. Black clouds were sweeping over the crests of the ridges and gusts of wind tore at the vines and olive trees. Marisa let out a cry and set off at a run, hair flying out behind her. Scully slipped and tripped over the rocks on the path as he tried to keep up. He swiftly realised he was not quite as fit as he had imagined that morning. His legs were complaining painfully as they passed Bruno's farmhouse and headed up a rise overlooking the village.

A thunder-clap split the heavens and reverberated along the valley like artillery fire, as the rain came down in a grey curtain. In seconds, Scully was soaked to the skin, the intensity of the squall taking him by surprise. Lancing rain stung him and blinded him, bouncing off the path and quickly converting it into a minor torrent. The hot, parched earth steamed a welcome. Starved of water since spring, it had been burned during the long summer months by a fierce, sub-tropical sun until it cracked and powdered. The drought had withered leaves until they disintegrated at a touch, shrivelled the grapes and tomatoes, turned wells to empty, echoing chambers. Now, the earth sucked greedily at this refreshment while thunder and lightning joined in a symphony of celebration.

Cursing, Scully stumbled on. If that old witch was so damned clever, why had she not warned them it was going to rain? This downpour would cool his brain better than any of her evil brews.

Muddy water surged across the path, forcing him to leap from rock to rock. He paused to wipe his eyes and catch his breath.

"Don Carlos! Don Carlos!"

The cry came from somewhere out of the driving rain.

"Here! Here! Quick!"

Then he distinguished the outline of a low hut and a blurred, girlish figure waving from the door. He veered off the path and, slipping and sliding, gained the refuge. Marisa greeted him, laughing, raindrops in her tangled hair. In the gloom Scully made out some stalls and a floor covered with straw and animal droppings. Rain drummed down on the tin roof like a marching army.

"Better than a palace."

"Ramón keeps the goats here," said Marisa. "He milks them and either Bruno or one of the neighbours brings the churns back to the pueblo on their mule. Oh!" She pointed with concern. "You cut yourself."

Blood was leaking from a gash on Scully's forearm. He raised his arm and licked the wound.

"I slipped on the path. It's nothing. I'll get it fixed once we're home."

"But it's bleeding. Wait, I have a handkerchief."

Despite Scully's protests, she proceeded to staunch the blood with a corner of the handkerchief. Then she began wrapping the cloth around his arm as a bandage. Scully watched her air of concentration and noticed the gentleness with which she held his arm. He felt a thickening in his throat. He tried to speak, but no words came.

"There it is," said Marisa, deftly tying the ends of the handkerchief. "Mama will have some ointment for it. Does it hurt?"

The dark eyes scanned his face anxiously. Scully felt her closeness and her tenderness. Involuntarily, or so he told himself afterwards, he kissed her forehead. Surprised, Marisa coloured, drew back, then smiled, closed her eyes and tilted her head. Scully gazed at her innocent beauty and hesitated for long moments, the drumbeat of the rain hammering into his skull. He brushed his lips over the delicate nose before kissing her firmly on the lips. Marisa opened her eyes and gazed into his.

"Carlos!"

She pulled him closer and returned the kiss, with unexpected passion. She opened her lips to his, filling his mouth with rose blossom and honey, making the moment last, until Scully responded, sensing inside himself the stirring of something he had thought destroyed, gone for ever. Marisa's kisses tasted of spring. They were generous and giving. He thought of Amelia and her bitter-sweet spinster lips clinging to his as though to a life-raft. He squeezed Marisa's waist.

"Maybe it would be safer if I stayed Don Carlos," he said.

"Was it all right?"

"It was beautiful."

"You must have kissed thousands of girls."

"Thousands. But none like you. You're so tender, so fresh." Scully smiled. "And how about me? Was I okay?"

Marisa pouted mischievously.

"All right. Quite interesting, in fact."

"Interesting? That's all? Well, I suppose I can't compete with the lads of the village. I expect you've kissed them all."

"Of course. You don't think I'm totally ignorant."

"Ah, a woman of experience."

Marisa blushed and rested her head against Scully's chest.

"To tell the truth, this was the first time in my whole life. Isn't that awful? Seventeen, and no boy ever kissed me. Please don't laugh at me. You could tell, couldn't you?"

"That it was the first time? No way. I thought you must be very experienced. You kissed like...like an angel."

"Honestly?" She giggled. "Oh, Carlos, did you really think I was experienced? Truly?" Then she frowned. "Is it wrong what we did? I mean, we're not engaged, or anything."

"You don't have to be engaged to kiss, Marisa. Even so," He assumed a serious air. "I somehow don't think your mother would approve."

Marisa put a hand to her mouth.

"Oh, you wouldn't tell her?"

"Why should I? It's a private thing, between us."

"Yes, private."

She studied his face. It was a long time since a woman had looked at Scully with that mixture of trust and desire. It both pleased him and produced a twinge of alarm. He was not certain that he needed this sort of devotion, not when it came from the landlady's daughter. Marisa stroked his brow.

"We could try once more," she whispered.

"We could."

This time was not like their first embrace. He lightly kissed her closed eyes, caressed her cheeks, held her tightly as he brought his lips to hers and thrust his tongue into the sweetness of her mouth. She sighed and wriggled. But it was not the same. He found he was coldly observing himself, a cynical witness to the technical skill of Charles Scully. Cocktail party tricks were fine for cocktail party flirtations, for cocktail party people. But now he held innocence in his arms.

Angry at himself, he kissed Marisa brutally, as though bruising her would salve his conscience. She gasped and pushed him away, hurt and shocked. Unable to explain his emotions, even to himself, Scully turned and gazed out at the driving rain.

"We have to get back to the village."

His voice was bleak and empty. Marisa did not answer. Instead, she squatted down against a wall, looking at Scully in puzzled fashion.

"Are you coming? Marisa?"

"No, the rain is too heavy. We must wait until it lets up. It won't be long."

"I can't wait. I'm going now."

The words came out harshly, as though uttered by somebody else. Marisa was pale, frightened.

"Marisa?"

"I'll wait for Ramón."

"All right. I'm going. Until later."

He plunged into the deluge, his head bursting. He ran recklessly along the waterlogged path, stumbling and almost falling, rain drops coursing down his face and mingling with what could have been tears.

ELEVEN

When Scully awoke next morning, a cement mixer was grinding away inside his head and somebody had stuffed his mouth with sawdust and ashes. Fire burned in his throat. He felt more than a little unwell. Groaning, he picked up the jug of water on the table and, inclining his head over the bowl, poured coolness over himself. He towelled himself and staggered on to the terrace, sucking in air.

During the night, the rain had ceased, and a wind had swept away the clouds, burnishing the whole valley. The rain had scrubbed the air of dust so that the white cubes of houses, the olive trees, the craggy slopes leapt fresh and sharp to the eye. Across the valley somebody was chopping wood and the regular thwack of axe meeting timber travelled clearly to the pueblo. A man passed by in the street, singing cheerful coplas.

It was a magnificent day, one to savour. Not for Scully, however. Blinded by the sun, he reeled back inside, the sound of the chopping hammering at his skull. The physical pain over-ruled all else, crushing all thought. He felt almost grateful to that unknown axeman. Somehow he dressed and went down. There was no breakfast awaiting him, so he knocked on Dolores's door and entered. She paused from rattling the pans in the kitchen to eye him a little coldly.

"Don Carlos, I knocked on your door earlier but there was no reply."

"Señora, is there the possibility of a cup of coffee?"

She sniffed, but motioned him to sit down. At that moment Marisa appeared. She halted abruptly when she saw Scully, then lowered her gaze and walked swiftly into the kitchen. Dolores poured out some coffee, studied Scully intently, her lips pursed, then retired to the kitchen. He heard her conversing with Marisa, about flowers they must buy to take to the cemetery. Marisa replied in muted tones.

This morning Scully did not care about the burnt barley flavour. He gulped the black liquid, content only that it was hot. Dimly, despite himself, he recalled the previous night, returning to the village soaked and near-exhausted, ordering a brandy in Sebastián's bar, followed by many more. There had been half understood conversations with other clients, boisterous arguments, singing, more drinks. He recalled Felipe the mailman arm-wrestling on the counter with Cristóbal the lottery ticket-seller. He remembered being lectured on life's vital truths by a gnome who claimed to be the oldest man in Benamargo. It all dissolved into a blur of faces and lights, until somebody had been yelling into his face: "Don Carlos, it's time to go home." He had sat on somebody's front step for a time, then bounced off whitewashed walls that miraculously had directed him to his bed.

Scully took one more swig of the black brew and shuddered. Disgusting stuff. Sebastián, he remembered, had a coffee machine. Jowly face unshaven, the barkeeper was sitting at a table, reading a three-day-old newspaper. Scully recognised his shirt as one recognises an old friend. A glance at the neckband confirmed that it was the same one Sebastián always wore.

"Coffee, Don Carlos?" Sebastián tried to focus blood-shot eyes on him. "The machine will take time to warm up. Here, have an anise while you're waiting."

He went back to reading his paper.

When Sebastián served the coffee, he peered closely at Scully.

"Hombre, what you need is a sol y sombra."

"What the devil's that?"

The bar-owner winked.

"Sun and shade. Works wonders."

He mixed generous servings of brandy and anise, one for himself and another for his customer. Scully shrugged. He finished the drink in one and immediately felt better. He ordered another. Caffeine and alcohol coursed through his body, numbing the nerve-ends satisfyingly. The morning, if not exactly rose-coloured, had begun to improve. The headache had gone and he no longer tasted ashes. He grinned, floating pleasantly as he pushed his glass forward for another fix. Sebastián grinned back, proposing a toast.

"Health, money and strength in your flies!"

"Health, money and strength!" echoed Scully. God, he was beginning to feel good. In fact, he felt bloody good. Old prissy-mouthed Dolores and her giggling daughter could go screw themselves, and so could the priest and that pedantic son-of-a-bitch the schoolteacher and his frustrated sister, stupid bastards the lot of them, shit, he felt good, fuck 'em all. And as for Stella and that black-enamelled bastard Klease, well, they could screw themselves silly for all he cared. A lot of good it might do them, a lot of good. Klease! Christ, the very thought of that asshole! Hell, he needed another drink. Another of those sol y sombras or whatever they called them. He gestured at Sebastián, who swiftly obliged.

"Are you going to the cemetery, Don Carlos?"

"The cemetery? Do they serve drinks there? Why the hell should I go to the cemetery? I'm not dead yet, y'know, though I may look it. Ha, ha, I may look it."

He chuckled. That was good. Not dead yet, though he probably looked it. Not dead yet.

"It's the Day of the Saints. Everybody goes to the cemetery to lay flowers on the family grave. Didn't you know? They clean up the tombstone and light candles. Everybody will be there this evening. It's a sight to see, truly."

"Sounds bloody depressing to me," muttered Scully. "Don't much go for tombstones. Think I'll stay right here. Best place in town."

"That's true. You'll hear more commonsense in this bar than anywhere else, and that includes the church and the school." A thought struck Sebastián. "Hey, is that right you've taken up with the schoolteacher?"

"I've talked with him, sure. Why do you ask?"

Sebastián spread his hands and stuck his tongue in one cheek. It was a vain attempt to look innocent.

"Oh, nothing important. But, you're a man of the world,

Don Carlos, what do you reckon of Don Baldomero?"

"He's a cultivated man."

"Ah, cultivated, yes, he is that. Very cultivated. Knows more than the rest of us put together, too much maybe."

Sebastián closed one eye and rubbed a finger against his nose.

"Too much? How do you mean?"

"But, hombre, don't you know?" Sebastián beckoned Scully closer and, even though the bar was deserted, put his lips to his ear. Stale breath engulfed Scully. "They say he likes small boys."

"May God strike me down if it's not true," said Sebastián, as Scully gazed at him in a mixture of bleary disbelief and disgust. "Why do you think he came here, if he is so clever? Why, eh? Because they kicked him out of some fancy school up north. He couldn't get a job, not anywhere, except here, in Benamargo. We hadn't had a teacher for two years. They were going to close the school for good unless we found one. So we ended up with this son of a whore."

"But, if he was guilty of what you say, aren't people worried about his looking after their children?"

Sebastián looked sly, not too difficult a task for him, reflected Scully.

"Benamargo is his last chance. He knows that and we know that. If we kick him out, he has nowhere else to go. And anyway what I told you is confidential, just to put you in the picture. I'm not one to spread gossip, heavens no. Mind, I'm not saying that he has actually, you know, fiddled with young kids, not here anyway. It would be more than his life's worth, understand?"

"The people must be suspicious of him."

"Ha! You could say that. Don Baldomero is a bit of a joke, to tell the truth, him with his high-and-mighty ways when we all know what he really is. Why, he'll hardly speak to you, he thinks he's so superior. He's got a nickname, you know, El Elegido, the Chosen One. The way he struts about you'd think he was one of the 12 apostles. And Juanito, you've met him, the carrier, he's composed all sorts of coplas about him. They'd make you die laughing."

Two villagers who had entered the bar nodded in agreement.

"El Elegido? He's nothing but a stuck-up fascist," said one, a sharp-featured man with a limp. "They say he got the job through Don Ernesto, he who owns half the sierras. Trust him to be friends with the big noise. You won't see Don Ernesto. He lives in Granada. He only comes here to go hunting."

"Talking about nicknames," put in Scully. "Why do they call my Dolores 'La Caída'?"

Sebastián laughed and indicated the man with the limp.

"You better ask Antonio. She's his cousin."

Antonio had strange eyes. He appeared to be looking over Scully's shoulder as he addressed him. And then Scully realised that one of the eyes was of glass.

"La Caída? The Fallen One? Don't get the wrong idea. She's a very honourable woman, very religious. She got the name on her wedding day, if you want to know. Coming down the church steps, what did she do but trip up and fall head over heels. Right to the bottom. From that day on, they called her La Caída."

"And her husband? Is it long since he died?"

"Died? Well, in a manner of speaking I suppose you could say he was dead. Francisco was a wild one, always in trouble. He ran off to join the guerrillas trying to start a rebellion against Franco after the Civil War. It was hopeless, of course. The soldiers and the Civil Guard used to chase them from dawn to dusk.

"Bad times," muttered Sebastián. "Bad times. They would creep down at night to the village or the farmhouses to get food. You hadn't much choice but to give them something, but if the Civil Guard found out they would beat the shit out of you. You weren't safe from either side. And the hunger! Nothing but potatoes and chick peas to eat. Once I took a fig off one of Don Ernesto's trees and the guards caught me and beat me until I could hardly walk. Just for one fig! Hombre, those were bad times."

The others nodded.

"But what happened to Francisco?"

Sebastián shrugged and began washing glasses behind the counter.

"They got him in the end," said Antonio. "They got them all. And they nearly all died."

His companion, a slight man whose eyes darted about like a ferret's, laughed sardonically.

"Shot while escaping. That was often the way it happened. A lot of folk here lost a son or a husband. There was treachery too. Betrayals and double-crosses. Just like in any war."

"Exactly," said Antonio. "That's how they got Francisco. He came down to the pueblo one night for food. Perhaps he wanted to see Dolores as well. She was his novia, his promised one, understand? Well, a squealer had given him away and they were waiting for him. You could say he was one of the lucky ones. They knocked him about a bit but he survived. They sent him to jail. When he came back, he seemed to settle down. He married Dolores and managed to scratch a living. But it couldn't last. He wasn't the settling type. He got into all sorts of scrapes and then he just disappeared. They say he went to Barcelona. Anyway, that left his wife on her own with two children."

"But she's a strong woman, La Caída," put in Sebastián. "She managed. She always said that her fall was an omen. And maybe she's right. It was a bad marriage, right enough."

They all gazed moodily into their glasses for a time.

"I lost my brother," said Antonio. "They called the outlaws Reds, but not all of them were. Not Alvaro."

"Of course not," agreed his friend, "But we can't forget what those Reds did. We all paid for it. They put a curse on this village."

"There were terrible things done on both sides," murmured Sebastián, injecting some barman's diplomacy.

"That's true. But here, in Benamargo..." The ferrety man shook his head. "I mean, I never had much time for the clerics. They used to hobnob with the rich ones and get girls in the family way. They always had plenty on their table when we hardly had two cents to rub together. All the same, what happened, I mean, it was a barbarity, hombre, a barbarity."

"And how would you remember?" demanded Antonio, his one good eye already bloodshot after two glasses of brandy.

"Cojones! I remember! I was only a kid, true. But you don't think you could forget something like that. It's burned on my memory, I swear to God."

"Hey!" Sebastián beckoned them to the doorway. "Look. Ay, what shapes! What beauties!"

The others crowded to the door, too. Two young girls were passing, their arms full of white chrysanthemums. Although they were modestly dressed, their youthful freshness, the grace of their movements brought whistles of admiration from Sebastián and his clients.

"Blessed be the day that your mother gave birth to you! How pretty you are!" called Sebastián.

Both girls blushed intensely, biting their lips as though to stifle any giggles as they tripped past. Scully, peering blearily from the depths of the bar, realised that one of the girls was Marisa. Nose tilted proudly up, she was resisting the temptation to look around. Sebastián elbowed him.

"What luck you have! Seeing that vision every day. It's enough to make any man have evil thoughts."

Scully scowled.

"I don't need to rob cradles."

The barman only laughed.

"I thought you were going to say you were married. Juanito has at least three wives, but it doesn't hold him back." He sighed. "There's a fellow living in paradise. He carries stuff to and fro from the coast so he has plenty of opportunity. He has one of those foreign pieces down there, a Dane he says, and she'll do anything for him. Then he's got another one in Cerrogordo. That's why he always looks shagged out. You'll recognise Juanito when you see him, for sure. He's a real macho."

Scully drank again. His brief period of reckless elation had gone. The ill humour that had erupted in response to Sebastián's leers had surprised him. Why should he care?

He was not involved with anybody. An emotional attachment was the last thing he needed, especially in this village. He did not need righteous fathers nor furious brothers hunting him with shotguns. He did not need anybody, least of all a naive teenager mooning over first kisses. He did not need it.

"What was that, Don Carlos?"

Scully started, realising he had spoken aloud.

"I said 'Another brandy'."

Oblivion closed in. Scully had no recall of staggering back to the house and slipping into unconsciousness. When he awakened, it was already dark. His mouth tasted even fouler than before and his head and throat ached. He drank several tumblerfuls of water. Then he came across the herbs given him by Celestina. He shrugged. Anything was worth a try. He found a pot and set the bunch to stew over the solitary gas-ring. Soon a pungent, sweetish smell pervaded the house. He stirred the liquid. It looked decidedly evil. But Scully was past caring. He strained some into a glass and, closing his eyes, gulped it down.

Jesus! It tasted worse than it looked. Cursing La Bruja, he tossed the rest down the drain and went in search of air. He lurched towards the church square. A slight breeze stirred the leaves of a lofty eucalypt and bats were fluttering in and out of the light from a street lamp. Scully slumped on to a low wall. After a while he noticed that his head no longer ached. And the burning sensation in his throat had eased. He felt restored. Maybe Celestina was not so crazy after all!

At that moment, he became aware of a dull thumping. He listened intently, but could not detect its source. Then the noise grew stronger, sharper, and he saw that a side door in the church had opened. Figures were emerging and he remembered that it was All Saints' Day. Presumably a service had just finished, but there was none of the usual hum of conversation, only the insistent throb of a drum.

Peering across the plaza, Scully could make out 20 to 30 people, all garbed in black. They were pairing off under the command of their leader, who held an oil lamp. By its light

Scully saw that he and the others all had their features concealed by tall, conical hoods in the same style favoured by the Ku Klux Klan. He recalled a long-ago visit to Seville at Easter, when a mixture of religious fervour and pagan revelry swamped the city. Members of the brotherhoods who accompanied the images of Christ and the Virgin through the streets wore the same medieval costumes. He had thought the fancy dress only came out during Holy Week, but Benamargo, it seemed, had its own customs.

The man carrying the lamp, distinguished from the others by his bulk and the white cross blazoned on his tunic, led the way across the plaza. The others followed, the long staves they carried click-clicking on the cobbles. At the rear, the drummer kept up a steady, funereal beat as the strange procession marched off down the main street. Both curious and vaguely disturbed, Scully began to follow. Since most of the villagers had apparently gone to the cemetery to pay respect to the departed, the street was deserted. There was only the hooded group shuffling along to the monotonous rhythm of the drum and the click of the staves, a procession of silent black phantoms. It occurred to Scully that he was a privileged witness to a scene that had endured down the centuries, a scene straight out of Spain's past when the Inquisition struck terror into the heart of anybody judged a heretic.

After several sharp curves, the main street petered out at the point where mule and goat sheds marked the beginning of irrigated farmland. A track wound upwards past terraced fields to the cemetery, planted on a knoll.

Lights glowed from the cemetery which was surrounded by a high wall and shaded by mighty cypress trees. The hooded marchers headed towards it at a steady pace, as Scully trailed about 50 yards behind. When he reached the cemetery entrance, he saw that the procession had entered a small chapel just inside the gate. The marchers had taken up position in the pews, heads bowed in silent prayer, while the leader stood before the altar on which he had deposited the lamp. A chalice and an engraved silver bowl stood on a side table, as though ready for Mass.

None of the other villagers were in the chapel. They were moving about amid the tombs, most of which consisted of narrow niches in the cemetery walls. Some had brought ladders to reach the higher levels. A candle or an oil lamp burned before many of the plaques that sealed the niches. Some women were wiping down the plaques or arranging large bunches of chrysanthemums in plastic or earthen-ware containers. Others knelt in prayer. But most of the villagers stood about in groups, chatting together. Several small children played amid the tombstones.

Scully noticed Marisa and her mother, heads bowed, be-fore one of the niches. Carmencita, the vixen of a shop-keeper, was holding court to a coven of women. Several held scarves over their mouths, as though to ward off the evil humours of the night. Sebastián treated him to a wink. The bar-owner was almost unrecognisable. He had changed his working shirt for an impeccable, freshly-ironed one and had donned what must have been his wedding suit. He was even wearing a black tie. He was listening obediently to the words of a dumpy, gray-haired woman with a severe mouth.

Reading the inscriptions on some of the niches, Scully could guess at a little of the village's recent history. One plaque, dated 1898, paid homage to an 18-year-old who had died at sea in the Caribbean in the service of his country, presumably a victim of the war with the United States that ended with Spain shorn of two prize colonial possessions, Cuba and the Philippines. He saw that in the early 1900s many children had not lived beyond their first or second birthday, and around 1915 some sort of plague was blamed for the death of several men and women in their prime.

A slot in the wall was the final fate of Benamargo's inhab-itants, except for the members of one family. They enjoyed eternal peace in an elaborate marble mausoleum. While some graves bore no more than the roughly painted names of the dead, this monument carried finely chiselled classical allusions and biblical quotations. It was clearly the resting place of the ruling dynasty, of Don Ernesto, owner of all the sierras, and his relatives. The dates went back 200 years and the same names occurred and recurred. Next to this pantheon stood a solitary iron cross. Scully bent to read the words carved on the granite base.

The light of a candle just enabled him to make out: "To the memory of Father Salvador Torres, priest of Benamargo from 1922 to 1936, who died a martyr at the hands of the Marxist hordes when, with great valour, he tried to protect the House of God. Glory to his name. Rest in peace."

"We have a bloody history, as you can see."

Bruno stood there, watching Scully with a wry smile on his lips.

"What a pueblo! When I think of what has happened here in my lifetime! And before that... Uf!"

"What happened to the priest?"

"Better not to ask. I was too young to know anything about it. But I heard stories. It was a shocking thing, I know that."

"But why?" asked Scully.

Bruno shrugged.

"Man's strongest emotion. Hate. When it takes over, we're no better than animals. Worse, I suppose. Animals don't kill for greed, or vengeance." He sighed. "Anyway, it was a long time ago."

"Yes, long enough."

"Things have changed. Spain was a different country before the Civil War. Hardly anybody in a village like this could read a newspaper. We knew nothing. There was just us, the poor scraping a living, and the caciques, the landlords, the fat ones. We were the slaves. But kids get an education now and the caciques don't get it all their own way any longer. It's all changed. Progress, you see. It takes time and the old-timers are set in their ways, but the youngsters won't be content with things as they are. They'll make this a better place, you'll see. Especially now that Franco's gone."

They wandered through the cemetery. A brisker wind had brought cooler air down the valley, fanning the candles and oil lamps. Near the entrance huddled members of the hooded brotherhood, as though in a football scrum. Scully nodded towards them.

"Who are they, Bruno?"

"You've heard of the Cofradía de Las Animas? Well, that's them. They always make a big thing of this particular night. They hold a Mass and stand vigil over the graves all night." Bruno examined one of the niches. "My grandfather lies here. Well, I have plenty of work tomorrow. I'm off home. Are you coming, Don Carlos?"

Bruno and Scully walked back together down the track. In the moonlight the flat, whitewashed terraces scattered among the tiled roofs of the village looked like polished stones and the leaves of the olive trees shimmered like silver coins. With the dwellings nestling about the church tower, the village dreamed snugly on its ridge.

"I live down here," said Bruno, indicating a side-street. "Good night, Don Carlos."

They shook hands and Scully continued on his way. But he had only taken a few steps when he heard a sharp cry. He doubled back quickly, rounded the corner and came upon Bruno standing as though transfixed.

"What is it?" demanded Scully.

The stocky farmer was unable to speak. He lifted an arm and pointed. The moon was bright enough for Scully to make out something suspended against the wall. It was Bruno's dog, hanging from a beam. Its coat was matted with blood and its teeth were set in a death snarl.

"Why? What does it mean?"

Bruno did not answer. He was trembling violently.

"Who would do this?" demanded Scully.

"The swine!" Bruno sank down on his doorstep and put his head in his hands. "Swine! They haven't the guts to face me. But to do this! Cowards! Cowards!"

Scully gripped his shoulder.

"But, for god's sake, man, who?"

Bruno lifted his head and gazed at him with a tortured expression.

"You don't know?" He was about to say more, but stopped himself. "Count yourself lucky. If you were from Benamargo, you would not need to ask."

CHAPTER TWELVE

Since his last encounter with Amelia at the wedding, Scully had contrived to avoid her. But on a November Sunday he rounded a corner and bumped straight into her. They stood smiling at one another, she with obvious pleasure, Scully in an attempt to conceal his embarrassment.

"Oh, Carlos." She was flustered. "How are you? I haven't seen you around."

"I've been doing lots of walking."

"But why haven't you called?"

"I didn't want to trouble you."

She studied Scully earnestly.

"Trouble? Please, we like your company."

Scully pondered how he could tell her he just did not want to see her.

"Amelia, it's not that I don't want to see you. You're a charming person. And I like your brother. And the food at your house is marvellous. But I have my own problems and I don't want to bother you with them." He was getting rusty. The lies came lamely, unconvincingly. "When I'm feeling low, I can be rather depressing company."

"But Carlos, that's what friends are for. To help out. You must call whenever you want." She was girlishly eager. "I missed you, Carlos."

"Well, I missed you too, Amelia."

"You're not going to church? I'm on my way. Oh, but of course, you don't believe in the power of prayer."

"I'm sure it works sometimes," said Scully with a smile. "I'll walk you there."

The golden light of late autumn threw into relief the details of the street, the balconies and barred windows, crumbling stonework over the doorways, the uneven paving-stones, the deep lines in the faces of the old, shrouded women who watched and commented. Amelia walked alongside Scully with a prouder tilt to her head, occasionally greeting a villager. The church bell was tolling and Scully could see Dolores and Marisa heading in the same direction, both in black with scarves about their heads.

"All the women seem to be going but where are the men?" he queried.

"The men find reasons not to go. They have to work in the fields. The animals have to be attended to. They're getting ready to pick the olives. I think that's the way it is in most of these villages," said Amelia.

They halted at the church steps. Amelia smiled again.

"You're coming for lunch today, aren't you? After the service? Baldomero will be so glad to see you."

Scully hesitated. She touched his arm. Her eyes were pleading.

"Please! You'll be welcome."

Reluctantly, he nodded.

"All right. After the service. Thank you."

The bell had stopped ringing and Amelia hurried up the steps. Scully circled the plaza, avoiding Pepe, a retarded youth with a Neanderthal aspect to his features, who was playing an invisible bull. He stood defiantly with his body arched and hips thrust forward, while waving a rag at the end of a stick.

"Olé!" cried a mocking group of children, as Pepe spun and capered, missing death by centimetres from the horns only he could see. Drunk with imagined glory, Pepe leered and laughed, then dropped to his knees to challenge his adversary once more.

"Pepe! Pepe!" chorussed the gallery. "Torero! Torero! What balls you have!"

From the church rang out the deep baritone of the priest's voice followed by the chanted responses. Scully decided to drift inside with the latecomers. Most of the seats were occupied by women, except for a small male group near the front, among whom he noticed Ramón and Antonio, the one-eyed cousin of Dolores. Scully joined those standing at the rear. Somebody shooed out a stray dog which had wandered in. A baby was bawling, but it was no competition for Father Saturnino. Scully was surprised to note that the rites were being conducted in Latin. He had thought that Catholic services were conducted in the language of the country. Was not that one of the reforms introduced by Pope John? He struggled to remember. It had been so long since he had heard the Catholic liturgy or any other.

"There are those among us..."

Day-dreaming, Scully refocused his attention on the priest, who had switched to Spanish and was pacing up and down before the altar.

"There are those among us who are deaf to the word of our Lord. They can put forward no plea of ignorance for they know his teachings, yet they choose deliberately to go against Him. Even worse. Not only do they reject the church by their own actions but they incite others to follow their example."

Saturnino's thunder quelled all disturbance in the church. He gazed grimly about him.

"It is easy enough to fall into the trap. Just a few days ago I witnessed something that testified to the weakness that lurks within us, in this village. One of our daughters appeared in a public place, dressed in an immodest manner. When I remonstrated with her over this flagrant affront to decency, what was her reply? She told me that it was 'the latest fashion'. The latest fashion! If that is the fashion, then Lord help us all! Daughter, have you no shame? Don't you see the dangerous path that you are treading?"

The priest was gazing fiercely at one particular pew midway down the church and the whole congregation craned to catch a glimpse of the culprit. From the back, Scully could only see that one of the village girls appeared to be the object of the priest's wrath. Her head was bowed as Saturnino stormed on.

"A single brazen act may seem unimportant. But remember, one small sin makes it so much easier to commit the next, and the next. One more cobblestone is laid on that terrible road that leads to damnation. Look at the world today and you will see where tiny acts can lead. Everywhere we look there is strife, between nations, between neighbours, between man and woman. Innocence has been lost. Evil is winning."

Scully stared beyond the priest, at the damp patches on the whitewashed walls and at the heavy cross watching over the scene. The timber was chipped and battered, stained black in patches. There were holes where nails had once secured the image of Christ.

"...avarice, lust, hate. They rule in this world where even the holy sacrament of matrimony is spat upon and even an unborn child, yes, an innocent unborn babe, can be sentenced to death."

Terrible in his anger and scorn, Father Saturnino thumped a weighty fist into his palm.

"And there are those who call this progress. There are those in Benamargo who preach this progress. Adultery, divorce, the murder of the unborn — they tell us that is progress. They would permit our young to read immoral literature and to watch pornographic films. Because that is progress. They would allow our womenfolk to parade like strumpets. Because they say — and they know best — they say that is progress."

Father Saturnino paused, lowered his head and covered his face with his hands, as though overcome by the follies of the world. When he raised his head, his face wore an expression of profound sadness and he spoke in barely a whisper, but a whisper that reached all four corners of the church.

"Progress, they say. They have the effrontery to tell us that that is progress. Well, do you know what I say?" His voice rose, climbing to a crescendo. "Do you know what I say? Better that we should live in poverty and ignorance if that is what progress means. Better to do without the trappings of this wonderful civilisation, if progress means taking Satan as our brother and flouting the Holy Word..."

Scully edged outside. The sun was blazing down and he walked across to the edge of the plaza, gratefully inhaling the air. He stared out at the pristine beauty of the mountains and wondered at the blueness of the sky and shook himself. Even out here, even though this was not his church and not his village, he felt the power of the priest's words and will. He strode away, into the countryside.

When he arrived at the schoolteacher's house for lunch, Amelia welcomed him inside.

"Baldomero will be back soon. He has gone to see one of the parents." She led the way to the living room. "Would you like a sherry?"

As she handed him the drink, their eyes met, but Amelia swiftly looked away and in a distracted fashion began clearing away books and papers that drifted over chairs and floor.

"Is anything the matter, Amelia?"

"Not at all. Why should there be?"

But her voice betrayed her. She turned towards him. She clenched a bunch of withered flowers and he could see the white of her knuckles.

"You didn't come...these past weeks."

"Well, I explained," said Scully, pretending to examine his sherry.

"Not once! I waited, but you didn't come. Perhaps it was stupid of me. Reading too much into things." Scully remained silent. "Was it my fault? Because of what happened, you know, at the wedding?"

"At the wedding? Don't be silly, Amelia. Why should that make any difference?"

Amelia's shoulders sagged.

"Yes, why should it? You're right."

"We just acted like schoolkids, didn't we?" Scully kept his voice cool, dispassionate. "Nothing to worry teacher."

The mocking tone of his last words stung Amelia. Spots of colour flamed on her pallid cheeks and she flung the flowers to the floor.

"So that's it? For you it's just a joke, Carlos. A woman kisses you and it's nothing, nothing!"

"Please, Amelia —"

"Nothing!" She looked as though she would strike him. "Don't you feel anything? Don't you care about my emotions? Or am I just somebody you can play games with?"

Her bitterness provoked a response from Scully.

"No games, Amelia." Scully sighed. "Please understand. You're a fine person, but right now I don't need your kisses. I don't want entanglements."

"You think I'm just a silly spinster, don't you? Desperate for a man!" Amelia was sobbing. "You don't even think of me as a woman, with all a woman's feelings."

"I'm sure you're a woman. Amelia," said Scully quietly, wondering how the devil he was going to extricate himself.

"You! You don't even know what a woman is!" She was quivering with fury, tears splashing, arms waving wildly. "I'll show you what a woman is, you Englishman! I'll show you!"

She tore at her blouse and, before Scully could make a move, had ripped it open to the waist.

"For god's sake!" he groaned.

She was clawing at her bra, a pink construction embroidered with rosebuds. Then the hook came undone and her breasts tumbled free before Scully's horrified gaze.

"Do you see? Am I not a woman too? Carlos, Carlos, don't you see?"

He had to admit that there was considerably more to the schoolmaster's sister than he had imagined. She held out her arms to him. Scully tried to draw back, but she clutched at his sleeve, pulling him into her bosom. She smiled.

"You see now. Oh Carlos, I've dreamed of this, ever since we first touched. God help me, but I wanted you all these weeks."

"Father Saturnino isn't going to like this," muttered Scully weakly.

Amelia did not seem to hear. Her eyes were shining and she stared at Scully with what he feared was adoration.

"God help me!" she cried.

"And me too," he echoed.

He struggled in her embrace and his hand came into contact with naked flesh. He found himself kneading those spinster breasts that swelled and burned at his touch. Amelia gasped and sucked his mouth into hers. Their thighs collided and, despite himself, Scully felt a surge of desire.

Amelia breathed faster. She pulled him towards the couch. Somehow her skirt had come loose and fallen to the floor. She was pulling off a corset, of a style that Scully thought had gone out with his grandmother. She dragged him down on top of her and Scully's nostrils were filled with lust and lavender. His hand plunged between boney embankments.

"Amelia!"

They rocked on the couch as though at sea.

"Amelia! Where are you?"

Scully and Amelia gaped at one another.

"My brother! God save me!"

Scully crashed to the floor as Amelia, panic-stricken, leapt up and ran blindly around looking for her clothes. She tripped over a chair in her haste to make an exit through the door leading to the kitchen. Scully was just doing up his shirt buttons when Baldomero wandered in. He halted in surprise when he saw the Englishman.

"Hello, Carlos. I didn't know you were here. Have you seen Amelia?"

Scully noticed Amelia's skirt-belt lying near the couch. He edged towards it.

"She's preparing lunch, I think. How are you, Baldomero?"

"What? Oh, fine, fine. Where has she put all my papers? Don't tell me she's been clearing up again."

He peered around him.

"What's that on the floor?"

Scully glanced anxiously at where Baldomero was pointing.

"Those flowers, man. How did they get there?"

Like a bird of prey, Baldomero pounced on the faded blooms, giving Scully the chance to nudge the belt under the couch with his foot.

"...Lope de Vega, Moliere, Unamuno, Dickens, did they have to put up with this?" The teacher brandished the flowers angrily. "How is a masterpiece ever produced when a writer has to run an obstacle course of frustrations and domestic problems? How many works of genius have been sabotaged by a baby's nappies? One really wonders."

Baldomero muttered away, whether in jest or not Scully could not tell. Then he shrugged.

"Never mind. Have a drink. It seems ages since you were here, Carlos."

"I met Amelia on the way to church and she invited me."

"Ah, good girl. Church did you say? Don't tell me you've been converted?"

"It was curiosity. I thought I would find out what the good father had to say."

"And?"

"My head's still ringing. Everything seems to add up to guilt and damnation."

The teacher snorted.

"Guilt! Part of the cursed conspiracy. They crush us with guilt so that we cannot think straight, then we're so much easier to manipulate. Religion is a stick and carrot business. I went off it years ago. I don't believe in guilt any more, only in my books."

Sitting on the couch, Scully decided it was time to change the subject.

"Did you hear about Bruno's dog?" he asked.

"I told you this place was full of barbarians."

"But who would do something like that?"

Baldomero cocked his head like a world-weary eagle.

"Don't you know? I thought you would have plugged into the village grapevine by now. It was those idiots Las Animas, of course."

"But why?"

"Why indeed? They're our local government, that's why."

"What do you mean, Baldomero? I thought they were a charitable group, concerned with the Easter processions and that sort of stuff."

"So they are. They raise money to dress the Virgin in finery and to gild her throne and they give handouts to poor widows. That's the way it started, years ago." He sniffed. "But they've grown too big for their boots. They see themselves as the watchdogs of the pueblo. In fact, they have set themselves up as arbiters of public morals. Ridiculous, I know, but let a girl bare her arms or wear a short dress in public and they'll create a scandal. And the same when a widow tries to remarry. They disapprove of that too."

Scully frowned.

"But why should anybody take any notice?"

Exasperated, Baldomero clicked his tongue against his teeth.

"Haven't I been telling you? These are ignorant folk and they know only one set of rules, those of the village, of social custom. They are rigid commandments, set in concrete. And Las Animas are the enforcers, pretty merciless ones too. There was a girl, for instance, who became pregnant by a fellow from Cerrogordo. They made her life hell, scrawling things on her door, calling her a whore. They shamed and hounded her and her family until in the end she fled the village."

"Didn't her family complain to the police?" demanded Scully.

"There are no police here and, in any case, they don't want to get dragged into what they see as petty village squabbles, especially if the Church is involved. Besides, the villagers don't put much trust in authority. It's always stood for oppression. Authority means trouble and tax collectors. Best keep away from it. And Las Animas know how to put the fear of God into them, with all that religious mumbo-jumbo, parades through the village at night beating drums, and barbarities like Bruno's dog. Kids' stuff, but it works. It's amazing how much power such people can wield in a place like this. Sometimes they will call an offender to a special court. If he goes on his knees and repents, they may be merciful to him, as long as he is ready to do penance and pay for a dozen masses or some nonsense of that sort."

"That sounds like blackmail to me. Surely the priest should stop it?"

Baldomero sighed.

"Yes, maybe he'll walk across the River Guadalquivir too. The priest believes the Church should wield a flaming sword and Las Animas are his crusaders. He has said as much.

He puts them up to these damn tricks. He has done such a good brain-washing job that belonging to the Cofradía is regarded as an honour. And you have plenty who would like to join for their own protection."

"Ramón, Dolores's son, is a member," said Scully, accepting a refill.

"Ramón? Yes, it's understandable, I suppose. He's so young and idealistic, just the fodder that prejudice feeds on. He's a bright lad too. I had considerable hopes for him, even went as far as arranging a scholarship for him to attend school in Granada. A pity."

"What's a pity?"

Amelia had entered the room. She carefully avoided meeting Scully's gaze.

"The lunch is ready if you want to come through."

Baldomero stood up.

"We were talking about Ramón. An unusual boy. Intelligent, and sensitive. He could have bettered himself."

"But if he is happy as he is?" ventured Amelia timidly.

"What? Spending his days with the goats and his nights saving souls with that bunch of half-witted bully boys?"

Amelia bit her lip.

"Is it so bad to try to save souls? I mean, it's better than damning them."

"Pah!" scoffed the teacher, looking at Scully and spreading his hands in a gesture of hopelessness. They sat down at the table where Amelia had already placed a tureen of soup. She was making a great effort to appear unflustered, but she could not help banging the ladle awkwardly against the tureen and, as she set down Scully's bowl, she narrowly missed knocking over his wine glass. Scully glanced at Baldomero. He appeared to have noticed nothing.

"Er, tell me," said Scully, trying to switch attention from Amelia's trembling hands. "The priest who was here at the start of the Civil War, what happened to him? I couldn't help noticing the plaque in the cemetery."

Baldomero shook his head.

"I have heard stories about it, each one different. Anything was possible in those days. Such hatred was unleashed, you know. It was the same everywhere. In Cerrogordo, they burned a nun alive. In another village the women took revenge on a Civil Guard by literally tearing him to pieces. In Granada hatred murdered our greatest poet and dramatist, García Lorca. And the executions, by both sides, they could not be counted."

"I suppose we should be grateful that things have changed," said Scully drily. "Now they are only hanging dogs."

"Dogs today. Who knows what tomorrow? Hate, envy, guilt...they are like maggots gnawing away inside us and sometimes it all spills out. Even in peaceful little Benamargo."

"For goodness sake, dear, things aren't that bad here," interjected Amelia. "This is just about the sleepiest village one could imagine. Nothing ever happens."

"I would have said the same," said Scully. "Still, there was the dog."

Baldomero smiled cynically.

"You see, Amelia, Carlos is a true Englishman. His heart bleeds over a dog. Soon he will be setting up a Benamargo branch of Her Imperial Majesty's Society for the Prevention of Cruelty to Animals, mark my words. Ah, the English." He laughed. "No, please do not misunderstand me. I respect you English for what you are. You can teach us a lot."

At the end of the meal, Scully did not linger. He sensed tension in the air. Baldomero was more obstreperous and argumentative than usual, and Scully wondered whether he suspected something. Amelia followed him on to the doorstep, out of her brother's earshot.

"About what happened, I'm so ashamed." She rubbed her thin, pale hands together as though trying to wash them clean. "It was only that I thought you were mocking me. I've never done anything like that before, never."

Scully spoke earnestly.

"There's nothing to be ashamed of. You reacted like any woman."

It was the right thing to say. She watched him until he had turned the corner.

CHAPTER THIRTEEN

A nagging tooth took Scully to Granada. Since a dentist made only occasional visits to the village, there was no alternative. It took two visits to complete the treatment and, when he took the bus back to Benamargo on the third day, the weather had changed abruptly. The light had a cold, metallic quality and the mountains looked black and ill-humoured.

But Scully felt only relief. He was glad to be returning to his mountain sanctuary, where there was nothing of the past to torture him, where there was no challenge, where he could just be, as adrift as the clouds that floated over the amphitheatre of the sierras. Back to the womb.

As soon as he stepped off the bus he felt as though he had never left. Walking down the narrow street to his house, he remembered he had left the heavy old iron key with Dolores.

"Don Carlos, you're back."

Marisa stood in the doorway, her full unpainted lips curved in a smile. Her face was shining and eager. She had plaited her hair and a dark coil fell over one shoulder. Scully smiled too.

"It's so good to see you, Marisa." He leaned forward and kissed her lightly on the forehead. "How are you?"

"Oh, the same as ever. Here we are. You know, nothing ever happens in the village. And you, did you do exciting things?"

"The most exciting thing was getting off the Benamargo bus just now. I'm glad to be back."

She fixed her frank gaze upon him.

"I thought you might not come back. And I was afraid that your friend had come to take you away."

Scully opened his eyes wide.

"What friend?"

"An Englishman. He arrived a day or so ago. He said he was anxious to see you."

A cramp gripped Scully's stomach.

"Did he say his name? Where is he?"

"He said he would wait for you. I think he's staying with Carmencita of the shop. She rents out rooms sometimes. He seems a very nice man, so polite. A real gentleman. Shall I run and find him?"

Scully shook his head slowly.

"Don't bother. He'll find me soon enough."

And so he did. Scully was in his room pouring himself a Scotch when he heard steps on the staircase.

"Save some for me, Charles." The smirking face was only too familiar. "Run to earth at last! And looking guilty as hell. Hand in the till? Up the wrong skirt? Same old Charles, eh?"

Scully gaped at his visitor, refusing to believe the evidence of his eyes. A nerve began ticking on his forehead.

"Klease!"

"Right first time. I just dropped in for a little chat."

Scully stepped close to the intruder.

"I've only one thing to say to you, you bastard! Fuck off, back to where you belong."

Mock surprise blossomed on Klease's boyish features.

"Come on, Charlie boy! That's no way to greet an old amigo."

Scully was possessed by a cold rage.

"Get the hell out of here! Or I won't be responsible for what happens."

"Managing director speaking, is it? All staff to attention? Sorry, Charles, I'm not on your payroll any more. And you're not in a position to give orders, to anybody. Take a look in the mirror, Charlie boy. You couldn't win an arm-wrestling match with Mickey Mouse."

Klease was younger than Scully, by at least five years, and he kept himself in shape. His effete air had fooled many a victim. Scully knew that everything about this man was deceptive. Klease was expert at putting the knife in, physically and figuratively. Three years in the US Marines had taught him plenty of nasty tricks. The rest came naturally. His accent suggested upper-class England, except when a harder, nasal pitch betrayed his North American origins. He wore a permanent tan and looked like a professional tennis-player, but his true profession was blackmail. He treated women barbarically, but they loved him. Maybe it was the sensual twist to his lips. Scully hated those lips.

"Thanks, Charles, I will have one."

Klease picked up the whisky bottle, framing a smile, though his blue eyes remained as cold as ever.

That was when Scully hit him, or attempted to. It was a miserable failure. Klease swayed easily out of range and, still holding the whisky bottle in his right hand, hit Scully twice with his left fist. The blows came so fast that Scully did not even see them, merely felt the agonising pain in his solar plexus. He doubled up on the floor. For a moment Klease seemed about to follow up, with his feet this time, but then he merely laughed.

When Scully could catch his breath, he saw that Klease was sitting on the bed, watching him and grinning. Just like the last time, except then Stella had been in the bed. And she too had laughed.

Klease raised his glass to Scully.

"Here's to Mickey Mouse!"

Scully eased himself to his feet and slumped on to a rickety chair.

"How the hell did you know where I was?"

"How, Charles?" Klease studied him like a cat which has cornered its prey. "It was easy. So easy that I'm tempted to wonder whether you really wanted to be traced. Could that be so?" He drank some of Scully's whisky. "The word was that you were in Spain. So where else but the Costa del Sol? You know, Charles. Birds of a feather. They all flock to the good life in the sunshine."

Scully glared at this man. He and Klease were themselves birds of a feather, he recognised that. They had wheeled, dealed and connived together. But that belonged to a world so distant he could hardly credit what was happening.

Klease had no right to be here in Benamargo, resurrecting the past. Scully could not think of anybody he detested more.

"Then, whom should I bump into but an old flame. A neat chick, if she didn't yak quite so much. And whose name comes up? Why, that of my old buddy, Charles Scully. Rumoured to be living in some benighted village in the sticks. Well, a few inquiries here and there and Bob's your uncle. Naturally, I couldn't wait to renew our acquaintance. I guessed you'd be delighted to see me, Charles."

Scully felt nothing now. He just wanted to get rid of the man.

"All right. What the hell do you want?"

Klease beamed.

"Ah, that's better. Patient sitting up, showing interest." He paused. "Charles, I want you to know I bear no grudges, none at all."

"That's big of you, Klease."

"Indeed it is. You were the one who left everybody else to hold the baby. Or have you forgotten?"

"My memory is perfectly okay," snapped Scully. "And I remember perfectly well the last time I saw you — with Stella."

Klease laughed scornfully.

"Stella? As if you gave a shit about her." He wagged a finger. "Pride, Charles. One of the deadly sins. And, may I say, damned hypocrisy too, knowing your record with the ladies."

"At least I restricted myself to one sex!"

"What a puritan you are! Charles Scully setting moral guidelines! Christ, is that one for the record!" Klease leaned across. "So you're Mr Clean? That's a joke. They'll die laughing at Scotland Yard. They want to talk to you, Charles. A heap of outstanding business to be cleared up apparently."

"And what about you, Klease?"

Klease opened his eyes wide.

"In the clear, Charles. Only the guilty run, you know that. And I stayed to face the music. Why, I even offered my cooperation. You know how they like that."

"You screwed your friends. Well, at least you're consistent."

Klease showed his teeth, but it wasn't a smile and his baby-blue eyes were frosty.

"Law and order, Charlie. It's a citizen's duty to do his little bit. But I kept the hot stuff in here." He tapped his head. "Too valuable to give away. Yep, your secrets are safe with me. But they are looking for you, my friend."

"Let them find me. I've nothing to fear."

"Plimpton kidded himself too," said Klease. "They grabbed him for tax evasion, business fraud and all the rest. No more Havanas for Plimpton."

"In jail?"

"Dead."

Scully's colour had been returning, but now he paled again.

"I don't believe it."

"Locked himself in the garage, car engine running. That put the story back in the headlines, I can tell you. The cops had been grilling him about his friendship with Reynolds."

"So?"

"So, they seemed perplexed about how our tame Member of Parliament, Mr Reynolds, suddenly acquired a country house and began taking vacations in the Bahamas. You know the Fraud Squad. Suspicious bunch. They started putting everything together, that killing we made on currency exchange rates, rumours about a high-level leak in the Treasury Department, talk about kickbacks on some of those construction contracts... Pure fantasy, of course."

Scully remembered the last time he had seen Plimpton, all joviality gone, already broken, muttering "We're done! We're done!".

"I came to this village for some peace, not to receive visits from acquaintances who persist in talking over old times. Stop boring me, Klease. We all know the party's over. There's no more to be said."

"My opinion too. But Charteris, Charteris sees it differently."

Scully stiffened. Charteris was somebody who never

moved without precisely calculating the consequences. Diamond-sharp, an expert in legal loopholes and escape clauses in small print.

"Charteris would never lose his nerve."

Klease flashed those well-formed teeth again.

"Who's talking about nerve? The subject on the agenda is weasels. I always thought Charteris was one and so it's proved. Your chum has been spilling his heart out to the Fraud Squad. The North Sea oil business, the Cayman Isles set-up, the Singapore investment trust...it has all been coming out, anything to save his miserable skin."

Klease knocked back his whisky.

"And, so I'm told, he has been handing over bundles of paper tied in pretty red ribbon that were lodged in some bank deposit. I can't imagine what interest they would be to the police, can you?"

"Charteris would never do it."

"But he is doing it. He's turned what you Limeys call Queen's evidence. He's talking his head off and coming out pure as a virgin. That's what you get for having a goddamned weasel on the payroll."

Scully scowled wearily at Klease.

"You've come all this way just to tell me this? You could have saved yourself the trouble. Post-mortems don't interest me."

"Any more of this stuff?" asked Klease, examining his empty glass. He lolled back nonchalantly on Scully's bed, smiling while Scully glowered.

Klease, trouble-shooter and trouble-maker. It could be as dangerous to have him on your side as in opposition. Scully recalled his first contact with him. A million-pound computer deal had been virtually sewn up when abruptly, inexplicably, the purchasing company began to lose interest. The deal had been about to slip through Scully's fingers. Just in time, he discovered why. Klease, working for a rival group, had simply bought off two of the company's directors and hinted to their chairman that his sexual preferences could hardly stand the glare of publicity.

The contract was being stolen from under Scully's nose.

But, as Klease had cheerfully admitted when Scully cornered him for lunch one day in a discreet country pub, nothing is immutable. They had talked long over the cognac and, shortly afterwards, Scully clinched the computer deal and Klease switched employers. The association had been profitable, but Scully had always been careful to keep his back covered when dealing with Klease.

"Spit it out, Klease, for god's sake. What do you want?"

"Want? Jesus, we're old comrades-in-arms. The least I could do was look up my old buddy and offer him some help."

Klease glanced around, wrinkling his nose.

"And it sure looks as though you could do with some. I mean, what in the name of creation are you doing in this god-for-saken hole? Screwing the goats? Having it away with the village maidens behind the haystacks? It's not you, Charles. You always loved the good life. This fucking place is prehistoric. It's knuckles-on-the-ground territory. These people, they could get parts as gargoyles if they ever remake The Hunchback of Notre Dame. All interbred, I expect, to judge by the looks of them. Incest behind every door." He smiled at Scully. "Maybe that's it, Charles, you've turned kinky."

"Just go away, Klease."

"But then, you're Don Carlos, the local celebrity! They all know you. I met a charming boy who said you were actually staying in his family's house. Not bad detective work, right, tracking you to the end of nowhere when I hardly know a word of the lingo. Maybe I've been in the wrong line all along."

Scully said nothing.

"The point is, Charles, if I could find you, so can others. Your little secret is out."

"The bus goes back to Granada this afternoon. I'll buy your ticket."

"Costa Rica, that's the place. Pacific breezes, easygoing natives, welcome mat out for investors, no questions asked. And no extradition, Charles, no extradition. You could be safe there."

"I feel perfectly safe here, thank you."

"You surprise me. All those Cockney conmen may think they can take vacations in the sun for ever and nobody can touch them, but there are ways and means for chums like you, Charlie boy. One word from Scotland Yard and the Spanish cops will be shipping you home to face the music. Fortunately, Scotland Yard does not know where you are — so far."

"What do you want? Spit it out!"

Klease sighed and adjusted the blue silk cravat at his throat.

"It's Stella. She wants a divorce and a settlement. For the children, naturally. You left them all with hardly a crust. When the inquiry started and the creditors moved in, naturally all the company assets were frozen."

"Don't expect me to cry over Stella's plight. She has the house and enough jewellery to sink the QE2."

"The liquidators are poking around. They may well seize the house. And what about the boys?"

"There is enough money in trust to cover their education. Nobody can touch that. As for Stella, it's about time that bitch scrubbed a few floors. Anyway, as you're so concerned for her welfare, why don't you help her, Klease? You two are on quite intimate terms, after all."

"I'm broke, Charles. The crash caught me at the worst moment. I don't like living near the breadline. You know me, Charles. It puts me in a foul mood, makes me talkative too. Of course, my name's not Charteris, but..."

Klease rose and stretched himself, dusting off his white linen pants, all pretence at amiability wiped away.

"Two hundred thousand would be enough," he said. "Two hundred thousand good old British smackers. Peanuts."

"You have to be joking," snapped Scully.

"You have it stashed away." Klease raised a hand. "Don't deny it. I know all about those Swiss and offshore accounts. All I'm asking for is a little severance pay."

"You are misinformed. I have no money. And, even if I had the cash, the answer would be the same — get lost!"

"Don't be hasty, Charles. You need my help. How are you

going to get out of Spain to a safe spot? You need somebody
who knows how to fix you a passport, visas, all the rest.
And I'm not going back to London empty-handed. Stella
would be very displeased. The lady's turned a mite bitter
since your sudden departure. She's threatening all sorts of
things. You wouldn't believe it."

"Wouldn't I?" asked Scully sourly.

Klease laid a hand on his shoulder.

"Think about it, Charles. You want peace? You can have
it. You won't help your old sparring partner and your family? Things could turn nasty, very suddenly. Think about it.
I'll be around."

"Idiot! You're wasting your time!"

Scully yelled the last words. By then Klease was opening
the street door. For a long while afterwards, Scully sat gazing into space. Klease was wasting his breath if he hoped
to blackmail him, for he had no money, not real money. He
had drained those foreign bank accounts in a desperate attempt to buy time when the whole deck of cards had been
crashing about his ears. Klease would never believe it, of
course. But he could threaten as much as he liked, it would
not alter the facts. There was nothing left.

That evening Scully ate the usual meal with Dolores and
her family. The fare was the same as always, a thin broth,
followed by rice and cod fish and a salad, but it did not
bother Scully. He was content to be back, eating simple rustic food.

Marisa and her mother bustled about, while he contem-
plated the goat cheese and debated how little he could eat
without exciting comment.

"Hola, Don Carlos. Back from the capital?"

Ramón grinned at him and sat down for his meal. He was
usually in good spirits, except when his sister teased him,
and this evening he appeared as exuberant as ever.

"Have you heard the latest about Alejandro? He went
down to Cerrogordo the night before last and got in a fight
with a gypsy. They threw both of them in jail. He just got
back. Phew! You should see his face!"

"That boy's brains are in his fists," sniffed Dolores.

"Ramón, you better talk with Gonzalo the postman. He wants a baby goat for Sunday. The family's visiting from Barcelona."

"Sure. But this time he has to pay on the nail. Remember how long it took him last time?" He glanced at Scully. "And Granada? What's happening there?"

Scully shrugged.

"Plenty of people, plenty of noise, too many cars. It's good to be back in Benamargo."

Ramón chuckled.

"I could have told you that. The only time I went any-where was when the schoolmaster organised a special excursion. First we went to Granada and then up to Madrid. Madrid! You've got to be careful there. Nothing but thieves and tricksters. And the country! It's awful, flat and so cold in winter. They don't even know what a good tomato looks like up there. And wine? Ha! The wine of Benamargo has no equal, that's for sure. Nor the air, nor the water, nor the ham... In fact, I used to write poems about Benamargo."

"Poems? I didn't know you were a poet, Ramón."

"I'm not, but I used to try. Don Baldomero encouraged me. He wanted me to go to university. Can you believe it? Who goes to university from Benamargo? All those degrees and titles, they're not much use when you're trying to save a sick goat."

Dolores nodded her head in agreement.

"What good does all that learning do, except confuse people? It just makes folk discontented. That's why the Reds are always talking about education."

"But do you still write poems?" asked Scully.

Ramón frowned.

"No, not now. But I read a lot. I've got all the works by Machado and Lorca and Alberti. And Aleixandre — he won the Nobel prize, you know that? Nobody can write better poetry than the Andalusians."

"You're right," said Scully, smiling. "This is the land of poets. I studied them when I was at university. And this is Lorca country, isn't it? He came from Granada."

"Baldomero knew his family," said Ramón, his face shining. "Once we went to Granada and he introduced me to them. García Lorca was assassinated, you know. At the start of the Civil War. They killed a man like that, a genius. What a barbarity! In that war, the whole of Spain went crazy, crazy."

"Don't talk about it," interjected his mother. "It's all right for you, but I lived through it. I don't want to hear any more about those evil times in this house."

"But it's marked us all, mother, you know that," protested Ramón. "It's impossible to rub it out. It's written on our souls. It's what the priest says, we all have to do penance for the sins committed in our name. You can't escape the past."

Scully shifted in his seat.

"You believe that?"

"Of course," said Ramón. "The past always catches up with us. If we do somebody a bad turn, retribution always comes, sooner or later."

"I don't believe in retribution," said Scully. "I don't believe that the evil always get their deserts. I wish I did. Life would be a lot simpler. I think we just stagger on from day to day and hope that things go right. From what I've seen of this life, there's no justice, just good luck and bad luck."

Dolores shook her head as though shocked and Ramón was obviously surprised by the firmness of Scully's tone.

"Then I'm sorry for you," he said. "Because I know somebody is watching over us. Don't you believe in anything, Don Carlos? Protestants have a god too, don't they?"

"I believe that this is fine wine. That's what I believe. And I prefer not to think about yesterday or tomorrow. It's all I can do to cope with today."

Ramón chewed a piece of cheese and eyed Scully in puzzled fashion.

"I met your friend, the blond Englishman."

"He's no friend of mine. He's a ghost from the past and I prefer not to think about him."

"But he seems such a gentleman. He helped me yesterday when one of the goats fell down a crevice. I couldn't reach it, but he climbed down and fixed a rope so I could haul it up. He told me that he has climbed some of the biggest mountains, covered in snow and ice, in the Alps. Is that right?"

"That's true. He's almost as good a climber as he is a talker."

"Yes, he talks plenty, even though he doesn't speak much Spanish. He told me some crazy jokes. I couldn't stop laughing."

Klease the charmer. Even in an alien tongue he could win friends effortlessly, it seemed. God rot his soul! Why was it Klease who had to find him here?

"Señor Klease is a very amusing person, but be on your guard, Ramón. Don't trust him too far."

Ramón stiffened. All his macho pride came to the fore.

"Don't worry about me, Don Carlos. I can take care of myself. I've always been a good judge of character. Ask anybody. Isn't that so, mother?"

"It is so," confirmed Dolores. "Ramón was a man by the time he was 15. He knows his mind. Nobody can play tricks on him, I can tell you."

"That's good," said Scully quickly. "You need to have your wits about you in this world."

"Your countryman was very respectful towards you." Scully sensed Ramón was chiding him. "He said you were an important man and that he was an old family friend."

A family friend. Well, that was true, Scully noted bitterly as he prepared for bed. He tried to sleep, but for hours the images of Klease, Stella, Plimpton, Charteris, his children flickered before him. Stella and Klease appeared again and again, in bed together, laughing. Always laughing.

CHAPTER FOURTEEN

Sebastián pulled down the handle of the coffee machine and the pungent smell of the roasted grains drifted across the bar. A huddle of customers was gulping brandy and anise to protect themselves against the frost that had spread its rind over the cobblestones overnight. A mule shifted restlessly outside, nostrils steaming. Between the houses Scully glimpsed the high sierras where scree and grey rock had been powdered with white.

Two Civil Guards stood at the counter, sipping large cups of coffee and dunking lengths of greasy fritters into the hot liquid. The older one sucked at his moustache and knocked crumbs from his olive-green uniform.

"Por Dios! It's cold enough to freeze your balls off!" he said. "This pueblo is like the North Pole. You'll have snow soon enough."

"That's okay," said Sebastián complacently. "It's snug here in the bar. You're the unlucky ones. That Land-Rover must be like an icebox."

"We were lucky to get through this morning. Ice all over the road. Just as well we don't have to come up here too often."

Sebastián uncorked a bottle.

"Here, have a brandy. On the house. That'll keep you warm. Alcohol and women, you need them in winter."

The younger of the policemen, with the fresh face of a farmboy, guffawed and downed the brandy. His companion, a corporal, looked severe but accepted the drink.

"I wish every village were as quiet as this one."

Sebastián shrugged and winked.

"We're all law-abiding, types here, you know that. The priest frightens the life out of anybody who steps out of line."

"How about strangers? Any around?"

"None at all, unless you count a couple of English. The gentleman at the end of the bar and his friend."

The Civil Guard turned and studied Scully.

"English? Staying long?"

"A few months. I'm taking a rest."

"Ah, a rest."

"It's a good place for a rest."

"That so?" The corporal wiped his moustache with the back of his hand and smoothed his hair. His eyes were watchful. "Do you have your passport, señor?"

"It's in my lodgings."

"I see. Well, do you happen to remember the number?" He noted it down laboriously with a stub of pencil. "And the name?"

"Scully, Charles Scully."

"Ah, Escooly, yes. Very good." He turned to his junior. "Time to go."

They picked up their shiny black patent-leather hats and the younger man rescued his sub-machine gun from the table where it had rested.

"Adiós a todos."

The corporal saluted Sebastián and they walked out, creaking polished leather. The bar-owner grinned at Scully.

"Much respect. I feel much respect for the Benemérita, as we call them. It's one of my rules. Always respect a man carrying a gun."

Sebastián gazed over Scully's shoulder.

"Here comes your friend."

Wearing a tweed jacket and well-cut corduroy pants, with a woollen scarf nonchalantly wrapped around his neck, Klease breezed in, a wide smile on his face.

"Hola, Sebastián. You are well? Antonio, amigo! Federico! Bruno, how are things? Gonzalo, you ugly old sonovabitch!"

Shaking hands, embracing, back-slapping, Klease moved through the bleak little bar as smoothly as he would through his club in Boston or Mayfair. Already he seemed to know everybody and they greeted him as an old friend.

"And you, Charlie boy, good morning to you. In good spirits?"

He beamed at Scully, who scowled back.

"Bloody marvellous, isn't it, to be among friends?" exclaimed Klease, as though oblivious to Scully's ill humour. For the past two weeks he had haunted his former colleague, trailing him to the bar, ambushing him on his walks, butting into Scully's conversations. Scully had adamantly refused to speak to him, except to advise him that under no circumstances was he going to give him any money. Klease had only smiled and said he could wait. He appeared to be extracting a twisted pleasure from hounding Scully, provoking him into boorishness.

"Sebastián, trot out some of that old rotgut you have. You know, el wheeskee español. That's it."

He turned back to Scully.

"Bumped into a couple of odd characters in funny hats outside, Chas. Must have been pals of yours, their clothes were so badly cut. Puke-making shade of green. Definitely won't catch on. Carrying a lot of artillery. Wonder what they're hunting. Thought it was off-season for big game. Anyway, they wanted to see my papers. I was glad to oblige, especially after I saw the elephant gun. But no sweat, they could see I was a caballero, and I put in a good word for you too. One good turn, you know."

Scully turned his back.

"Hey, Don Rubio!" The locals had taken to calling Klease after his blond hair. "Tell us one of your jokes."

"Sorry, didn't catch that. Ah, a joke. Yes, funny thing you should say that. Goddamned weirdest thing happened to me this morning, while I was on my way here."

The bar customers gathered around as Klease launched into a tale in colourful pidgin Spanish, interspersed with graphic pieces of mime.

"This hombre, understand, looking for something in the street. On his hands and knees, like this. Most distressed. Eyes down at ground level, peering that way and this. So I asked him 'Something lost, perdido?' 'Sí, sí,' he said. 'One thousand pesetas. I was crossing the plaza and I dropped it.' Plaza, dropped it ...comprenez? Anyway, I said 'If you lost it in the plaza, porque you look for it aquí in the street.' 'Very simple,' he says. 'The light's better here.' Get it? Más luz aquí! Más luz aquí than in the plaza! Well, come on you thick bunch of ass-holes. Laugh! For godsake, laugh!"

For a moment the customers looked blankly at one another, then they all burst into laughter.

"Very good, Don Rubio, very good."

They slapped him across the shoulders and ordered more drinks. Klease grinned and raised his glass to Scully.

"That's what I like about this place. People have such a sense of humour. All except you, Charles, all except you. Can't even raise a giggle from my old comrade."

"Your jokes stink, Klease, and so do you."

"Is that right? Well, listen, Uncle Charles, the biggest joke around here is yourself, the whizzkid asset stripper trying to ape the peasants in this godforsaken hole. What a spectacle that is! Absolutely hilarious. I can't wait to tell the folks back home."

"Then why don't you piss off now and leave me in peace?" hissed Scully.

A veneer of bonhomie clung to Klease's features, but his cold blue eyes glittered menacingly as he leaned closer to Scully.

"I'm not leaving here empty-handed. Unlock those vaults and give me what I want."

"I've already told you. I'm as broke as you are. Don't you understand? And let me tell you something, Klease, even if I had some cash, I'd rather toss it into that ravine out there than let you get your paws on it."

Klease laid a heavy hand on Scully's arm.

"Don't fuck with me. You've had your chance. My patience is finished. I want that money now! Get it? Two hundred grand!"

Scully shook off the hand, which had been steadily exerting stronger pressure.

"There's nothing for you and that's final!" he insisted angrily. "Now get out of my life!"

He saw Klease's eyes open wide, a familiar danger sign.

"Two hundred grand now or I can promise you a fast trip to an English jail cell. Christ, I know enough about your activities to put you away for years. What good will your Swiss bank accounts do you then, you creep?"

"Do your worst!"

"That I shall, Charles, that I shall. Have no fear. This is your last chance, you dummy. The easy way out. Stella and I won't trouble you again. Or do you want to spend the rest of your life on the run?"

Scully sighed. Couldn't Klease understand? He didn't care. He couldn't give a damn about his threats, about anything. They were empty gestures that could not touch him. They came from another world.

"Klease," he said, speaking slowly and deliberately as though explaining to a child. "Do you remember when we had that lunch together, a long time ago, at one of those expense account places on the Thames, when you decided to change jobs? Remember? You said something that has stuck in my mind. You said: 'When it's time for a break, it should be done cleanly and without compunction. There's no room for all that emotional crap about loyalty or gratitude.' Well, can't you see? I've made the break. Stella, you, all that mess don't exist for me. I have cut the shit out of my life, for ever. And not you nor anybody is going to bring it back. So you know where you can put all your threats and sneers, don't you?"

Klease had paled. His fingers drummed on the bar counter. The other clients had halted their conversation and were watching them, uncomprehendingly.

"All right! Have it your way." Klease spoke swiftly, in a whisper that was like a razor. "If you won't see sense, then by god you're going to suffer. I'll see to that. This little paradise of yours is going to turn into a nightmare for you before I've finished."

He laughed sourly. "Do you know what the people here think of you? Your tame peasants think you're a very odd bird, that's what they think. A miserable fucking eccentric!"

"I'm not interested in your warped ideas."

"Not my ideas, old buddy. Ramón, for a start." Scully raised his eyebrows and Klease appeared gratified. "Yes, pretty boy Ramón. He told me you are half loco, possessed by the devil. And he's not far wrong, is he? You've got all the devils of creation gnawing inside you."

Klease smiled at Scully, as though a thought had struck him.

"Like Ramón, do you? A good boy, isn't he? The face of an Adonis. And what a body! Sturdy, lean, full of the freshness of youth."

The blood throbbed in Scully's head.

"Touch that boy and —"

"Choosing my friends now, are you, Charles? It so happens that Ramón and I get along fine. He's a nice boy. He's got a lot to learn, of course. But I think I can help him."

"Nobody here needs your help!" declared Scully, anger welling up within him.

Klease was mocking, his lips curling scornfully.

"Aren't you getting your share, Charles? You must be the only one who isn't. Sheep-shagging and buggery are what this place is all about. Fuck all else to do, is there? So why not join the fun. That's always been my motto. If in doubt, get it up."

Pale with rage, Scully glared at Klease.

"Shut up or I'll kill you, you bastard!"

Sebastián looked alarmed while the customers were gaping open-mouthed.

Klease laughed loudly.

"Hit a nerve, have I?" He smothered a yawn. "Well, I can't stay here idly gossiping all day. I have a date." He smirked. "No, don't bother to ask me with whom."

Scully cracked then, all self-control gone. He hurled himself at Klease before he could raise a hand in defence. The two of them crashed to the floor in a clatter of falling chairs and broken glass. Momentarily, Klease, the breath knocked out of him, was at a disadvantage and Scully smashed a fist into his face. He was not aware what he was doing. He just wanted to obliterate that sneer once and for all. Again he hit Klease.

But, before he could get in a third blow, he felt himself gripped by powerful hands and pulled to his feet.

"Please!" implored Sebastián. "We can't have this. Two English gentlemen fighting. It won't do."

Other hands had hauled Klease up and he stood glowering at his attacker. A trickle of blood dribbled from a cut on his lip.

"All right," he said, rubbing his cheek. "All right. You asked for it, Scully. You're going to pay, one way or another. Before I'm finished, you'll be coming to me on your knees."

He gazed at the surprised faces around him, then grinned.

"The ingleses are all locos, right, amigos? Here!" He pulled a one-thousand-peseta bill from his pocket and slapped it on the counter. "The drinks are on me, on El Rubio. Vaya con Dios, amigos."

He stomped out of the bar. Sebastián stared curiously at Scully.

"A bad business, a bad business. What happened, what got into you?"

Scully shook his head.

"It's all history. Just give me a drink."

He slumped in a corner seat. The fury had subsided. He tried to raise a glass of brandy to his mouth but had to put it back on the table. He was trembling too much.

CHAPTER FIFTEEN

The snow came that night, a wild night when the wind howled down from the sierras and Benamargo no longer belonged to the Mediterranean but to the frigid north. A fusillade of hail drummed against tiled roofs and shutters and then the snow came in large flakes, swirling down to glue themselves to doorways and roll themselves into drifts against the house walls and the stone terraces on the hillside, choking the village streets, deadening the tread of man and beast, pressing down on aging rooftops until they groaned, smothering the road to Cerrogordo.

It was the worst he had known in 20 years, said Sebastián. It was the severest winter since she was a child, said Dolores. It must be a judgment, cackled the old witches clustered around the stove in Carmencita's shop. They all agreed it was exceptional. Usually the snow lingered only a few hours. But this time the temperature stayed stubbornly below zero and in succeeding days it snowed again. Juanito did not even bother to start his truck and the bus service was suspended.

Scully welcomed the snow. It postponed a decision. After his confrontation with Klease, which had quickly become the talk of the village, he had debated whether he should leave at once. Klease had poisoned the atmosphere. Maybe it was better to go. But where to? It would not be easy to shake off his resourceful one-time colleague, he knew that. And in any case, why should he leave?

He had already decided he was not going to run any further. Klease's blackmail was not going to change that. This was his village. If anybody had to go, it was Klease. Except that Klease was not planning an early departure. Even though he despised everything about the place, his greed would keep him here. And he never made idle threats.

Scully hated to imagine what this malevolent spirit from the past was cooking up as Klease moved in a cloud of good humour about the village, teasing the girls, joking with Carmencita and her coven until they rolled about in helpless mirth, entertaining Sebastián and his boozy customers, teaching the youngsters to play the tin whistle. Klease had swiftly converted himself into a popular character, buying young and old with a drink, a ready smile or a handful of sweets. In a few weeks he had gained more acceptance than Scully had managed in several months. It was a masterful performance.

While Klease continued charming the pueblo, Scully felt himself more and more an outsider. Mostly, he brooded and tried to keep warm. Old beams and still-green olive logs glowed and sputtered in the fireplace of his house, but the building remained an ice-box. It had been built to keep out heat rather than to maintain warmth. In summer, it functioned perfectly, the metre-thick mud and rock walls effectively sealing off the dark interior from an African sun. In winter, the walls and tiled floors were freezing to the touch. Scully wedged newspapers around the warped windows and exterior doors but draughts still whistled through innumerable cracks in the woodwork. He rotated before the fire like a chicken on a spit, occasionally doing a few vigorous exercises. At least once a day he took a brisk walk to restore his circulation.

When he saw Klease, he studiously ignored him. Once he called on the schoolteacher, Amelia answering the door. She flushed deeply when she saw Scully. He and Baldomero chatted about books, about politics and — inevitably — about the teacher's literary efforts. Progress on the definitive work about Felipe II appeared to be agonisingly slow and Baldomero admitted that, after 15 years, he could see no end in sight. While Baldomero showed off his erudition, Amelia sat silently. But Scully could feel her eyes on him.

Scully's interest in the Duke of Alba's repression of the Low Countries and the perfidy of Queen Elizabeth I was extremely limited, but it only needed one question to set Baldomero off on an enthusiastic monologue. When Scully tried to divert him with a query about the Moorish occupation of Spain, he seized on the subject.

"Hmmph! One more example of the intolerance and lack of vision of our rulers. And how we've suffered for it! The Moors cultivated the arts and tolerated religions other than Islam and they created great wealth in this region. Andalusia was a garden. So naturally those benighted Christian monarchs of ours ordered them out at the first opportunity. They expelled the Moors, even those who converted to Christianity, just as they expelled the Jews, from which our commerce has never recovered. Stupid, disastrous. It's the story of Spain. Why, in Moorish times even Benamargo enjoyed a certain prosperity."

"But where did the wealth come from?"

"From the ingenious irrigation system, and from the silk worms. Merchants came from Granada to buy the silk. Don't remind the good Father, but his church is built on the foundations of a mosque. And you know those old walls up behind the cemetery? They are the ruins of a Moorish water-mill."

Baldomero paused.

"I saw your countryman up there, just before the snow came, with Ramón. Chatting away."

Scully grimaced.

"He's no friend of mine, believe me. I wish to hell he would go away."

"There's a story going around that your friend has come to persuade you to go back to England," put in Amelia. "You know how this place is for gossip and their tongues have been running away with them since some incident in the bar. They're saying you owe a lot of money to this other man and that's why he came. He did you a good turn in the past and somehow you have let him down."

She paused and looked anxiously at Scully.

"I'm sorry. That's what they're saying, Carlos."

"Christ! This is absolute nonsense."

"I knew it was," said Amelia. "I knew it couldn't be true."

Baldomero smiled sardonically.

"Truth is irrelevant here. Gossip is our main industry and our only entertainment. Facts? Investigation? Forget it. The gossips rule. All the same..." He looked hard at Scully. "This fellow isn't helping. It worries me a little, his friendship with Ramón. He's a sensitive, idealistic type. I wouldn't want him to get hurt. You know what I mean?"

"Don't worry, my so-called friend won't be around for long," said Scully, with a conviction he did not feel.

Later, in the entrance hall, Amelia caught his hand.

"And you, Charles?" Her lips trembled. "Will you be here long?"

He smiled and pressed her hand.

"Why not? This is my village."

But things had changed in the pueblo. Klease was spreading his poison. A not-so-subtle shift had occurred in Ramón's attitude. Whereas previously he had always been affable and talkative, now he spoke little to Scully, and when he did it was sometimes with an air of defiance. An undercurrent of tension invaded mealtimes. With growing frequency, Ramón was absent.

After visiting the schoolteacher, Scully tramped carefully along the main street. Following a brief thaw, sharp frosts had turned the village into a skating rink. The farmers were complaining that most of their olive crop had been ruined. A bulldozer had blazed a path up from Cerrogordo, but the road was still open only to four-wheel-drive vehicles. One night Scully could have sworn he heard the distant cry of a wolf. He told himself it must be a dog. Wolves had long been wiped out in this part of Spain, although they must have been common once. He remembered the name of the distance pass, Puerto de los Lobos.

Passing Sebastián's bar, he was about to enter but passed quickly on after a glance through the steamy windows. Inside, the man he least wanted to meet was holding forth amid a laughing, admiring group.

Near the house, Marisa approached from the opposite direction, wrapped in a long black coat, a woollen scarf around her head. Her cheeks glowed pink from the cold. She greeted Scully brightly. Then she frowned.

"Don Carlos, are you all right? Your face looks so black. What has happened?"

"Wolves, Marisa. I just spotted one."

She laughed.

"There are no wolves. They killed them all long ago. Is it warm enough in your house? There's more firewood in the outhouse. Come, I'll help you carry some in."

"It's all right, Marisa. I'll do it."

But she was already scooping up logs. The two carried the wood into Scully's living room and laid the logs in a corner near the hearth. The fire had almost gone out and Marisa knelt before it, piling on smaller branches and breathing new life into the embers with an old bellows.

"There!"

She stood up and turned towards Scully with a toss of her dark hair, which had slipped free of the scarf. Her skin was flushed by the flames and her eyes shone in the soft light. Scully experienced a thickening sensation in his throat. How beautiful she was! It struck him with renewed impact. So beautiful, so ingenuous. Instinctively, he raised his hand and ran a finger down her cheek.

"You are so beautiful."

Marisa giggled in embarrassed fashion and lowered her eyes.

"I mean it."

She stopped giggling to stare gravely at Scully, then wrenched her gaze away and walked to the window.

"How long will this last? It's never been this cold before." She laughed nervously. "You brought the snow with you, from up there in the north."

"Maybe it's time I went and took it with me. Then the sun could come back to Benamargo."

"No, don't say that. You're not leaving, are you?"

Marisa stoppped herself abruptly, biting her lip.

"You want me to stay?"

"Yes."

"Then I shall."

"Don Carlos —"

"Carlos! Remember?"

"Carlos, there's something I want to ask you. You won't be angry?"

"How could I be angry with you, Marisa?"

"You may be. It's about your friend." Scully groaned. "Do you know how long he's staying?"

"I've no idea. The sooner he goes the better as far as I'm concerned."

"I think so too."

Scully was surprised.

"You? But why? He seems to be very popular with every-body."

For a moment Marisa looked near to tears.

"What is it?" demanded Scully, putting his hands on her shoulders.

"It's Ramón. He has become so friendly with that man that he seems to have no time for me and Mama. When you ask him anything, he snaps your head off. He has started ridiculing the pueblo, saying cruel things. He's just so different these days. Mama is worried out of her head. She stayed in bed today. She said she has a cold, but I know what it is. She doesn't know what to do about Ramón. He goes out and we don't know where he is. It was never like this before."

"Have you tried talking to him?"

"Me? I'm just his baby sister. He never listens to me. But you, Carlos, couldn't you say something to your friend? Ask him to leave Ramón alone."

"Quite honestly, I'm the last person to have any influence with him."

Marisa looked embarrassed.

"He has been saying things about you, you know that? Bad things. He says he came here to remind you of your duty to your family. It's not true, is it?"

Scully sighed.

"No. That man will say anything to serve his purpose. He is very cunning and he can fool anybody. I feel bad about his coming here. It's my fault, and I know he will only cre-ate trouble."

"Why don't you tell Ramón that?" pleaded Marisa.

"Your brother is a fine fellow, but he's very proud. I don't think he wants advice from me. I tried to warn him off Klease once but he acted as though he were insulted."

Marisa nodded.

"You're right. He is so proud. It runs in the family. He hates to lose face. If somebody insults him, he is ready to fight them no matter how big they are. Mama says that when he was small he was always coming home bruised and his clothes in rags because he wouldn't give way to older boys. Once a boy threw him in the irrigation channel. But he climbed straight out and made the boy apologise. The trouble is he will never admit he is wrong. Mother says he gets it from his father."

"Your father," Scully warmed his hands before the fire. "Do you remember much about him?"

"Vaguely. He was big and handsome and always joking. I can remember him picking me up and hugging me and laughing so much. But he had a terrible temper, just like Ramón." Marisa shivered. "They had awful rows, father and mother. It used to terrify us kids. I always hid under the bed. His face would be so red and he yelled at mother and threatened to beat her — I think he did once or twice. She told him that he drank too much, that he was no better than a gypsy, that he was irresponsible and godless. He would laugh at that and say he had no need for her god. At least that's what Ramón says he said. I was too young to remember. And when he had calmed down, he would say 'A man has to live'. He always said that. 'A man has to live'."

"You miss him, don't you?"

She gazed listlessly at the fire.

"I used to, very much. It didn't seem fair that all my friends had fathers and I didn't. I dreamed that there would be a knock at the door one day and he would be there, handsome and laughing, and I would run to him to be kissed." The tears glistened. "But it was worse for Mama. She had no money and she had to raise us. There wasn't much to eat. Every day we had potatoes or chick peas. She says that, even if he did come back, she would not let him in the house."

Marisa had slumped down on to a sheepskin stretched before the fire. Scully squeezed her shoulder and sat down on the old wooden armchair. Resin hissed from the burning pine logs. It was a hushed, cotton-woolled afternoon, with the snow-muffled village turned in on itself, hugging itself against the cold, more like a womb than ever. Marisa leaned back against Scully's knees, her head to one side, eyes closed. He could feel her steady breathing through her thick coat, her slender frame against his legs.

His thoughts drifted as he enjoyed the warmth of the blazing logs and of Marisa. If only this peace would last and somehow the world out there would resolve itself. He wanted only to float, inert, letting events take their course. He wanted to wipe out all trace of the obnoxious past. A clean slate, that's what he wanted.

A log shifted in a flurry of sparks and he blinked his eyes open. Winter twilight was invading the room. Marisa had shifted her position and was gazing at him with a mixture of frank curiosity and tenderness. Encountering his glance, she dropped her gaze. He cupped her chin in his hand and she smiled and raised her face. He bent until their lips touched. Their mouths formed a kiss, the gentlest touching of lips that was hardly a kiss at all. But it was enough.

"Marisa?"

"Yes, Carlos, yes."

This time it was fierce, wild, and the demanding came from Marisa. Her lips scoured Scully's skin, her tongue thrust into his mouth flooding it with sweetness, her flesh was burning. Hell, thought Scully, I want this woman, I want her, I need her, I could swallow her whole, this yearning child-woman, to hell with it, she is crying out for me, I've thought about her every day since I first set eyes on her, why have I been kidding myself? If it hadn't been for her, I would no longer be here. I want her, I want her now.

Marisa pulled him down on to the sheepskin, helping him free herself of the coat and her thick sweater as his kisses caressed her face and neck. She was trembling with anticipation, arching her body as he struggled with her blouse. To Scully it seemed that touching her was like plunging a hand into hot cream, soft, smooth, scalding.

"Please, please," she cried.

"I'll be gentle, so gentle," he promised, and her woman's breasts expanded in his hands like blossoming rosebuds and he kissed her dark nipples.

"Marisa, Marisa!"

"Please, please!"

She moaned and shook as his caresses aroused her further. And, when he finally entered her, she let out a piercing scream which shocked both of them. Frightened by her own reactions, she stared up at Scully. Then they both broke into laughter and Scully took her, gently as he had promised, in slow, lunging movements as Marisa caught her breath and bit her lip and gasped, her body convulsed by sensations beyond her knowledge or control.

"Too much, too much. Please, I can't...oh, please."

When she came, in a frenzy of cries and spasms, her muscular young body bent to his like a steel bow. Then she slumped back, spent, shaking her head unbelievingly, her arms pinned around his back, unwilling to release him. Scully rested his weight upon her, drained but exuberant. The fire sputtered, licking them with warmth and a golden, flickering light, and Marisa stroked his chest and neck with her full lips. He smiled and pulled the overcoat to cover the two of them.

A long time later he opened his eyes. Marisa was looking down on him.

"Is it always like that?" she asked.

He smiled.

"Once in a lifetime."

"Oh!" She was disappointed. "Then I'll never know it like that again."

"It's different, every time."

"It was incredible. I was flying like a bird. I flew right through the fire and up to heaven. Everywhere there were stars, all around me. I was so far above the earth. Flying through the stars and the music growing louder and louder. You can't imagine how beautiful it was.

"I can, because it was wonderful for me too." He touched

her nose, her lips. "They say that the only way to make love is as if every time is going to be the last. And that's how it felt."

"What? Don't say that, Carlos! This was only the first time. I love you. Did you know that? I love you. I want to be with you always. I want to marry you. Please say yes."

He laughed.

"Perhaps I shall have to marry you, to make an honest woman out of you."

Her eyes opened wide.

"But I am an honest woman. I shall always be honest with you, always."

She shifted her position to lean on one arm and Scully marvelled how a woman could convert an apparently clumsy movement into a thing of grace.

"I've sinned, haven't I? How can I ever go to confession and tell the priest?" She smothered a giggle. "Just think of Father Saturnino's face if I told him. But I don't care. Surely it cannot be a sin if it is so beautiful. You know, Carlos, I feel different already. I suddenly feel like a real woman. Thanks to you, Carlos. I want you, do you know that? Do you want me?"

"More than you can imagine," whispered Scully, pulling her down to cuddle against his chest. "You can't realise what you do for me."

CHAPTER SIXTEEN

A hammering at the door roused Scully. He lay in bed, gathering his thoughts. The sun was shining through a crack in the shutters and he could hear the drip, drip of thawing ice and snow. The hammering came again, and Marisa's voice. He sat up and rolled out of bed. In bare feet, a blanket wrapped around him, he descended groggily to the ground floor. Marisa stood on the doorstep, her eyes wide with anxiety.

"Carlos, you haven't seen Ramón?"

"No, why should I have?"

She stepped inside.

"He never came home last night."

Scully felt something move in his stomach.

"Well, he's a big fellow. He can look after himself," he said.

"But where would he go? It's never happened before. Mama is out of her mind." She clutched Scully's arm. "I'm so worried. I'm sure something has happened."

"Don't be silly. Ramón can handle himself. He'll be out with his goats."

"Not all night."

Scully tried to block a recurrent image of Ramón and Klease together, talking, laughing. Perhaps they had gone off somewhere. With his silver tongue, Klease could persuade the Pope himself to go to the devil. But he banished the thought. It was ridiculous. And in any case the route down the valley was virtually impassable. Marisa was worrying about nothing. Ramón was a man, not a boy.

"Don't distress yourself, Marisa. He must be around. What could happen to him, here in Benamargo?"

Marisa shook her head. She was unusually pale.

"I don't know. But I have a feeling. Ramón would never leave us alone all night. It's the way he is. Something's wrong."

"I'll get my clothes on, and then we'll see," promised Scully.

When he entered his landlady's living room, he found Dolores slumped at the table in a dressing gown. The only heat in the room came from the traditional brasero, an iron bowl filled with hot embers, which was placed beneath the table. Dolores looked dully at Scully and did not speak. Marisa poured him a coffee.

"I'm sure he will turn up," said Scully. "Don't you worry."

Dolores stared at him.

"I don't understand it. It's not like Ramón."

Hell, he's only been out on the tiles all night, thought Scully. It's not the end of the world.

"He must be checking the goats. Maybe one was giving birth and he had to stay with them."

"None were due," declared Marisa firmly. "And he would have let us know."

"Well, let's go and see," said Scully. "I'll bet you're worrying over nothing."

He and Marisa walked down the street, dodging the puddles left by the melting snow. Overnight the brief winter had ended. A wave of warmer air surged over the valley and the sky was as clear and blue as Scully had seen it. From all sides came the music of hurrying water. It sang in the roof guttering and chattered through the irrigation channels. Miraculously, it seemed, the almond trees had burst into blossom, as though another snowstorm had clothed the fields.

As they passed a man loading a mule, they caught the words of a song. It was one of the couplets with which a young man would serenade his girl.

"En tu puerta da la luna
Eres guapa y Dios te guarde."
(The moon shines on your door
You're pretty and may God protect you.)
Scully and Marisa exchanged glances. The man's voice

was strong and cheerful and the words seemed to hang in the clear morning air as though waiting to be picked. Scully could not recall such a beautiful morning.

Marisa plodded on. Several times she stopped villagers and asked if they had seen her brother. They all shook their heads.

"He must be in the goat stable," she declared.

They took that path that led out of the village towards a huddle of tumbledown buildings where Ramón kept his 60 or so goats. Marisa outpaced Scully, ignoring the slushy snow and the mud that splashed her. She halted at the entrance to the stable.

"Ramón! Ramón! Are you there?"

Some goats were browsing amid chopped straw in a small yard while the rest could be heard moving about under cover.

"Ramón!"

They opened the crude gate and pushed through the goats to the interior. Bawling animals scattered, some of the younger ones playfully nudging them with their unformed horns. It took some minutes to discern anything as they peered into the gloom and the sharp ammonia odour of decaying dung assaulted their nostrils.

"There's nobody here, Marisa. He must be about the village or up the mountain."

They walked outside.

"He may have gone to cut wood."

"In the snow?" said Marisa sceptically. "Look, there's plenty of wood over there."

She sat down on an old mill-stone already warmed by the sun.

"They used to grind corn here, a long time ago," she said. "See. A channel led from the stream over there and the water turned the mill."

They listened to the tumbling stream. Scully kissed her on the forehead and wandered around the side of the building. As he relieved himself against the moss-crusted wall, a bird perched in a nearby olive tree directed a torrent of song at him. His heart lifted and he breathed deep of the mountain air. He thought about Marisa, spreading her limbs to the sun now and how she had been the previous day, opening to him like a fresh wild flower. He experienced a wave of tenderness. For the first time in — how long? — he felt good to be alive. Marisa had awakened something in him. He shied away from putting a name to it. Some words were no longer in his vocabulary. Hell, he had better tread carefully. Next he would be having really crazy ideas, like some silly teenager. Remember, lust is lust and nothing more. Remember that.

Scully was about to return to Marisa when he noticed a shred of colour amid the soaking weeds at the foot of the wall. He approached and picked it up. A red neckerchief. He recognised it. And when he turned the corner he saw that the search was over.

At the back of the stable a thick beam jutted from the crumbling wall and a length of cord had been tossed over it. Touched by the first sunshine of spring, the body swayed gently in the slight breeze. The bird still trilled brightly away and there was a strange tranquillity about the scene, unless one looked at the face, contorted and black, twisted to one side by the tightened noose biting into the neck-flesh.

Helplessly, Scully reached into his pocket for a knife he knew was not there and knowing it was too late anyway. Later, he could not recall his first reactions. But it did not matter. It was all too late. He remembered Marisa's face crumbling when she saw his expression. He tried to restrain her, but she broke free and ran to the body. She gazed dumbly at the inert flesh, until he found a sickle, hacked at the rope and lowered the corpse to the ground. Then she threw herself on her brother's neck, weeping uncontrollably.

Men came from the village and picked up Ramón and laid him on a rough stretcher and carried him slowly in silence down the path, while Marisa sobbed and stumbled alongside. The old men and the women and the children came out of the houses to watch as they bore Ramón home. The streets were hushed. The men panted and slipped on the cobbles but they never spoke. They carried Ramón up to his door where Dolores stood waiting. She watched them approach impassively, as though frozen by her grief. The men stopped before her. Then, when she could see Ramón's features, she collapsed.

"Ramón! Hijo mío! Hijo mío! My son! My son!"

Her wails echoed throughout the pueblo as the men, wooden-faced to stem their own tears, carried Ramón inside. Soon her cries were taken up by those of the other women who flocked to the house to offer their condolences and to share in the pain. They dressed Ramón in a white shirt and in the suit and tie he had said he would wear on his wedding day, and they laid him out on the brass bedstead in the big bedroom, where he had never slept. The women embraced Dolores, joining in her keening, and the men filed in to view the body and shake the mother's lifeless hand in commiseration.

In the evening, Scully too went to the house. He passed between the murmuring, black-clad women who fluttered like ravens at the front door and passed into the living room with its hand-painted family portraits and lamp glimmering at a tiny shrine in the corner. There was hardly room to move or breathe so many people were squeezed in there. The low hum of conversation and the anguished cries were unceasing but, little by little, as the mourners caught sight of Scully, the noise died. Everybody's eyes turned to him.

Dolores alone did not move, sitting as though turned to stone. She seemed not to recognise him when he approached her.

"I'm truly sorry, señora," said Scully awkwardly in the hush. "Ramón was a fine boy, a fine boy."

Dolores made no reply. Instead she began rocking to and fro, staring into space, muttering over and over to herself:"My son, my son."

Marisa, calm, like a ghost, touched his arm.

"He is in the bedroom. Come."

He followed her along the passage. The room was in darkness except for a candle which burned near the head of the bed, casting a flickering light on Ramón's face. He lay in a plain pine-wood coffin. Death had drained his dark complexion, burnished by sun and wind, of all colour so that it matched the grey, ill-fitting suit into which they had packed him and contrasted sharply with the clean white shirt he wore. Scully could hardly recognise him. This marble statue could not really be Ramón.

"He's so handsome, isn't he?" said Marisa, her voice washed of all feeling.

"Yes, he is...so handsome."

He wanted to get away from this icy room with its odour of death, but Marisa could not tear her eyes away from the empty vessel that had been her brother.

"I think I should go," he said.

"Yes, you must go."

Her voice was flat.

"I'll see you tomorrow."

"I mean, " She hesitated. "from the village."

"From the village?"

"It would be better, wouldn't it? After this."

Scully had to struggle to speak.

"That's what you want? You want me to go?"

"I did not say that."

Marisa did not meet his gaze. She had been standing, head bowed, before the bed. Abruptly she turned and brushed past him, tears spilling down her cheeks.

"But you must go — soon! Please!" she said, her voice broken by sobs.

She pushed blindly through the door into the living room and Scully followed her. The murmuring women made way for him and he blundered out into the keen night air. Pacing along the empty street, he was filled with a mixture of rage and despair. He could not rid himself of that last vision of Ramón. That pathetic arrangement of dead flesh in its Sunday best had no relation to the lively spirit he had known, the proud young male, the agile goatherd who wrote poetry and feared nothing. He had been robbed of his essence, the life prematurely sucked out of him.

Murderous rage gripped Scully. Intent only on unleashing it, he strode towards the village shop. He pushed through the shop-door into the dim interior, banged his knee on a crate of vegetables, cursed fiercely and gazed wildly about. Carmencita, veiled in black, stopped in the act of slicing Manchego cheese.

She squinted at Scully from behind trailing festoons of sausage. Her sharp eyes, buried in folds of fat, were challenging in the gloom, like those of a rodent surprised in its lair.

"Where is he?"

She stared, as though not understanding.

"You know, the foreigner, El Rubio, or whatever you call him? Where is he?"

She gestured towards the rear of the shop. He ran up the stairs and pushed open the first door. Klease looked around in surprise. He was about to place a shirt in his suitcase which rested on a sagging bed.

"Leaving town?" snarled Scully. "Well, that's the day's best news. Though, after what you've done, you deserve to be lynched."

Klease smiled faintly.

"I, Charles? You're getting melodramatic in your old age. Yes, I am leaving. If I spend another day here, I shall die of boredom. This place is suffocating me. You can have it all to yourself. But not for long, I think. Your days are numbered, Charles. I warned you. Unless, of course, you've come to your senses. Where's that cash?"

"If ever I could kill somebody, it's you, Klease."

Klease raised his eyebrows.

"But you couldn't kill anybody, Charles. I figured that out a long time ago. Ruthless you could be. But you always had a certain squeamishness, an unwillingness to go all the way. Your old buddies might laugh at the idea, but you're too soft, Charles. I've even known you show mercy once or twice. A fatal weakness. One I never suffered from."

"I'll grant you that, Klease." Scully's voice was thick. He clenched his hands. "You didn't have much mercy with Ramón, did you, you bastard?"

Klease shrugged.

"Ramón? Unfortunate. He was such a sensitive boy under all that macho bullshit."

"You killed him! You drew him into your dirty little game just to spite me, just to show your power. You shamed him. And you killed him!"

"Why are you so concerned, Charles?" demanded Klease in a scoffing tone. "Did you have designs yourself on the simple goatherd? Or couldn't you make your mind up between him or his sister?"

Scully had heard enough. He made as though to seize the man by the throat, but Klease stepped quickly aside and grabbed a heavy wooden candlestick which stood next to the bed. He waved it threateningly.

"Try anything, Charles, and I shall break your skull open. I owe you something for the last time."

For long moments they stood glaring at one another, breathing heavily. Finally, Scully gritted: "Just get out and leave me and this village alone."

"You think that will solve anything? Do you think I'm really the source of all evil around here?" He shook his head wonderingly and tossed the candlestick on to the bed. "For god's sake, Charles, I didn't kill Ramón. This fucking village killed him. He was murdered by ignorance and prejudice and superstition and guilt, all the crap that should have gone out with the Inquisition. He died of shame when he should have been proud of something beautiful. That's the truth."

"You drove him to this, didn't you?" retorted Scully. "Because he couldn't face his own family."

"Do you think I wanted this to happen?" demanded Klease.

"If you hadn't been here, he would still be alive."

"Half alive! Half alive! I tried to show him there was a little more to the world than Benamargo, that's all, to expand his mind. Not that you could ever understand, Charles. You're as screwed up as the rest of them."

"If you mean that I don't like queers and two-timers, you're damn right!"

Klease smiled pityingly. He made a gesture of hopelessness and sat down on the bed. He rubbed his hands over his face.

"Don't you see, Charles? I genuinely had a soft spot for that boy. He had a simple sort of nobility about him, a directness and a sincerity. We got on together. It may sound nonsense to you, but he believed in me, respected me. Not many people have ever respected Graham Klease. To him I was some sort of guru, I suppose. It wasn't just a case of the dissipated philanderer and the innocent goatboy, Charles. There was much more to it. He taught me things I didn't know about myself. We understood one another, Ramón and I. We moved to the same melody."

"You seduced him."

"Seduced? You're one big cliché, aren't you, Charles? All hackneyed thoughts and worn-out values. Don't try to give me a morality lesson, you of all people. We had a truly beautiful relationship. But it was poisoned by ignorance, the same goddamned ignorance that strangles these people from birth. Sure, at first I was just out to embarrass you, but — " Klease looked almost wistful. " — it was a lot more than that in the end, a lot more."

Scully's expression mixed scepticism and distaste. He was used to the glib, sneering Klease, not this one.

"You don't believe me, I know that. Because you haven't learned anything, Charles, about people or their feelings. You know nothing. Ramón had more emotion, more humanity in his little finger than you have in your entire body." His voice had acquired an unaccustomed tenderness. "He gave me this. He said he wanted me to keep it."

Klease produced a sheet of paper.

Scully looked at the paper. It was a quotation from a Lorca poem he vaguely remembered, carefully written out in a copperplate hand. He made to pass it back, but Klease stopped him.

"Read it to me, will you?"

"Read it?"

"That's what I said, goddammit!"

"For Christ's sake, I didn't come here to read you poetry, Klease."

"Read it. Tell me what it means in English. My Spanish is so lousy I can only get half it."

Scully scanned the lines that Ramón had copied out. They were from a poem entitled Canción Otoñal, or Song of Autumn. He groaned.

"Look, I'm not sure I understand this."

"For god's sake, man, tell me what it says!"

Scully scowled and, muttering to himself, began a stumbling translation.

"It starts 'Se deshelerá la nieve cuando la muerte nos lleva?' That's something like 'Will the snow melt when death carries us off?'."

Klease gestured impatiently.

"It says more than that. Go on!"

Scully glared at the poem.

"Or after death will there be more snow that is more perfect? Will there be peace like Christ says, or can the problem never be solved? That's what it says."

"Go on."

"Then it says 'Y si el amor nos engaña?' And if love tricks us? That's it. And if love tricks us?"

Grabbing the paper from Scully, Klease stared at it as though seeing something beyond the lines.

"And if love tricks us? That's all? And if love tricks us?"

He gazed into space, a stricken expression on his face, repeating the line again and again.

"Y si el amor nos engaña?"

CHAPTER SEVENTEEN

A bulldozer came up the road from Cerrogordo and blustered aside the rocks and earth that the winter storms had dislodged. Teams of men went out to start rebuilding the retaining wall which the run-off had washed away at several points along the highway. Juanito brought up loads of canned goods and fresh fruit and vegetables and carried away cured ham and rounds of goat cheese. The bus lumbered up the treacherous, curving road once more and rattled back down it in the afternoon.

It could have been spring in Benamargo. Mild air currents surged up the valley, persuading the almond trees to scatter pink-white petals over the awakening landscape and luring a lone peach tree sheltering below the plaza to explode into blossom. North of the sierras, the bleak plains of Castile and the rest of Europe still cringed before gale and frost, but sunshine caressed the pueblo. Only the snow on the distant peaks hinted that winter had not quite said farewell, that and the chill that reigned over Benamargo.

The first available bus had carried away Robert Klease, breathing contempt and menaces to the last. He had gone, but his shadow lingered. It lay like a shroud over Scully. He could not shake off the depression created by recent events. The circumstances of Ramón's death had reinforced his feeling of alienation. He had thought he had found a bolthole but his hopes of peace had gone up in flames.

Then there had been the funeral. It took place in late afternoon, following a night-long wake, and was attended by only the men of the village. That was the custom. They gathered in small groups outside the house of Dolores, gossiping in low tones, while the women sobbed within. They wore clean, threadbare jackets and newly pressed, ill-fitting pants and frayed, open-necked shirts. Some of the closer

relatives had donned black armbands. When Scully appeared, nobody met his eye and the men murmured and
shuffled uncomfortably.

The wait seemed interminable, but finally the coffin was
carried from the house. It was a simple affair, surmounted
by a cross. Six of the younger men hoisted it on their shoulders, steadied themselves, and then, with firm steps, began
the walk through the narrow streets. The men followed, others joining the procession as it wound its way towards the
village edge. At its head walked a grey-haired man, an uncle
of Ramón, bearing a large wreath. Scully saw that a lanky
youth had occupied the position by his side. He recognised
the spiky hair, the Neanderthal jaw and limbs that never
seemed to be quite under control. It was Pepe El Tonto, the
village simpleton, frequently mocked by other teenagers but
also tolerated in a peculiarly protective way by the village
as a whole. He was the despair of his widowed mother who
trailed him about, rescuing him with angry shrieks when
the customers in Sebastián's bar tried to get him drunk.

He was gesticulating wildly at bystanders on the route,
pointing to the coffin and indicating they should cross themselves. Nobody paid him any attention. He was so much a
part of the scene that they did not notice him. Pepe could
indulge every whim. He lived in a private world, unfettered
by convention or custom. The mourners continued to whisper among themselves during the progress through the village, but fell silent as they climbed the winding path to the
burial ground. It was cooler up here. A breeze got up as the
sun dipped close to the horizon and their faces set harder
the closer they approached the swaying cypresses and high
walls that crowned the ridge.

Father Saturnino waited at the entrance, hands folded
around his stomach, cassock fluttering in the wind, granite
severity emanating from every pore. He turned slowly and
led the way into the tiny chapel, followed by as many of the
mourners who could squeeze in. Scully heard the priest's
voice booming out, as the cypresses creaked an accompaniment and shreds of white cloud flew out like banners above
the mountain-tops. He wondered how a traditionalist like

Father Saturnino would get around the awkward fact that Ramón had taken his own life. Perhaps the fact that he had been a member of Las Animas would be enough to guarantee him a place in sanctified ground. In any case, the priest appeared to make his own rules.

Emerging from the chapel, the coffin-bearers trudged through the cemetery, followed by the priest and mourners. In a far corner, they prepared to slide the coffin into a vacant slot high in the wall. With surprising strength, they raised the heavy burden at arm's length above their heads and heaved it forward into the waiting cavity. Halfway in, however, the coffin wedged against some obstruction and would go no further.

A sigh went up from the men. Several people offered advice while the coffin was eased out and laid on the ground. After some delay, a man with a hammer and chisel mounted a ladder and began chipping away at the edges of the cavity. Gusts of cold air rustled the dried flowers laid before some of the tombs. The men stamped their feet impatiently and thrust their hands into their pockets. Scully noticed Bruno among them.

"Does this always happen?" he asked.

Bruno shrugged.

"Only when the coffin does not fit."

He stared intently at Scully.

"And your friend?"

"You won't see him again."

Bruno scratched his head, as though embarrassed.

"He said things about you, in the village."

"So I heard."

"I didn't believe them myself, but you know how this place is. It's easy to make trouble. And after this..." He gestured at the open grave and the coffin. "The bad tongues are at work. They are saying it's the strangers who are to blame, and their friends. That's how it always goes. When some dung falls, there's always somebody ready to pick it up and throw it around so that everybody gets dirtied. I'm just telling you this, Don Carlos, so you know."

Scully nodded grimly.

"But they are right, aren't they? If I had not come here, if this acquaintance of mine had not followed me here, this would never have happened."

"You can't blame yourself," said Bruno. "It's god's will."

"A socialist doesn't believe that, surely?"

Bruno produced a bleak smile.

"A Spanish socialist, yes," he said, without irony.

The man came down the wobbling ladder and nodded to the priest. Saturnino uttered a last blessing and the pall-bearers picked up the coffin once more, eight of them this time, and in one easy motion raised it and pushed it smoothly into its home.

The wreath was laid inside too and a bunch of lilies and then the bricklayer carried up a bucket of plaster and a trowel and began sealing up the niche, walling in the dark box and the white lilies, brick by brick.

Outside the cemetery gates, the male relatives waited in line. Scully recognised most by sight. Juanito, a second or third cousin of Dolores, was there. And Emilio, a shell of a man who chewed tobacco endlessly and liked to reminisce about the days when he carried produce on his mule to market in "la capital", as he called Granada. Each mourner shook hands with the relatives and murmured his condolences.

"Que en paz descanse...en paz descanse...May he rest in peace ...may he rest in peace..."

The relatives accepted these commiserations impassively. All emotion had been spent at the wake. Their duty done, the mourners began drifting back to the village. Scully felt something of an interloper in this ritual, but at the same time he did want to express his sorrow over Ramón's death. Mechanically, he uttered the appropriate words as he moved along the line.

He saw that the youth in fifth place was Alejandro, the excitable wedding guest who had been scolded for hurling rice about too enthusiastically. Alejandro already had his hand extended. Then he raised his eyes and saw Scully. His expression switched to one of undisguised hostility and he abruptly withdrew his hand. For several seconds they stood confronting one another, then Scully moved on. As he strode away from the cemetery, he heard a clamour of muffled comment.

Tramping back down the hillside, he studied the huddle of dwellings below as the first lights flicked on. The pueblo was the same as ever, a haven of security in the dark void of the sierras. Self-contained, engrossed in itself, cosy. Even so, he could not avoid feeling a tremor of unease.

CHAPTER EIGHTEEN

The house of Dolores was like a tomb. Death's heavy odour seemed to have crept into every corner. Dolores rarely moved, except to go once a day to mass. Her very life-blood appeared to have been squeezed out of her. She sat in the gloom, her vacant eyes fixed on Ramón's portrait on the wall. The large, hand-tinted photograph had been draped in black crepe. Day and night, the shutters remained closed. Dolores was oblivious to the coldness of the room, alleviated only slightly in the evening by the brazier of glowing embers beneath the table. Her pallid, immobile features floated in the obscurity, like a disembodied piece of sculpture. She permitted no light in the room, except that from a candle guttering before the plaster Virgin.

It was left to Marisa to do the cooking and clean the house and negotiate with a cousin who wanted to take over the goat herd. She served Scully his meals in the kitchen. But she rarely spoke. It was as though, since Ramón's death, both she and her mother had taken a vow of silence. When Scully asked Marisa a question, she replied in monosyllables and avoided his gaze. If they ever encountered one another outside the house, Marisa would hurry past him as though he were not there. The situation was untenable and Scully decided he had to make a move. He could no longer stay in Dolores's house. Before he could announce his decision, however, Marisa told him her news.

"Don Carlos, I have to tell you something," she said, making more noise than usual as she gathered up the dinner things one evening. "It's about the house. Mama says she doesn't want to rent it any more. I'm sorry, but that's what she says."

She busied herself at the sink.

"I'm sorry too," said Scully. "But I understand."

"She was keeping it for Ramón, you see, for when he got married. But now there's no point. So she's talking of selling it. We have no use for it now. But it's not as though you have to go straight away, not tomorrow, I mean. Maybe at the end of the month, when you're ready..."

She was talking quickly, the words tripping over one another, her back to Scully. He rose and touched her on the shoulder.

"It's all right, Marisa. I understand. I knew I could not stay here any longer."

She made no reply and then he saw that tears were coursing down her cheeks.

"Marisa." His voice was soft. "I'm so sorry for what has happened. But that doesn't change anything between us, does it? We're still friends, aren't we?"

She shook her head miserably.

"I don't know. I only know that it's best you should go."

Scully cupped her chin with his fingers.

"Marisa —"

She pulled away from him.

"Please," she said, in a whisper. "Don't touch me."

All right, then go he would. He had known that there was no choice after the incident in the cemetery. He could not pin down any overt antagonism towards him in the village, but he thought he detected a distinct change of attitude. People looked at him or addressed him with a wariness that had not been there before. At first, he tried to convince himself that he was imagining it, but he had to admit that things were not the same. Klease had done his work well, poisoning the atmosphere as only he knew how and leaving somebody else to face the consequences.

"Of course things are not the same, my dear blind Englishman," snorted Baldomero. The schoolteacher was at his most irritatingly pompous. "A young man has killed himself. Was it that accursed Christian sense of guilt that drove him to it? Never mind. The people demand a scapegoat and lo and behold they have one, a member of that perfidious, masochistic race whose favourite sports are chasing foxes and whipping one another. Degenerates to a man."

"I can't be blamed for the sins of the whole British nation," said Scully, in feeble protest. He had bumped into the teacher between classes.

"Why not? Somebody has to face the music. You're the most convenient target, the only one of Her Imperial Majesty's subjects that anybody around here is likely to meet. So naturally we have to castigate you for holding on to Gibraltar or for the sins of those awful British football fans who insist on beating up such defenceless citizens as the Spanish police. And we have to blame somebody for what happened to Ramón."

Baldomero shook his head.

"Poor Ramón. It's not difficult to feel bitter."

"How do you think I feel?" demanded Scully.

The teacher shrugged.

"I can guess. But it doesn't make any difference. Our prehistoric cleric rules here and he has been thundering away against all outside influences. He started at the funeral service. The way he's talking, you might as well have cloven feet and horns sprouting from your head. Ask Amelia. Now, I have to pound some culture into the heads of these young ruffians."

Baldomero's sister was preparing a meal in her kitchen. She jumped when Scully spoke to her.

"Oh, I didn't hear you."

"Are you well?"

"As well as can be expected." There was a tautness in her manner and she wiped her hands nervously on a dish cloth.

"I was talking to your brother. He tells me that I have become the black sheep of the village."

"I wouldn't say that."

"Well, the priest has been having a go at me, hasn't he?"

"He was very fond of Ramón, you know. I think he looked on him almost as a son. And Ramón was a member of Las Animas too. So there's bound to be some reaction."

Scully grimaced.

"But that doesn't mean I have to get the blame. What happened was nothing to do with me."

Amelia spread her thin, bony hands.

"I know that, Carlos. I know that you're a good person behind all that cynicism. But not everybody knows you as well as I do."

"The priest is turning the village against me, isn't he?"

"There has been a lot of talk." She looked anxious. "Oh, Carlos, I'm afraid for you."

"Afraid? Of what?"

"I think you should leave the village."

"You too?"

"Heavens, I don't want you to go, I swear it. But..."

"But what?"

Amelia bit her lip. Twin spots of pink flushed her drawn face.

"For your own sake, you should go, get away from here, although I would hate it, not to see you again. I would miss you so much."

"So much?"

She took a step forward and clutched his arms.

"Carlos, kiss me. Please, kiss me."

"Amelia..."

"It's all right. Baldomero is in class." She was tense, her breath coming in short gasps. "Kiss me!"

Scully leaned forward to give her a brief peck on the cheek, but Amelia quickly twisted her head and their mouths collided. Her lips were dry but demanding. She kissed him feverishly, caressing his hair and neck. Then she laid her head against his chest.

"Carlos, it will be so lonely if you go. I know this sounds crazy, but please, listen. If you go, would you take me with you? I don't care where we go. It doesn't matter. As long as we can be together, somewhere else. Please, will you?"

"Who said I was going anywhere?" Carlos played for time. The thought of running off with the teacher's sister was too much for him to grasp. "And I thought you had to be here, to support your brother and look after him?"

"I've got a right to live too, haven't I?" Her tone was fierce. "I've given, given, all my life. It's my turn! It's my turn! I want to live too. Take me with you, Carlos."

"You amaze me, Amelia. I never expected this. We hardly know one another. I would drive you crazy within a week."

"You don't want to take me, do you?"

"Take you where, Amelia? I'm not going anywhere yet." He sighed. "Why does everybody want me to leave? Why should I? Just because Father Saturnino thinks my breath smells?"

"We could live anywhere. I don't mind travelling. I'm more adaptable than you might think."

"Where would it lead, Amelia? Let's be realistic. We're not teenagers."

"It would be marvellous, Carlos. We could do so many things together." She ran a hand over his face. "Carlos, say yes. Don't you see I love you?"

"I can see you want to leave Benamargo, but things are not quite that simple," said Scully. He disentangled himself from Amelia. "I think I should go."

"I've got some money, an inheritance. I could get a job too. It would work out, Carlos." She was pleading, grabbing at a lifeline. "You'd never regret it, never, truly. Think of it. We could go to the theatre, to concerts, good restaurants. Can you imagine? It would all be so different from here."'

"This isn't the sort of thing you just jump into," said Scully, alarmed at her desperation, at her pathetic pleading. "And what about your brother?"

"Baldomero?" Her lips set in a thin line. "What has he ever done for me? He was always the spoilt one, the brilliant student. He always got all the privileges. My mother and sisters used to wait on him hand and foot. Clever Baldomero! So smug, so arrogant. He laughs at everything I do. Let him find out for himself what it is to live without me, without a servant."

Her sudden vindictiveness surprised Scully. Baldomero and his sister had seemed to form a perfect partnership, with never a sour word between them. He edged towards the door.

"Promise me, Carlos! Promise me! It will work out, you'll see. The two of us. Please, you'll think about it?"

He smiled, and escaped. He took a long, hard walk

through the countryside, deliberately trying to burn himself out as he sweated up gorse-covered hillsides and scaled precipitous buttresses. Everybody, it seemed, wanted him to leave. Nothing difficult about that. He could just walk away. But why should he? Where could he run to this time? He was being hounded out of the village by this idiotic priest and, wherever he went, Klease could be relied on to turn up, snapping at his heels. There was nowhere to run to. And then there was Marisa. To run from Benamargo would be to run from her too. Soft, sweet Marisa, the only sympathetic human being on this goddamned earth. She alone was reason enough to stay. He could not desert her. But what about Amelia? My god, he had to avoid that woman.

"What a bitch she is!" Sebastián was on his favourite subject, women. "A vulture. She's killed off two husbands, nagged them to death, and ended up with all their land."

With difficulty, Scully found out that the bar-keeper was talking about Amparo, a shrivelled little lady who had begun making frequent appearances at Dolores's house.

"She's Dolores's sister," explained Sebastián. "She hasn't spoken to her in 20 years. But now she sniffs some profit she's on her doorstep all the time."

"Why haven't the two spoken for so long?" asked Scully idly.

"Because Amparo thinks Dolores stole her man. She was going to marry Francisco, Ramón's father, or so she thought, but he picked Dolores instead. She never forgave her. In those days, I suppose you could say Francisco and I were rivals. I was as handsome as the devil then. I didn't have this."

He patted his belly.

"Trouble was I couldn't make my mind up between Amparo and Dolores. Then, son of a whore if Francisco didn't sweep Dolores off her feet and I very nearly fell into Amparo's net. What an escape! I'd rather have been stuck with Celestina up there in the hills. She's an angel compared to Amparo."

"Hombre," said one of the customers. "They say this is a man's country but don't you believe it." The other drinkers solemnly nodded agreement. "The women rule. Give them a centimetre and they devour you and spit out the bones. That poor fellow from Cerrogordo will find out, soon enough. I don't envy him, taking on Inmaculada."

Sebastián winked at Scully.

"You'll see a bit of fun tonight. Inmaculada is a widow. She's getting married and they don't let that sort of thing pass unnoticed in Benamargo." He winked again. "You'll see."

He did, indeed. Walking home along the main street, Scully became aware of an unaccustomed noise. It sounded like somebody unloading a truckload of scrap iron. As he rounded a corner, he discovered the source. A group of youngsters advanced towards him. Virtually every teenager in the village was there, plus most of the smaller children and a sprinkling of adults. Each was carrying some metal object, an old saucepan, a kettle, a tin mug, a sheet of iron, a cow-bell, and was beating it energetically and remorselessly. The din was painful to the ears.

Scully saw that Juanito was one of the leaders. He was carrying the rusty remains of a kitchen sink, which he was bashing with a spanner. His face shone with merriment as he swapped wisecracks with the villagers who came to their doors. Behind him, a young boy hauled a length of rope tied to a clattering bundle of old iron. Next came a bizarre-looking couple. One wore a crumpled top hat and a ragged frock-coat and carried a cardboard suitcase. The other, a grotesquely made-up youth with lavishly applied rouge and scarlet lip-stick, sauntered along in a long gown, swinging his hips and pressing a baby doll to his mighty bosom with hairy forearms.

The villagers fell about with laughter as the couple pouted and swaggered. A group of children added to the pandemonium by pumping away at zambombas, earthenware pots with goatskins stretched across one end. Attached to the skins were sticks and, when the children ran their hands up and down the sticks, obscene noises were emitted by this strange instrument.

Scully spied Bruno standing with Javier, a small, mole-like man with some claim to legal training. As secretary to the village council, which never seemed to meet, he occupied a tiny, flyblown office. It was hard to distingish Javier from the mountains of dusty files which rose all around him to ceiling height. He spent his days burrowing through these papers, issuing forms and writing letters in longhand, since Benamargo lacked even a typewriter. The one belonging to his office had been sent away for repair and never returned.

"What on earth is happening?" asked Scully, above the din.

Javier chuckled.

"It's what we call a cencerrazo. It's a custom that goes back centuries."

"Hmph! That's where they should have left it, back in the 15th century," snapped Bruno. "It only encourages the ignorant. They should ban these things."

"That's what you'd like, I suppose," retorted Javier. "There's the typical reaction of a Socialist. If somebody's having a good time, ban it. You're no better than all those Francoists."

"And what about the widow? How do you think she feels? No, they should ban it for good. This sort of nonsense gives us a bad image all over Europe. It's tercermundista, that's what it is."

Bruno rolled "tercermundista" around his mouth as though chewing it. It was one of his favourite words. Scully knew that in modern, progressive Spain there was nothing worse than being judged part of the underdeveloped Tercer Mundo, or Third World.

"What is it all in aid of?" he asked.

Javier explained.

"The widow Inmaculada is getting married. El Canario was her first husband. A widow remarrying! So she has to be serenaded. It started a couple of nights ago, but tonight is the climax. Everybody joins in. Juanito there, he's a great one for inventing witty rhymes. He's composed some about the couple."

Bruno sniffed.

"What it is," he said, bellowing into Scully's ear to make himself heard. "It's an excuse to do no work and get drunk. And the rhymes, the coplas, they can be very cruel. It just provokes mischief. It's all rooted in prejudice, you see. Widows and widowers are not supposed to marry again, you understand. It's not thought right. So they make them suffer. Pah!"

Javier gesticulated in exasperation.

"Do you think Inmaculada cares a jot? She's so pleased to be the centre of attention she'll put up with anything. Lucky for her she found a fellow from Cerrogordo," said Bruno. "There aren't many in this village who would dare to go against the custom, or the priest. He would never perform the ceremony. Nobody ever remarries in Benamargo. So they're off to Cerrogordo. Anything goes there."

The racket intensified, vibrating the windows of the houses, reverberating through the mountains and echoing back, frightening dogs and mules so that they set up their own accompaniment. From all points in the village the people descended on Inmaculada's house. It was a test. If she or her husband-to-be, who had arrived to fetch her, should lose patience and show ill-humour, then the noise and merciless leg-pulling would continue indefinitely. Shouting, laughing, chanting, the villagers serenaded the bride with anything that came to hand. Somebody had found a large oil drum, dragged it to Inmaculada's door and was beating on it with a heavy stick.

"Drink! Drink!" insisted the revellers. And Scully drank with them, as the bottles passed from hand to hand.

Amid the cacophony, Juanito whirled like a carrousel, his face reddened and swollen by alcohol and exertion. Occasionally, he would launch into one of his coplas, full of slanderous allusions and double meanings. Scully strained to catch the words as, voice cracking, Juanito related in ululating flamenco style the story of a shepherd meeting a maiden by a well and asking her if he could dip his spoon. The crowd rocked — "Ay, Juanito!" — and the jokes grew ever more ribald.

When a plump, middle-aged woman appeared at the

door, accompanied by a white-haired man in a new suit, the tumult reached new heights. Though close to tears, the widow smiled bravely, something her anxious partner found it impossible to manage. They were waiting impatiently for a taxi which had been ordered from Cerrogordo, where they would be married next day. As the couple retreated into the house, the party outside continued unabated.

Suddenly Pepe El Tonto appeared on top of a wall. Somebody had been plying him with drink and he capered joyfully along, a grinning gargoyle hovering above the gaping, upturned faces. A whoop went up, and then a shriek of laughter as the crowd saw the lighted candle planted on his head. To cheers and jeers, he began dancing a clumsy jig. Several times he almost toppled from his perch, only to catch his balance by a miracle, a feat that won renewed applause from the spectators. This encouraged two more youths to clamber on the wall, where they proceeded to demonstrate their limited mastery of flamenco, stamping their feet and flicking their fingers wildly.

Scully looked around at the villagers. A universal exaltation gripped them, a collective madness. They had forgotten where they were or who they were. All restraints were gone. They were beyond themselves, and Scully felt himself being sucked into the same vortex.

"Shameless one! Cursed be the day I bore you! Mother of god, to shame your mother thus! Home, get thee home!"

The villagers guffawed and cheered even more at the sight of the angry figure which had appeared out of the darkness and started belabouring El Tonto about the legs with a broomstick. He cried and yelled for mercy. But his mother continued thumping him, until he tumbled off the wall and fled down the street, sobbing in pain and humiliation, as she swung the stick again and again.

A klaxon and a battered trumpet had joined the chorus that swelled and swelled in clangorous discord, to a level where Scully felt his rib-cage vibrating like a drum. Next to him, a youth was pounding a lavatory cistern on the cobbles and a young man was walloping an ancient bicycle against a wall. When he dropped the bicycle, another picked it up, raised it above his head and hurled it full force on to the ground. Sparks flashed, but the bicycle remained in one piece. The man picked it up and repeated the action. This time a wheel broke loose.

Scully saw that it was Alejandro. He had a glazed, obsessive look about him, as though hardly aware of where he was. He picked up the twisted frame and swung it above his head, then dashed it down. He raised it and smashed it down again. Fragments of metal broke off. A cut had appeared on Alejandro's hand but he was oblivious to it. He leaped on to the mangled remains of the bicycle and his feet went through the spokes with a resounding twang. He beat what was left against the ground and the crowd laughed and cried encouragement.

Euphoria engulfed the villagers, and with them Scully. He laughed and sang with them. He found a mangled piece of metal in his hands. Once it might have been a tin washtub. It didn't matter. He smacked it down on the cobbles. It made a satisfying crash. He raised it and did it again. A madness gripped him. He wanted to break it, smash it into tiny pieces. And he raised it and flailed the ground with it, again and again. His eyes were blinded by sweat, his ears hammered by the uproar around him. He was laughing and crying at the same time. He didn't care.

CHAPTER NINETEEN

Benamargo slept late next day. Not until the early hours of the morning had Inmaculada and her groom succeeded in escaping from the village. The taxi-driver had sworn he would never return. Waylaid by some of the young men, he had been unable to reach the widow's house for several hours. Even when the couple had boarded the taxi, their ordeal had been far from over. The cavorting multitude had surrounded the vehicle, swarming over it, pounding on the roof and blocking its passage. It had taken a full hour to clear the village and take the road to Cerrogordo.

After the clamour of the previous night, an almost oppressive stillness cloaked the village the following morning. Scully took himself off to the sierras, with a couple of rolls, some home-cured ham and a bottle of wine. Climbing fast, he tried not to think about the details of the cencerrazo. It disturbed him, the craziness, the release of so much passion, his own reactions. Yes, that most of all. He had shocked himself.

Yet, after pausing to gain his breath and drink some wine, he could examine things more objectively. He had let himself be carried along by the mob, acting in a way that he never recalled doing before. Even so, it had served some purpose. He realised that he felt better for it. He felt purged. The poison of pent-up frustration and anger bubbling within him had been released. The boil had been lanced.

Returning wearily from his walk, he experienced both an unusual lightness of spirit and a sense of physical well-being. He began to think of comforts that for a long time had not mattered to him.

The first thing he would do when next he ventured into the world beyond would be to take a long leisurely bath. He would wallow for hours as the steam curled about him. He wondered if a bath actually existed in Benamargo. He had never seen one.

He neared the village and passed close to the spot where Ramón had kept his goats. He glanced towards the moss-grown walls of the barn, then swiftly looked away as he bumped into unpleasant memories. But he had seen a movement. He stepped off the path and approached. Marisa was shovelling grain out of a sack for the goats, her face flushed with the effort. She stopped abruptly when she saw Scully. Then she went on shovelling.

"Let me help you, Marisa," he offered.

She kept her head down, continuing to dig out the grain and spread it in the feeding troughs. Scully was irritated by her silence.

"Marisa, surely you can speak to me?"

She ignored him, concentrating on her task with greater intensity and gripping the shovel so firmly that her knuckles showed white. Impatiently, she pushed aside two baby goats scampering about her legs.

"Marisa!" Scully grasped her wrist and swung her around. She was breathing heavily. "What is it? You silly little bitch, answer me!"

For a moment she looked as though she would strike him with the shovel.

"Yes, that's what you think I am, isn't it? A silly little bitch, a stupid baby! Why should I speak to you? There's no point, is there?"

"What's wrong, Marisa?"

"Wrong?" She struggled fiercely to release herself. "You didn't tell me your wife was alive, waiting for you in England. I would never have known, except for your friend. He told me everything."

"Marisa, you're the only person I care about," said Scully earnestly.

"Why didn't you tell me?"

"My wife is dead as far as I'm concerned. She has no interest in me, nor I in her. It's finished. Believe me."

"What's the use? Everything's changed, ruined," she said, shaking her head hopelessly.

"It's Ramón, isn't it?" said Scully. "You blame me for what happened."

"He could still be alive," she said, in misery.

"Yes," he said. "He could be. But we can't change the past. You must not — "

"Ramón! Why, why?"

Scully held her by the shoulders and gazed into her eyes. He spoke deliberately, forcefully.

"Marisa, you have your life to lead and you're the only person in the world who matters to me. I need you. I need you. And I won't let anything come in the way."

"It's no good," cried Marisa. "It's no good. Leave me alone!"

She twisted herself free and ran. But Scully gave chase and caught her arm. He pulled her around.

"Listen to me, Marisa, listen to me."

She wriggled in his grip, her breath coming in sobbing gasps. For several moments they struggled. She was as wiry and fiery as a wild pony.

"Let me go!"

"Never!"

She fought to bite his hand to force him to release her. To prevent her, he pulled hard back so that she fell against his chest. He bent and kissed her forehead. Their lips met, reluctantly, but then, finally, with total yearning. And this time it was so different from that first time that it was as though two different people were involved. It was wanton and violent. Scully laid her on a bed of straw and attacked her body with a hunger that terrified himself, tearing at her thick woollen garments and crying her name. She accepted him feverishly, pulling him into her until they were united in a delirious climax.

Before the gouts of sweat could dry on their flesh, Scully made love to her again, as he wanted to, slowly, with infinite tenderness, touch responding to touch, kiss to kiss, caress to caress, skin to skin, entering her so gently, their passion answering to the same rhythm. Scully ploughed deeper, deeper into this earth-goddess, seeking to bury himself for ever as she wept and gasped and strove to absorb him into her own flesh. When the final surge came, her nails dug into his back, but he felt no pain, only the wish that this could last for eternity, and he thrust deeper, whipping her with his member, until they were no longer on the bed of straw but far beyond it, floating on their own cloud of senses and emotions.

It was the beginning of a madness. It was crazy and dangerous, and Scully knew it, but it made no difference. When they met, they were possessed by the same devil. They made love recklessly, whenever they could, wherever they could, with oblivious happiness and abandon. They made love in Scully's bed, giggling and whispering, until the house shook and they feared Dolores would come running to investigate. They made love in the barn, where the goats nuzzled their feet and the straw tickled their skin. They made love in a secluded hollow near the stream and washed themselves in its waters. They made love in a field of thyme and buttercups and gentian as a lazily circling hawk kept guard overhead. It was madness, and they wanted it never to stop.

"Carlos, what shall we do?"

It was almost dark and the chill of evening jabbed at his bare flesh. He threw on his clothes.

"We'll go home before it gets any colder," said Scully, deliberately misunderstanding. This must never end, he was thinking. This affair was total insanity, he knew, and he embraced it avidly. Sometimes he felt so cheerful and optimistic that he was alarmed. These were such unaccustomed sensations that he could hardly grasp what he was feeling. He could not, did not want to, analyse what was happening, for fear that it would disintegrate at the first touch.

"When you leave, I mean," said Marisa, biting her lip.

"Don't talk about it. I have a few days yet in your mother's house, to the end of the month."

"But you must go, Carlos." She was insistent. "You have to leave the village."

"No, I don't. Unless you want me to go."

"It's because I love you so that I want you to go. I'm afraid. There are people here who would do you harm. And if they knew about us..."

"This is our private thing and nobody else's business."
He stroked her cheek. "Do you know what I'm going to do?
I'm going to marry you. What do you say to that?"

"Oh, Carlos." She snuggled up to him, her tousled black
hair teasing his cheek. "Yes, yes, yes. But...it's impossible."

"I'll get a divorce as soon as I can. It doesn't take long."

"But what about my mother? She'd never allow it. And
you a Protestant too. There would be a terrible scandal."

"She'll come round once she sees we're serious. And, if
not, hell, I'll take you away without her permission. I mean
it."

Marisa shook her head.

"It would kill her, to lose me as well as Ramón. Since he
died, she has been so strange. She lived for him. Now she
just stares at his picture and goes to talk to the priest. She
accepts every word he says and he's against you, you know
that?"

"I know. But I'm not scared of him."

"No, but Benamargo people are," declared Marisa.

Scully squeezed and kissed her. He noticed she was shivering.

"Let's go. It's getting cold. Don't worry, we'll get permission
from your mother. I'll speak to her."

Her eyes opened wide.

"Please, Carlos, don't say anything to Mama, not yet. I
beg you! Keep our secret."

CHAPTER TWENTY

Some secrets cannot be kept. The people of Benamargo were neither blind, nor silent, as Scully soon discovered. The activities of The Disinherited One and the shameless daughter of Dolores La Caída gave the villagers more meat to chew on than they had enjoyed for some time. Entering Carmencita's shop one day, Scully caught the gossip in full spate. The witches nudged one another and whispered. "Shameless.. .shameless," they muttered among themselves. Their target was less Scully than Marisa. Men, after all, were expected to sow their wild oats. Women should conserve themselves intact until they walked up the aisle, and those who did not, well...

But Scully did not appreciate just how strong the undercurrents were until one night in Sebastián's bar. Sebastián leered at him and cracked some doubtful jokes. That was normal enough. The storm came over dominoes. It was not a game that set Scully's adrenalin flowing, but it was something to do to fill in the hours. A clutch of old-timers were usually huddled over a rickety corner table whose surface had been polished to a black gloss by the movement of the pieces. Sometimes Scully joined in. He had a formidable memory so that he could hold his own with most of the players.

This evening he was paying little attention, as his thoughts dwelled on the situation of Marisa and himself. Within a few days his tenancy of Dolores's house would be up. After months of inertia, circumstances were forcing him to make a decision. He shuffled the dominoes. He was in a group of four, with several bystanders offering advice as usual. At first, he did not register the arrival of a new player on his right. Then he looked up and saw it was Alejandro.

"Let's see who knows how to play this game!" said the

young villager, glaring at Scully. His eyes had a red glint and he spoke with a slur. Accustomed to heavy work as a bricklayer, he was a hefty fellow with arms like oak beams. "What do you say, Inglés?"

Scully grinned.

"May the best man win," he said quietly.

Alejandro grinned.

"And so say I!"

After picking up his pieces and examining them, he gazed around slyly at the other players.

"We've got 'em, partner," he told Rafael, the carpenter, sitting opposite. Rafael nodded sagely.

When Alejandro's turn came, he made a great show of raising his piece high and smashing it down on the table. One of the spectators slapped him on the back, crying: "That's it, young 'un. You show 'em." But Rafael and Scully's partner, a toothless pensioner with failing eyesight, carried on calmly, ignoring such theatricalities.

The game reached a critical point. Scully had one domino left in his hand. Alejandro looked around suspiciously as he debated which of two pieces to play, then with a dramatic gesture he slammed down a double blank, observing: "You won't get past this one."

Scully laid down his last domino, a three and a blank.

"Mierda!" Alejandro scowled and spat on the floor. Muttering to himself, he lurched to the bar as the other customers laughed and pulled his leg. His mood worsened during the next game as he made foolish moves, forgetting which pieces had been played, dropping easy ones for Scully to follow.

"That's it," said the pensioner, laying down the remaining pieces in his hand. "Game to us."

"What do you mean?" demanded Alejandro. "The game isn't finished."

"Sure it is," said Rafael. "Look at the fichas. With what he has in his hand, The Old One can't lose. Don't you see?"

"No, I don't!" Alejandro was furious. "There's something wrong with these pieces. One is missing. Let's have a look at them."

He began laying all the dominoes out on the table face up to check them. This caused hilarity among the spectators, and irritation among his fellow players.

"Get on with you, Alejandro! D'you think somebody has been eating them?" asked Rafael, shuffling the pieces. "Now, what are the stakes for this next one? Ten duros each, okay? One hundred points wins?"

"Ten duros nothing!" snapped Alejandro. He nudged Scully and gave him a bloodshot look. "Fifty miserable pesetas. That's a waste of time, eh, Inglés? What do you say?"

"It seems okay to me," said Scully.

Alejandro snorted.

"What! Let's play for real money." He dug into his pocket and pulled out a bundle of wrinkled bills. "Here, who's got some balls around here? All that on the table. Who'll match me?"

"Don't be stupid," remonstrated the carpenter. "This is just a friendly game. You can't afford to lose that."

"Who said anything about losing?" said Alejandro belligerently. "I can beat any man here, no trouble. I've been playing around up to now, but it's time to get serious. Come on, you lot, put your money where your face is."

One of the spectators had been counting the cash on the table.

"Hey, there are 5,000 pesetas here!" he exclaimed.

A gasp went up.

"Five thousand pesetas! You're crazy, Alejandro. What did you do? Sell the Virgin's robe?"

"I've got plenty," boasted Alejandro. He lolled back, enjoying the bemusement of his fellows. "Five thousand says nobody can beat me. Come on, you sons of whores, show some balls."

Rafael stood up.

"I've got more cojones than you'll ever know about, Alejandro, but I'm not playing. I can't afford to lose that much, and neither can you. You've lost your mind."

The pensioner sucked his gums and shook his head in agreement. Alejandro turned to Scully.

"That leaves you, Inglés."

Scully smiled at him.

"I don't need the money, Alejandro. Thanks all the same. I just need a drink."

He rose from the table, but Alejandro grasped his jacket.

"Wait a minute. What do you mean? You don't need the money? You think it's so easy to beat me? Is that it? Is that what you're saying, Inglés?"

The others muttered among themselves.

"Leave it, hombre. Nobody wants to play for those stakes."

"To hell with the lot of you," snarled Alejandro. "This is between me and the Inglés." He banged his fist on the table. "Right, Inglés? It's between us. Are you playing?"

"Some other time," murmured Scully. The wild light in the other's eyes warned him to keep cool. Alejandro grinned, showing chipped, nicotine-stained teeth.

"Why? Are you busy? Or are you like that friend of yours? A maricón, a queer, with no balls?" The bar went silent, shocked by Alejandro's outburst. "Five thousand pesetas say I've more balls than you. What do you say?"

Scully shook his head.

"Come on, Inglés. You've screwed everybody. Why don't you see if you can screw me too?" jeered Alejandro. "But, of course, you need balls for that."

Scully glared at the young man, inflamed by alcohol, swelling with bravado. All right, you asshole, he thought, you asked for it. I will screw you into the floorboards. He resumed his seat.

"If that's the way you want it," he said coldly. "Let's see what you can do."

Alejandro grinned again.

"Good, now we'll see who's got the cojones. Now we'll see."

As Rafael shuffled the pieces face down on the table, more spectators started drifting in. News spread quickly in Benamargo, as though it had a special smell which travelled without the aid of wagging tongues. Within minutes, the bar was full. Latecomers peered from the rear, demanding to know what was happening. Those nearest to the table breathed down the players' necks, trying to glimpse the pieces in their hands, offering advice.

The air was brittle with tension and Scully cursed himself for getting involved. In the first game, as he looked across at Alejandro's sneering face, irritation got the better of him. His concentration strayed and he made stupid errors, greeted by Alejandro with whoops of triumph.

"One to me, Inglés!"

In the second game, Scully hardly fared better. Luck was with Alejandro and he played as though the result was preordained, nonchalantly tossing down his pieces with only a brief moment of consideration. He smacked down his final domino and guffawed.

"That's how to play! With bravura, hombre. That's how we play the game here. Like we play the bulls." He scoffed. "But you know about that, don't you, about putting in the horns?"

Scully knew the expression. To put in the horns meant to cuckold somebody. He looked poker-faced at Alejandro.

"If it's a choice between putting in the horns or getting screwed, I know which I'd prefer," he said. "Stick to dominoes, friend, and forget about the bulls. It's safer for a little one."

The spectators chuckled among themselves, while Alejandro looked murderous. He snatched up his pieces for the next game. They had agreed to ignore points. The first to win three games would be the winner. Already two down, Scully smiled to himself. On the brink of defeat, he suddenly felt perfectly cool. That had always been his strength, coolness under pressure. He had to win this game and he was going to.

"Go ahead, Inglés, it's your move. This time I'm going to finish you off."

"You should do more thinking and less talking, Alejandro," said Scully.

Alejandro scowled through the thickening cigarette smoke. The spectators pressed closer. This was one to remember. There had not been a match like this in years. They commented on every move, whistling when they saw what seemed like an error or an unnecessary risk. This time, the mistakes were on Alejandro's side.

He could do nothing right and Scully took the game easily. Alejandro swore. Seeing that he was not selling any drinks, Sebastián began taking bets on the result.

His initial irritation gone, Scully was enjoying himself. Long in low gear, his brain had needed some cranking up. Now it clicked over with a familiar precision as it assessed which pieces must be in his opponent's hand and analysed the options. It was like setting a rusty computer to work out the two times table. He recognised a surge of exultation within him as though greeting an old friend. Whenever he had been at a critical point in clinching a deal or pulling the carpet from under a rival, there had been the same tingle of anticipation, the same ice-cold calculation, followed by the merciless coup de grace. That had been ages ago. Then he had been dealing in millions. Now it was a game of dominoes with a drink-hazed youngster, a ridiculous and uneven test of wits. It made no difference. The kill would come quickly and he would enjoy every moment of it. This young punk deserved to be humiliated and he would be.

Scully took the fourth game. It was not quite as easy as the third. Alejandro had been shaken by that defeat and was trying to regain control of himself. But he made silly blunders. He glowered at Scully, who grinned back.

"I make that two each," said Scully. "This one is the decider. You can call it quits now if you like. Just pick up your cash and go. I'm easy."

"Listen, Inglés," growled Alejandro. His face was scarlet and sweat trickled down his brow. "This is what I say." He dragged some dirty peseta notes from a pocket and scattered them over the table. "Let's double the stakes. Okay?"

"No, Alejandro, you're crazy! You're throwing away a week's wages."

An elderly man had forced his way through the crowd and was arguing angrily with Alejandro.

"Listen to your father," cried the spectators.

"Leave me alone! I'm not a kid. I know what I'm doing."

Alejandro shook off his father's restraining hand. "The money's there, Inglés. What about it?"

Scully shrugged. With deliberate calm, he reached into his inside jacket pocket and extracted some notes. He handed them to Sebastián, who was holding the stakes. "That makes 10,000. Now let's get on with it."

There was a flurry of new betting, while Alejandro disappeared to stick his head under a water tap. The hubbub only died down when Rafael the carpenter started shuffling the pieces. Scully and Alejandro drew to decide who would start. Alejandro drew the higher number and flashed a jubilant smile. Rafael swirled the pieces about again and each drew seven dominoes.

"Beat this!" said Alejandro, dropping a double five. Scully scanned his hand. He could not go and was forced to draw another domino from the stock pile of 14 remaining pieces face down on the table. The dominoes were running for Alejandro, and the villagers' loyalty to one of their own began to show. They encouraged Scully's opponent with loud cries, urging him on.

"Go to it, young one! Ay, you've got cojones, nobody can deny that!"

Cold water had washed away some of the alcoholic clouds from Alejandro's head and he played more cautiously, displaying a cunning that had not been there before.

He held the dominoes close to his chest, his eyes burning as he studied first them then Scully. He played by guesswork rather than careful assessment, making him more unpredictable. Scully was barely aware of the noise and people pressing in on him. Intuition and cold calculation would win this and he knew he was going to. He liked that feeling. That's what he had always liked, winning and watching the surprise on the loser's face...

Scully weighed the three remaining pieces in his hand. It was his move. One end of the game was blocked. The other required a five. There were two unknowns in stock and Alejandro had two pieces left. Scully grinned to himself. He had taken a risk. Now he would see if his gambling instinct still functioned as effectively as it had in the past. He dropped a five and a two. Without hesitation, Alejandro whacked down a two and a three. He was gloating, poised to finish the game. Scully stroked his chin. There was no hurry. His gaze flicked up to his opponent. Alejandro was fingering his last piece. He was convinced Scully could not match that three. The bar was suddenly quiet. Scully slid his domino along the table and paused, savouring the moment, before flipping it over. It was the three and six he had held back earlier. Alejandro could not believe his eyes.

"Mierda!" he exclaimed.

He stared at the dominoes as though paralysed. Scully matched his last piece with another six to end the game.

"That's impossible!" Alejandro whirled on him. "I shit in your mother's milk! You didn't have a three. This is a swindle!"

Scully smiled at him. He took the stake money from Sebastián and pushed it into Alejandro's hands.

"Here, take it," he said. "I don't want it."

Alejandro hurled the money into the air and leaped to his feet. He swept the dominoes from the table in fury.

"Son of a whore! You've swindled me!"

He lunged viciously at Scully.

"I'll kill you, you foreign shit!"

Scully just missed having his head knocked off by one of Alejandro's wildly swinging fists. Those around the enraged youngster grabbed his arms. He struggled fiercely.

"Let me at him! The son of a whore!"

"Shut up, man. Go home and sleep it off," yelled Sebastián, as he and the others tried to calm him.

"Why should I?" demanded Alejandro. Tears of anger and frustration spilled out. "This maricón! He killed Ramón and now he's fucking his sister. Everybody knows that. He's fucking Marisa, turning her into a whore. Fucking her in among the goats, the prettiest girl in the pueblo."

For a moment, Alejandro wrestled free. He thrust his livid face into Scully's.

"You think you can come here and fuck our women and get away with it, Inglés. Well, you're wrong. You won't get away with it, you son of a whore!"

CHAPTER TWENTY-ONE

"Hey, Don Carlos, are you going to be here for Holy Week?"

Scully looked up from his morning coffee and saw that Sebastián was pointing at a poster on the wall. "Semana Santa en Benamargo" read the uneven lettering. A crudely-drawn figure of Christ staggered along under a massive cross. The artist had dwelt lovingly on the crown of thorns, the agonised expression and the bloody wounds.

"It looks like fun," said Scully drily.

"It starts with Palm Sunday. That's when the kids have their procession. But the big ones are on Holy Thursday and Friday. Half the village takes part and the other half is watching. It's worth seeing."

Scully shrugged.

"I may be in Granada then."

"Ah, Granada. They put on a fine show there. I saw it once. They have the army and all the brotherhoods and the drums going. Ay, those drums! What a spectacle! And the Virgins! Beautiful enough to make your heart stop. You should see their robes, like something out of heaven. Velvet and jewels, and enough gold leaf to sink a galleon. But why don't you stay for ours?"

"Sebastián, you know how things are. I seem to have offended one or two people."

Several days had passed since the nasty scene in the bar. Nobody had mentioned it to Scully, but he knew it was the talk of the village.

"Ach!" Sebastián was scornful. "Any man worth his salt offends others. If you inspect every centimetre of the path before stepping on it, you'll never reach the inn before nightfall, right? You don't want to worry about that young crazy. He's always shooting his mouth off after a few drinks. It runs in the family."

"Maybe. But I think it's time to move on," said Scully.

He fingered the letter that had arrived that day. Gonzalo the postman had made quite a ceremony of delivering it personally, since it was the only mail Scully had ever received. It had been sent express from England and had taken a week to arrive. He had known it meant trouble. Only one person knew his address. The single page carried Stella's signature, but he had no doubt who had typed the carefully chosen words.

The letter oozed false concern, for his sons' education, for Scully's health and most of all for his future. He was surprised that "future" was not in inverted commas. Stella said she had been compelled to put the house up for auction and take the children out of private school. What was to be done? Heavens, cash was so tight she had even thought of applying for a job. But her nerves were too wretched, thanks to these constant interrogations. She was on the point of breakdown, she really was. Things were terribly fraught. Anything, anything at all he could do to alleviate matters would be so welcome.

"You are never out of our thoughts," insisted the letter. I'll bet, thought Scully grimly. A newspaper clipping was enclosed, just a brief item. Plimpton's obituary notice. As though as an after-thought, a postscript mentioned that Graham Klease had been subpoenaed to appear in court in three weeks' time. The date was underlined.

Time was of the essence, said Stella, as she was concerned about what he might say under cross-examination. They all knew Graham, a loose cannon if ever there was one. It was not too late to save the situation. It all depended on Scully really, suggested Stella. If he did "the right thing", it would be better for everyone. The word "everyone" was underlined.

Scully crumpled the letter in his hand.

"It's definitely time to move on," he said.

"Well, that's up to you. But the truth is," Sebastián produced one of his most lecherous winks. "The truth is there are some here who are jealous of you. Envy has always been one of our deadly sins. Folk can't bear others enjoying the fruit they would like to have picked themselves. Know what I mean?"

He treated Scully to such an evil attempt at a grin that he could not help bursting into laughter.

"You're a rogue, Sebastián. How come you survive here, the way they all criticise you?"

"Don Carlos, here they would criticise you if you lived like a saint, so I don't even try. I've always done just what I wanted. My father gave me the best advice. He said: 'Remember, la muerte viene sola. La vida hay que buscarla'."

Scully repeated the words to himself and smiled. Death comes on its own. But you have to go out in search of life. He liked that.

"So, you're a philosopher too?"

The bar-owner nodded complacently and ran a damp cloth over the counter.

"Have you got a match, Sebastián?"

Scully struck the match and held the flame to the letter. Sebastián watched, intrigued, as the paper flamed and charred. Scully ground it into an ash-tray.

"From the taxman? Or your mother-in-law?"

"From another life," said Scully. "And now, I'm going in search of a new one!"

He sought out Marisa, his mind made up. She bit her lip anxiously at his first words.

"Mama would never give permission. I know it." She looked appealingly at him. "You said you would keep our secret, Carlos. Please!"

"What secret? The whole pueblo knows about us. Alejandro is going around making filthy accusations. There is no secret, Marisa. I have to go to your mother before she hears about this from somewhere else."

The girl made a hopeless gesture.

"It's no use. She would just lose her temper."

She has to say 'yes' and, if she doesn't, we'll marry anyway," insisted Scully.

"But who would marry us?"

"Who? I'll take you to France, America, wherever. We'll have a civil ceremony."

"Oh no!" Marisa was aghast. "It has to be by the priest. It has to be a proper wedding."

"Don't worry. We'll fix it."

"I can't just leave my mother. My duty is to her."

"Duty?" Scully was impatient. "We're in love and that creates other duties. It's not betraying your mother to marry the man you love."

"The Guardia would bring us back. Maybe they would arrest you."

"They won't find us," declared Scully. "Marisa, in two days' time I have to leave the house. My time is up. But before then I'm going to speak to your mother and explain about us. I'm sure she'll understand, and then we two can go away together."

"You can't do it," said Marisa, fear in her eyes.

"I can and I will."

Even so, when the moment came, he felt anything but sure of himself. He would rather have suffered a tooth-pulling or a stormy shareholders' meeting than confront the stern, erect figure of Dolores in her mourning black. He considered every possible objection that she might present and the most telling arguments he could offer in favour of the match. Stiffened by two brandies, he considered his case convincing enough. He remained reasonably confident, until he actually banged the iron knocker on Dolores's front door. The knocker, shaped like a hand, sent echoes through the house. They sounded like a portent of doom to Scully. Only a total lack of realism could have brought him this far, he reflected. He was a foreigner, a non-Catholic, about to be divorced, years older than her daughter, blamed for the tragedy of her son. Hardly impressive credentials.

"Carlos, you're not going to —"

He waved Marisa, pale and distraught, aside.

"I have to see her," he said. "We're going to get this settled."

He marched with determined steps to the living room. Dolores's ghost of a face was just visible in the gloom. She was seated in her usual place, gazing at the portrait. Scully felt as though he had intruded in a chapel.

"Señora," he said diffidently. "Excuse me for troubling you. But I have to speak to you. It's most important."

There was a long pause, as though she had not heard him. She did not turn her head. Then she spoke.

"Is it about Ramón?"

"No."

"Then it cannot be important."

"I wanted to ask you —"

"Sometimes when I look at the picture, I'm sure he's looking back at me. Imagination, I know, but those eyes..." She spoke in a dull monotone, not addressing anybody in particular. "He didn't want to die. Even at the funeral, they said, he didn't want to join the others. It wasn't his grave, you see, it wasn't meant for Ramón, not for Ramón."

There was heavy silence. Scully could hear the nervous breathing of Marisa in the background.

"Señora, I do have something important to tell you."

Finally, the pallid features swimming in the twilight turned towards him.

"If it's about staying on in the house, that's out of the question," said Dolores.

"It's not about the house. It's about Marisa."

"Marisa? Don't blame her for anything. You can't put an old head on young shoulders. She can't be expected to do much about meals when she has the goats and everything to attend to."

Dolores resumed her vigil before the portrait.

"She's done nothing wrong, nothing at all," said Scully. "It's just that I have grown very attached to your daughter and she to me. In fact, I want to marry Marisa, señora." Dolores jerked around sharply. "That's what I wanted to tell you. We love one another and we want to marry."

Dolores gaped at him and clutched at her rosary with twitching fingers.

"I realise you may think I'm rather old for your daughter," said Scully, the words tumbling out. "But, from my experience, age is not the most important. And I would look after her well."

Inwardly Scully groaned. This was sounding like something out of Jane Austen. Dolores still said nothing, as though she could not bring herself to speak, and he plunged desperately on.

"I'm sure we both want Marisa to be happy. She's a wonderful girl."

"And what does your wife say to this?" asked Dolores. The words flew at Scully like ice daggers.

"That's all over. I am getting a divorce."

"Most convenient!" Dolores gazed at him with disgust. "To do this to me! To do this behind my back! How you have the face to enter this house!"

She called harshly: "Marisa! What have you been hiding from me?"

"Nothing, Mama," said Marisa, in a whisper.

"Nothing? You heard what this man said. And there's nothing between you? Tell me the truth!"

Marisa looked from her mother to Scully and back, but did not speak.

"Answer me, daughter!"

"I love him, Mama."

Dolores looked as though she would strike Marisa. She shook with anger.

"I don't believe it! I don't believe it! All this, behind my back. The shame of it!"

"Please, señora," put in Scully. "Marisa has done nothing to be ashamed of. We simply love one another and would like your blessing."

Dolores whirled on him.

"You talk about a blessing? After this, dragging our name in the mud. I welcomed you here as a guest and you betrayed my trust. The cura was right. All you have brought is trouble. He warned me about you, that you and your kind were sent by the devil. And now I see. Your friend stole my son and now you want to steal my daughter!"

"Mother! Please!" cried Marisa.

"You!" Dolores directed all her bitterness against her daughter. "You're no better than a whore, running after a married man twice your age. That you should do this to me!"

"But we're going to get married, Mama."

"Not while there's breath left in my body," snapped Dolores. Her eyes glittered with white-hot anger. "You will never speak to this man again, never see him again. You shameless one! Do you understand?"

Scully tried to keep his voice calm.

"Señora, Marisa loves me and I love her. You cannot part us."

"Oh, can't I?" said Dolores.

"No. We intend to get married as soon as we can. I would prefer to do so with your permission."

"Never! Never, never, never!"

Scully's patience cracked.

"I'm not giving her up!" he said hotly.

"Get out of my house!" Dolores flung out a hand dramatically. "Marisa is under age and still my daughter. You'll not steal her from me. Don't even go near her again. Go, viper!"

She was magnificent in her righteousness, while her weeping daughter slumped into a chair, pressing her hands against her ears as though she could bear to hear no more. Seething, Scully marched out.

CHAPTER TWENTY-TWO

Back in his room, Scully started packing his bag. It had been Victorian melodrama, worse than he could have imagined. The woman was impossible. There was no way to change such a closed mind. Dolores wanted him to leave. Well, by god, he would. But not alone.

Marisa was a part of him, part of a new Scully. She represented a fresh start. He would leave Benamargo and take her with him. Call it love or lust, call it what the hell you wanted, he was bound to that girl. He needed her. He did not need Dolores and her ranting, nor that damned priest.

Father Saturnino! He was the one who had stirred up all this feeling against him. He had poisoned the minds of Dolores and the rest of the village. He would have it out with him, right now. He was not going to leave until he had given a piece of his mind to the man whose tirades and narrow prejudices had made it impossible for him to remain here. He would tell this petty dictator a thing or two.

The priest's house was built against one side of the church. The maid came to the door, a slight, mousy girl who gaped at Scully as though unable to credit her eyes. For several minutes he stood waiting on the doorstep. Then she returned.

"The Father is dining," she said. "But you can wait in here."

She led the way along a corridor to a tiny, sparsely furnished room. A bookcase along one wall overflowed with well-worn catechisms and leather-bound theological works. It was cold in the room and Father Saturnino took his time in coming. When he appeared, he was brushing his cassock where soup or wine had stained it. He stood facing Scully, as stern as ever, dark eyebrows drawn together, yet with the air of somebody who had won a victory.

"Señor?"

He was an immense figure in this confined space and suddenly Scully felt awkward. His anger and frustration ebbed in the face of the priest's imposing presence. This was a futile exercise. What could he say to this man, so sure of himself and the rightness of his cause, backed by the might of Rome?

"I've sinned, Father," said Scully.

The priest's eyebrows shot up, but he said nothing.

"I admit it." Scully spoke calmly. "I've done some pretty nasty things. I've stabbed people in the back, I've committed adultery, I've lied, all of that. So you'd call me a sinner. On the fast track to hell. And I haven't even bothered to pave the way with good intentions."

The priest's lip curled. Scully plunged on.

"But one thing I'm not, Father. I'm not a hypocrite. And I don't spread poison. I haven't turned one man against another by sowing hatred and suspicion. I haven't enslaved people's minds with blind prejudice and fear. I haven't done that, Father."

"You have done enough," said the priest. Stern conviction emanated from him.

"You, Father, have done more than enough. I wonder how you can sleep at night, the evil you have done to this village."

"Evil!" The priest swelled. "You have the temerity to talk to me of evil. You who wallow in it! I am sorry for you, señor, for you have learned nothing. You show no desire to repent for your ways. The first time I looked into your face I was filled with a great sadness, for I could see how empty you were, devoid of scruples, faith, hope."

"You were against me from the start," said Scully fiercely. "Now you're even preaching against me from the pulpit. You have deliberately set people against me. Why are you doing this?"

"Because you're a shipwreck, man, that's why, a burnt-out hulk threatening to drag the innocent down into the depths. Your sterile soullessness infects others. You're a danger to my flock."

"And this is the tolerance and humanity of your faith, is it? Judging, condemning, punishing. By what right? Who appointed you god?"

"Tolerance?" The priest's eyes blazed. His voice rose. "You talk of tolerance. Should we show tolerance to fornicators and perverts? You brought your warped values to this peaceful community and, thanks to our tolerance, a young soul lies up there on the hillside, his eager spirit snuffed out. Toleration is all very well, but not in the presence of evil. Our church is not a supine one, señor. When necessary, we are ready to defend the faith with all the means at our disposal. And when my people need protection, I do not hesitate. Although perhaps you would not understand the word, it is my duty."

"You have a strange idea of duty," shot back Scully.

The atmosphere vibrated with tension as he and Saturnino confronted one another.

"You're not saving these people, you're filling them with medieval claptrap. Hellfire and vengeance, that's what your Christianity consists of."

"You should go on your knees to beg forgiveness for your blasphemy," said the priest. "I do not need to justify myself to you. You came here uninvited, Señor Scully, and nothing is stopping you from going. Why do you stay? Haven't you done enough harm?"

"You're anxious to get rid of me, aren't you, Father? What have I done to you? Why this personal vendetta?"

"Personal? You think I am moved by personal interest?" The priest turned away. He glanced up at the crucifix on the wall and sighed. "That is something I have always been at pains to guard against. In my impetuous younger days, no doubt I may have erred. We are all fallible. But we of the priesthood must always strive to quench these baser human emotions, to rise above egoism. It's part of our daily battle."

"Your fallibility is not in doubt," said Scully, sarcastically. "Nor is mine. But I find it intolerable the way you have slandered me in public and private."

"And I find it intolerable" said Father Saturnino, his

voice edged with steel, "that, not content with contributing to one tragedy in a family, you are now creating another."

"What the devil do you mean by that?"

"I am talking about Marisa. Leave that girl alone!" thundered the priest.

"That is no business of yours!" retorted Scully.

"It is every business of mine. We have no place here for pigsty morality."

Scully lost his temper.

"Don't lecture me on morality! For your information, I intend to marry that girl — as soon as possible!"

For the first time Saturnino appeared rattled. He glared at Scully.

"Marry Marisa? You?"

"That's what I said."

"Not in this church or any other. I shall see to that." Fearsome in his anger, Saturnino towered over Scully. "If you harm that girl in any way...God help you, señor, God help you!"

"We shall marry, whatever you may say, Father," said Scully. "You may dominate this village but not me. I'm not one of your gullible peasants and your hell and damnation don't worry me!"

But Father Saturnino had already turned away. He knelt before the crucifix and began intoning a prayer in a low voice. Scully regarded the massive wall of his back for a moment, then shrugged resignedly and strode from his presence. The wide-eyed maid, caught eavesdropping, pressed herself against the corridor wall as he passed.

He found Marisa at the edge of the village as she returned from milking the goats. She and a young cousin, who was helping her with the animals, were bearing pails of the fresh milk. Marisa set hers down abruptly.

"I told you it was hopeless," she cried. "I told you. It just made things worse."

"No, it had to be done. Now we know where we stand," said Scully.

"My mother will never forgive you." Marisa gestured at her cousin, who was listening curiously. "Go on, Paco. I'll see you at the house."

"Maybe your mother won't forgive me. Or maybe in time she will. But right now I don't give a damn," said Scully forcefully. "And tomorrow neither will you."

Marisa looked at him in alarm.

"What do you mean?"

"I mean that we're leaving, the two of us, tonight."

Marisa put a hand to her mouth.

"No! You're not serious."

"I'm deadly serious. It has to be tonight. If we tried to leave on the bus, your mother would stop you. I'll see if Juanito will give us a lift. If not, we'll walk. By tomorrow morning we shall be in Cerrogordo."

Marisa swayed. She tried to grasp the idea.

"Just walk away? Leave Benamargo for ever?"

"Some day you could come back. But we have to go now."

"I couldn't!"

"There's nothing to stop you. You're almost 18. You have the right to decide your future."

Scully pulled her close.

"We can go wherever we want."

"Anywhere?"

"To America, Australia, the moon. I don't have much money, but we'd manage."

"To Madrid? I always wanted to walk down the Gran Vía. Or to Paris? They say it's so beautiful."

"Why not?"

"Would we have our own house?"

"Sure."

"Where we could raise a family?"

"Absolutely."

"Would you mind that?" she asked anxiously. "If we had children?"

"Mind it? Marisa, I'd love you to have my children. Dozens of 'em!"

She flung her arms around him and they kissed, a long tender kiss in the darkness beyond the village lights.

"I love you, Carlos," she whispered.

"You'll come? Tonight?"

"All right."

"Oh, Marisa." He cradled her face in his hands. "Don't worry, some day your mother will understand."

"How shall we do it?"

"Wait until your mother goes to bed." Scully spoke slowly and deliberately. "Then come to my door. I'll be waiting. Don't carry too much because we may have to walk quite a way. Bring your identity card and whatever papers you have."

Scully wondered whether Marisa's nerve might fail at the last moment. She had lived all her life under the same roof, her world limited by the sierras and village custom, lectured by her mother, the priest, the schoolteacher. But not dominated. He should not have doubted her spirit. Shortly after the cracked tones of the church clock had sounded 10 o'clock, he heard a soft tap at the door. Trembling with excitement, Marisa embraced him.

"It will be all right, won't it, Carlos?"

He kissed her lightly, a feeling of exultation sweeping over him.

"Nothing can stop us now," he told her.

He picked up his shoulder bag, eased the door to, and they trod softly down the deserted street. He had been unable to find Juanito and his truck. The carrier was off on a trip and would be back that evening, or maybe tomorrow. His unreliability was a byword. On second thoughts, Scully had decided it was just as well. He had doubts about Juanito's trustworthiness.

Most of the road to Cerrogordo was unpaved, but it ran downhill for much of the way and both he and Marisa were fit. It was just a matter of several hours' steady walking, something they were both used to.

As they cleared the edge of the village without seeing more than a stray cat, Scully felt a splash of rain. Thunder growled distantly and lightning flickered over far-off peaks. He and Marisa hardly noticed. At the first bend, they turned to look back at the pueblo. It was wrapped in tomb-like silence, only a couple of street lamps silhouetting the houses against the blackness of the mountain. The two gazed at the scene, without speaking, for long moments. Then they turned their faces to the raindrops and, laughing like school-children, sprinted down the road hand in hand.

Later, Scully was to remember that instant as one of the happiest of his life.

CHAPTER TWENTY-THREE

An exuberant sensation of release enveloped Scully as he tramped through the darkness. Until they were actually out of the village and it was absorbed by the darkness, he had not appreciated how strong had been its grip. Then he forced the pace, anxious to put as much distance between them and Benamargo as possible.

The lumpy track to Cerrogordo cut like a wound across the steep mountainside, before looping through the trees over a ridge into the next valley. They walked steadily, Marisa easily keeping up with Scully. They had broken out of the womb. Thank god, they had got away. He began to appreciate how, unconsciously, he had been swallowed by the village. It offered security, but its embrace was deadly. Its rules were not your rules, but they could not be ignored. Its values were not your values, but they influenced your actions. If you defied them, you were a rebel and in making you feel a rebel the village had won again. Almost imperceptibly, you were moulded, suffocated. But no more. They were out, both of them, out of the cage.

Light-headed, he halted and stood, sniffing the air. Scent of pine trees in the heavy press of night. Water rambling over rocks far below. The weird, bleeping tones of a nightbird. Marisa tugged his arm.

"What are you doing?"

"Breathing."

"Nothing more?"

He laughed.

"It's enough. Breathing freedom. Smelling happiness. Drinking it all in."

Marisa laughed with him.

"I can smell happiness too. It has the odour of man, of you. Carlos, you'll never leave me? Ever?"

His answer was a long, deep kiss. The wind sighed up the valley and shuffled the tall trees, accompanied by distant rumblings and lightning flashes. A night for grand opera, mused Scully, as they resumed walking.

He smiled to himself. It was never too late to learn. He had arrived in Benamargo as an anonymous alien and he was leaving like a fugitive. Yet his only wish had been to merge into the background of this community which had given him sactuary. Enjoying a stranger's privileges, he had thought he could remain impervious to the local ways. Live and let live. But it had taken centuries to shape the village's character, to set its customs and its mores in granite. They could not be ignored. Sooner or later, he had been bound to collide with them and to find his fool's paradise confronted by reality.

Klease had been the catalyst, brutally jolting him out of his passive role. At the same time, his sneers had stirred an unsuspected loyalty. Benamargo had for a time become his village. Faced by an outsider's sneers, he found himself identifying with its people, defending them. Maybe it was a backward community, at the end of a road to nowhere, but it had been his community. He could understand Bruno's dreams of progress and the villagers' desperation and their apathy, born of centuries of poverty and hopelessness. In that upswelling of communal grief at Ramón's funeral, the lump had been in his throat, the tears in his eyes, in the eyes of Charles Scully who did not give a damn about anything or anybody. He had begun to understand why the villagers needed their rituals and rigid codes of behavior. In a perilous, hostile world, they represented continuity, security, stability. He understood, now, when it was too late.

They made good speed, until the storm abruptly arrived. As they cleared the ridge, a roaring as of a wounded beast enveloped them and the wind scourged them in fierce, ripping gusts. The pines bent and cracked and branches flew past their ears. Then the rain began in earnest, easing after a few minutes, only to return with alarming fury. They ran towards a clump of trees, through a battlefield of thunder and lightning, the flashes picking out their figures like soldiers under fire. But the downpour mocked their shelter, bludgeoning their heads and shoulders and drenching them to the skin.

"Come on! We might as well keep going!" yelled Scully.

He clutched Marisa's hand and dragged her onwards. Water was pouring down the track and their feet sank into ankle-deep mud, the rain flooding their eyes and nostrils. Lightning provided unreliable illumination. Twice Scully stopped just in time as he saw that his next step would have taken them over the edge of the road. Once they cannoned blindly off a rocky outcrop half of which had been blasted away to form a shelf along the sheer mountainside. It was an eccentric road at the best of times, following the meandering path that mule teams had once traversed.

"This is impossible," cried Marisa. "We can see nothing. We'll kill ourselves."

"We can see enough with this torch." The crashing, wind-driven rain all but drowned Scully's words. "There must be somewhere around here where we can shelter."

"A shack of the road repairers. There's one here somewhere. But I can't remember how far. And in this rain..."

They staggered on, tripping over broken branches, ruts, and stones which had tumbled on to the track. Scully's flashlight revealed only a short wedge of slanting rain, a wedge that diminished as the cloudburst intensified. Scully gritted his teeth. The raindrops were as painful as sharp gravel lashing the skin. He saw they were being battered by hailstones.

"Oh god! Oh, my leg!"

Marisa had tripped and fallen. She lay groaning, until Scully pulled her to her feet.

"What is it? Are you okay?"

Marisa was shivering uncontrollably, anguish leaching all colour from face.

"It's my leg. It hurts," she said. Tears mingled with the water dripping from her plastered hair.

Scully pulled up one leg of her soaked jeans and under the fast-fading torchlight he saw that a stone had gashed her calf. He searched for a handkerchief and tied it around the cut, trying to staunch the blood. When he pressed her ankle, she winced. It looked swollen.

"It's not broken. Can you walk?"

She hobbled a few steps and stopped.

"Carlos, we'll never get there. We'll never get to Cerrogordo in this weather. We must go back."

His reaction was fierce.

"Go back? Don't be crazy!"

Marisa was weeping, shaking with cold and shock.

"What else can we do? My leg hurts and we can't see where we're going. It's hopeless."

"There's no way we can go back, Marisa. I'll get you to Cerrogordo if I have to carry you or...or swim all the fucking way!"

"We could be back before morning. Nobody would ever know. If we went now."

"No way. I'm not going back," snapped Scully.

"You go on then. I'll go back."

Her head was bowed. She was drained, helpless. Go back? Scully hurled curses at the rain that scoured and chilled them to the bone.

"No. We carry on, together. Don't worry. We'll be in Cerrogordo before morning."

There was no resistance in Marisa. She accepted Scully's urgings and dully allowed him to pull her forward once more. After hailstones and sleet, the storm settled down to a steady downpour. The thunder claps and lightning were less frequent, but regularly returned to the assault. Scully plodded on as though in a dream, holding tightly to Marisa's arm, almost carrying her, cursing obscenely to himself.

A new sound froze him in mid-stride. He saw nothing but he could certainly hear something. It reached him above the drumming of the rain, a deep rumbling as though millstones were grinding in hell. The earth shook beneath their feet and there came the sharp crack of timber snapping. Then a flash lit up the scene. Man-sized boulders were skidding down the mountainside and across the road just a few yards ahead. Another moment and they would have been in the midst of it.

Marisa buried her head in his chest and they clung together, shock mixing with relief, as raindrops pummelled their chilled bodies and dripped into puddles at their numbed feet. They struggled on. Rocks littered the road, as though somebody had been batting them around for sport. Several times they had to wade through torrents foaming over the route. At one point, most of the surface had been washed down a gully, leaving a series of crevasses. No vehicle could pass.

"You see!" yelled Scully in Marisa's ear. He did not relish the dangers ahead, the possibility of slipping over a precipice or of being carried off into the darkness by a landslide. He talked to reassure himself. "You see. If we had waited until tomorrow, the bus would never have got through. But on foot we can do it."

Marisa did not answer. She limped on, her face set. Passing over a small stone bridge, they could hear the waters raging beneath. Just beyond, a lofty eucalypt had toppled across the road, completely blocking it. The flashlight had died to a useless glimmer and it took some time to find a way through splintered branches and to clamber over the trunk. What would have been a pleasant walk on a clear, starlit night had become a perilous obstacle course, and they were running it blindfold. Scully could tell by Marisa's pressure on his arm that she was close to collapse. How far had they come? Halfway? A third? Maybe less.

There was no lightning now. They were walking inside a black velvet bag. The eye of the storm must have passed on, for the thunder was growling away somewhere to the rear. But the rain kept up, sluicing down in an endless curtain. Their feet dragged and Scully, trying to make out the track, stared into the night until his head ached.

"There! I saw it! I saw it!"

Marisa had halted and was pointing into the darkness.

"Over there! A hut! I'm sure. I saw it."

Gingerly they moved forward. Black mountains, black clouds. It was impossible to discern anything. Scully searched for a silhouette, anything. The strain hammered at his forehead.

"Nothing! You imagined it," he said. He blinked his eyes and rubbed them angrily.

"No. I swear, by all the saints," gasped Marisa. "Mother of god, it was there!"

And then it was there. The sharp outline of something, a barn. They scrambled over a pile of rubble and Scully's fingers touched rough stonework, crumbling cement, a wall. Tears of relief welled. Marisa was laughing hysterically.

"It's the roadmenders' place. God be praised."

They moved around the walls. Their groping hands found a door, hanging off its hinges. Something flew past their heads as they crept inside and felt about for a dry corner on the rough concrete floor. The place smelled of urine and in the darkness something rustled. Sodden, out on their feet, they curled into one another on the cold floor. The rain continued to drum down, but it was no longer the hostile element it had seemed a few minutes earlier. The drumming on the roof tiles and the cascade spilling from them were now comforting reminders that they had found shelter.

Scully pulled Marisa closer in an effort to generate more warmth. They were both shivering, but almost immediately she had drifted into the sleep of exhaustion. He listened to the rain and the rustling of an unknown creature and the plish-plish of a leak hitting the floor and dozed...

Suddenly, Scully was awake. He opened his eyes to see a dirty cracked wall decorated with graffiti. At first he was unable to grasp where he was. Then he realised that the rain had stopped. Light was filtering into their refuge. Something had awakened him from his fitful sleep. He lay perfectly still, listening. There was only the sound of water dripping and Marisa's steady breathing. He smiled. In sleep she was truly a child, her face was so vulnerable, so innocent. He brushed his fingers over her cheek.

' A voice sounded, some distance away. Then another. Scully untangled himself from Marisa and struggled to his feet. He groaned. His body felt as though it had passed through a mangle. Every joint ached and his wet clothing chafed abominably.

"What is it?"

Round-eyed, Marisa gazed up at him from the floor.

"Somebody coming," said Scully, moving towards the door. He longed for hot coffee, for bacon, eggs, sizzling.

He peered out. A few shreds of mist clung to the hillside, but the rain had stopped. About 100 yards of the muddy track were visible.

"Can't see anybody."

Marisa looked frightened.

"You don't think they have come after us?"

"No, why should they?"

She grimaced.

"It's just that we've, well, gone against them."

"Against them?"

"Gone against the village. They'll punish us."

Scully laughed shortly.

"What are you talking about, Marisa? Nobody has any right to punish us, or to give us orders."

Marisa did not look convinced. She was a startled faun, ready to leap off into the undergrowth.

"My mother?"

"Your mother does not enter into it. You left the village of your own free will," he said. "We can do what we want. It's nobody else's business."

But Marisa's concern made him think twice. She was under 18. What did the laws of Spain say about that? Maybe, they should conceal themselves until the newcomers had passed. No, hell, why should they hide like delinquents. She came to him in the doorway, putting her arm about his waist. He felt her anxiety. Then she started.

"Look, there's somebody coming from Cerrogordo." Three figures had appeared, moving slowly. "It's Juanito. The road must be blocked. He's left his truck."

Lean and hawkish, with wicked eyes that never stopped moving, Juanito usually carried himself jauntily. But fatigue slowed his steps and his two companions trailed wearily behind him.

"That's Curro at the back, the one with the belly. He used to be the baker," said Marisa. "I don't know the other. He's a stranger, although he looks familiar."

When Juanito was almost up to the hut, Scully stepped out into the grey morning light.

"Buenos días!" he said, smiling.

Juanito halted in amazement. Then he grinned.

"Hola, Don Carlos." He came up and shook hands. "But what the devil are you doing here?" His gaze flicked to Marisa, who had stayed in the doorway. "And Marisa! Now that's a coincidence, sure enough. But are you lost? Has something happened in the pueblo? Tell me."

"No, everything's fine." Scully saw the wicked, black-shadowed eyes darting to and fro. "Everything's fine. We were out walking, that's all. Got caught by the storm and couldn't get back. Just by luck we found this hut."

"You look like two drowned rats," chuckled Juanito. He looked knowing and his scarred lip curled mischievously. "Just as well we came along or you might have mistook the way and ended up in Cerrogordo."

"How is the road?" Scully asked, too quickly.

Juanito grinned again.

"In a hell of a mess. It'll take a bulldozer to clear a path. I had to leave my truck five kilometres back. I couldn't go back nor forward. Even on foot we could hardly get through. What a night!"

Curro, trudging ponderously along, had come up. Far from having a baker's pallor, his face was pink and blotchy. Its eroded surface hinted at heavy drinking and unimaginable debaucheries. He leered.

"Old Juanito was on the spree again. Did we have a time! Then we got stuck in a ditch. That's the last night I want to spend in your accursed lorry, Juanito!"

Suddenly catching sight of Marisa, he leered again.

"I pollute the Lord! It's little Marisa! Out here all night? And with a stranger?" He caught sight of Scully's expression. "Begging your pardon, Don Carlos. But in the circumstances…"

He and Juanito exchanged glances.

"It's certainly the devil's own coincidence, eh?" said Juanito. He called to the third man, who had wandered off behind the trees and emerged now, smoking a cigarette.

"For the love of god, hombre? Are you blind? Or aren't you going to speak to your own daughter?"

Scully heard Marisa gasp.

"What do you say?" demanded the man, striding up. He was taller than most of the villagers, with a proud bearing and sleek black hair.

"Don't you recognise her?" asked Juanito.

The man gazed in astonishment at Marisa.

"Can it be? But you're a woman." He shook his head in disbelief. "And the last time I saw you, you were just a babe."

"It's really you, Papa?" Tears spilled down Marisa's cheeks. Her voice was choked. "I never thought I'd see you again. Papa!"

They stood staring at one another and then, awkwardly, she ran to embrace him. The stranger patted her on the head uncertainly. He appeared uncomfortable, as though he would have preferred to have avoided this scene.

"And I kept thinking of you as a wee girl. Who could believe it?" He examined her at length. "Who would believe it? And pretty too. But what's happened to your hair? Where have you been?"

Marisa began to stutter.

"It was the storm. We got got caught. You could see nothing. So we couldn't get back to the pueblo. We couldn't get back."

Francisco glanced towards the hut and then at Scully. He had the same fine features as his son but marred by hard experience. His face was coarser, harsher. There was a cynical twist to his lips and an air of stubborn rebelliousness about him. Not a man to trifle with.

"And this gentleman is your friend?" he asked.

"Yes," said Marisa nervously. "This is Don Carlos. He...he helped me...when we...I got lost..."

Francisco inspected Scully gravely, but made no move to shake hands with him, like a wolf biding its time. Suspicion lurked in his eyes.

"Come on!" Curro slapped his belly. "Are we going to stand here all day. I'm dying of hunger."

"To the village!" exclaimed Juanito. "Come on, Paco. Have you forgotten that you have a wife waiting for you?"

Francisco scowled at Juanito.

"I have forgotten nothing. I know exactly what awaits me." His lips tightened. "Everything but a son. I know that." He turned to Marisa. "I heard about it, about Ramón. I've come back to visit his grave."

For a moment the tough features softened. He turned his face away and picked up the battered holdall he had brought with him. Then, not waiting for the others, he strode off along the road.

Marisa looked helplessly at Scully, her face displaying turmoil. Scully shrugged.

"We better head for the village," he said. "I'll catch you up. I've got some things in the hut."

He ignored the meaning looks that flashed between Juanito and Curro and dived into the hut. Marisa's bag lay against one wall. He quickly searched through it.

Apart from some clothing, it contained only an old biscuit tin , which he guessed held some keepsakes. He stuffed the tin and as many of Marisa's clothes as there was space for into his own shoulder-bag. He carried Marisa's bag into the rear room, where several rotten beams had crashed down, and concealed it beneath a pile of esparto grass. It could be picked up some other time. Then, slinging his bag over his shoulder, he hurried after the others.

There was little conversation as they tramped along, apart from a few prodding questions from Juanito. Curro appeared past speech, wheezing unhealthily, his face growing ever redder. Francisco strode ahead, ignoring everybody, including his daughter, in a world of his own. Scully and Marisa moved as though in a dream, retracing the steps which they had made with such difficulty the night before. Back, back to the pueblo. Half dead with fatigue, 14 hours after they had said goodbye to the village, they plodded back into the narrow streets of Benamargo.

Church bells were ringing and children were running about with leafy fronds in their hands, preparing for the procession. It was Palm Sunday, the start of Easter Week.

CHAPTER TWENTY-FOUR

There was no escape. Every day Carmencita seemed more like Scully's jailer. He had not wanted to go to her place, but there was no choice. It was out of the question to return to the house next to Dolores and his queries about other accommodation in the village had been met with head-shakings. Only the grim little room above the grocery shop, along with the gossiping witches, was available. Every night, when he retired and the sagging bed springs played a discordant symphony, he remembered that this was the room where Klease had stayed. Every morning he awoke with a sore head and a stiff back.

Several times a night Carmencita, or her crippled sister who lived with her, lurched panting along the corridor to use the toilet. Then there would come the prolonged flushing of water and the rattle of pipes for a further half an hour. Scully also had to endure the shop. Every time he passed through the witches murmured behind their hands and ran reptile eyes over him.

But there was no escape. Benamargo was sealed off from the world. The road to Cerrogordo had been so badly damaged by the rains that local gossip predicted it would be at least a week before communications could be restored. At several points the telephone lines had been washed away and electricity pylons toppled. Somewhere down the valley they were trying to repair the power lines, but the village lights continued to blink out at odd moments.

Shrugs greeted Scully's questions about when the road was likely to reopen. Even at the best of times it would have been a major task, involving heavy earth-moving equipment, and this was Semana Santa. In Semana Santa everybody went on holiday and it was difficult to find a plumber let alone a highway repair gang. In any case, other roads had been washed out. They had to be repaired too and Benemargo always came last. That was the way it was. Nobody gave a damn about Benamargo.

"Don't you want to see the processions here, Don Carlos? You'll find them interesting," said Carmencita, chuckling toothlessly as she sliced home-cured ham in the musty recesses of her lair. Her customers chuckled too, their cackles filtering out from behind the piles of canned sardines and boxes of decaying vegetables.

"It's fate," decided Sebastián. "Somebody up there," he jerked a thumb skywards. "has decided you must stay. So don't fight it. Only a goat could get out of Benamargo the state that road's in. Mind you," He looked Scully up and down and leaned closer so the other clients could not eavesdrop. "From what I hear, you're quite a walker. Day or night, it doesn't stop you, right?"

Scully smiled sourly. He had been surprised that nobody had asked embarrassing questions about his sudden departure from the village and his return. But then, he had no doubt that the village had made up its own mind about events and did not require any contradictory information from him.

"Don't get me wrong," said Sebastián. "You've got more cojones than most of this lot, I can see that. If I were 20 years younger, I'd do the same, so help me. By god, I would."

"I'm not sure what you're talking about," said Scully coolly.

Sebastián paid no attention. A mixture of envy and admiration suffused his countenance.

"Young blood, that's what we all need. Instead of being sucked dry by these old hags. But I'll tell you one thing, Don Carlos, and this is for free." He was suddenly earnest. "Don't get on the wrong side of Paco, Francisco I mean. He's a bad one. He always was wild — they reckon he killed a few when he was up in the sierras. He had a terrible temper and I don't suppose the years will have changed that. He's capable of anything."

"I've nothing to fear from Francisco," said Scully.

"No? Don't be too sure. He's got bad milk in him. And

they say he's out for vengeance. Who knows for what? But it's best to avoid him."

"How can I avoid him?" blurted out Scully irritably. "I want to marry his daughter."

The barkeeper looked aghast.

"Marry Marisa? Just as well you said this to me and not to somebody else or it would be around the whole village and then your goose would be cooked. Francisco is a very proud man. If he heard you, a stranger, a man of your age who has been married already, talk about his daughter like that, he'd take offence straight away. I mean it. For heaven's sake, man, if you want a woman, there are plenty of willing little beauties on the coast. Don't jump into a hornets' nest."

Scully reflected that Francisco had treated him to a somewhat hostile scrutiny when they had encountered him on the road to Cerrogordo. Yet at the same time he had been offhand, almost cold in his welcome to his daughter. Since then he had caught only glimpses of him. They had passed in the street, but Francisco had given no sign of recognition. Marisa he had not seen at all and he had thought better of calling at her house.

By the Thursday of Holy Week, with no sign of the road being re-opened, Scully found himself engulfed by pessimism. He began to doubt whether he and Marisa would ever get out of the place.

He found the atmosphere increasingly oppressive. Grey clouds glowered over the mountains, blotting out the sun, and the village was bathed in a thin, metallic light. Hostility seemed to lurk around every corner, behind every shutter. The black women halted their conversations as Scully passed and he sensed their gaze knifing between his shoulder-blades. Benamargo was one great whisper. He tried not to think about what it was saying. Curro and Juanito would have seen that there was no shortage of material for the gossip mills. Previously, Scully's presence had been tolerated. Now he knew that he was unwanted, an intruder snared in an alien web.

On Thursday afternoon the village stopped work. The

men plodded back from the fields with their loaded mules and washed and put on their white shirts and wedding suits. The children, scrubbed and combed, ran excitedly about, competing to be the first to soil their uncomfortable, immaculate best clothes.

At 6 o'clock the cracked bell rang for mass, drawing the villagers towards the church plaza. Women trooped into the church. Most of the men either stood chatting outside or headed for Sebastián's establishment or another, rather more primitive bar, run by El Tuerto, The One-Eyed, at the pueblo entrance. Sebastián's bar was considered the sophisticated spot since it boasted a coffee machine. Even so, women never set foot in it, except the most daring ones whose husbands escorted them there at fiesta times.

Scully lingered outside the church to see if he could get a word with Marisa. But when she emerged, her mother was firmly arm-in-arm with her. Pale-faced, head bowed, Marisa walked past him as though fearing to meet his eye. Behind her came Amelia, in a severe, dark blue coat, a prayer book clutched in her hand. She noticed Scully but made no acknowledgment. Instead, she pursed bloodless lips and hurried away.

Scully remembered that among his things he had found a book loaned by the schoolteacher. Seeing Amelia reminded him that he should return it before finally shaking the dust of Benamargo off his feet. Now was as good a time as any. He made his way to the schoolhouse as night came on, an early darkness due to the lowering clouds. Baldomero answered the door. On seeing Scully, he appeared disconcerted.

"You're still here?" he said, with surprise.

"For the moment, yes."

"I thought you had left the village."

Scully shrugged.

"Unless somebody lays on a helicopter service, I shall be here for a while yet."

Baldomero glanced beyond Scully as though to see whether they were being observed. He made no attempt to invite him in.

"I brought you this book back," said Scully. "It had some interesting passages. How's your research going?"

The teacher did not reply but took the volume with a distracted air and moved back as though to close the door.

"Is there something wrong, Baldomero? You look worried."

"Er, worried? No, no, not at all." Baldomero tried to smile and succeeded in looking even more ill at ease. "I'm just surprised you're still here. You should have left, really."

"Well, I tried. But these rains..."

"It would have been better, Carlos. Under the circumstances."

"The circumstances?"

The door closed and Scully walked, away, irritated and puzzled. He tried to divine that expression on Baldomero's face. He had not just been surprised to see him. Annoyed perhaps? No, there had been something else. If Scully had not known the teacher of old, with his cynicism, his scathing tongue and his superior airs, he would have said it was apprehension.

He returned, reluctantly, to Carmencita's. He longed for a decent meal. The best that Carmencita could manage was a thin broth in which shreds of chicken skin floated, followed by a plate of rice dotted with two or three pieces of salted codfish. Occasionally, she treated him to migas. This was a leaden, belly-filling concoction of bread-crumbs and garlic fried in olive oil. Scully had had quite enough of that. But there was nowhere else to go, so he suffered every evening and made his own sandwiches during the day.

"Everybody knows me for my cooking, señor," Carmencita assured him, as he tried to hide chewed-up pieces of gristle beneath his plate.

"Ask anybody and they'll tell you that the house of Carmencita has the best. Nothing fancy, but honest home cooking, yes, sir. This week though, what can I do? That no-good Juanito was bringing my stuff and there it all is, stuck on the road to Cerrogordo, rotting away. We've no fish, no fruit, no margarine. My customers are complaining. It's a scandal, that of the highway. You'd think they could afford a few pesetas to build us a proper one. Where do all our taxes go? I'll tell you!"

Carmencita, who had never paid a tax in her life, slapped a creme caramel sealed in plastic in front of Scully.

"Those *políticos* in Granada and Madrid. Living on chicken breasts and lobster. What hard faces they have! They with no shame! And us with no road! But no matter, here you'll always eat well. Everybody knows that..."

As she rambled on, Scully remembered the frugal meals at Dolores's. Already they began to seem like Bacchanalian feasts.

"...tomorrow's the big day. But it's worth seeing tonight's procession too. They bring out the Virgin. Ay, how pretty she is, and this year she's got a new cloak. And you'll see the Cristo as well. I swear you'd think he was alive, suffering there for all us sinners. Do they have processions in your country, señor?"

"Nothing quite like this, señora."

Carmencita pushed back a wisp of greasy hair and nodded complacently.

"We're all good Christians here. Not like in other places. The Lord rules here."

Scully had a feeling he had heard this before. He went up to his room and by the 25-watt bulb, which was all Carmencita allowed, he tried to read a book. But his thoughts were of Marisa. As soon as that road opened, they would catch the bus and leave, for ever. And they would leave in daylight, for all to see.

Then he thought about Marisa's father. What would his reaction be? He was not bound by village conventions and had lived many years away, so possibly he would be a little more open-minded. And, as he appeared to have no love for Dolores, perhaps the very fact that she was against the union would swing Francisco to their side. But his return had added one more uncertainty to a delicate situation. Scully could not forget the barman's words. Even allowing for Sebastián's exaggeration, Francisco sounded a dangerous customer.

CHAPTER TWENTY-FIVE

Just before midnight Scully heard the thump of a drum and the shuffling of feet. He wandered out to see what was happening and stepped straight into the Middle Ages. Hooded, black-robed figures lined each side of the narrow street. The only light came from the candles they carried. Scully examined the nearest of these figures. His long robe dragged on the cobbles and wax dripped from his candle. Eyes glinted from holes in the mask. They were those of a simple man of the soil, Scully knew, but the robes and the anonymity gave him an air of mystery, almost of menace. Some of the marchers exchanged whispers with villagers standing in doorways, while distantly the drum throbbed. At a signal they moved on.

"Here come the Apostles," murmured somebody.

One by one, 12 men wearing tunics and crude papier-mâché masks depicting the Disciples came into view, followed by a blaze of light at the end of the street. It shimmered from dozens of candles that ringed an image of Christ staggering under the burden of the Cross. The Christ figure shifted unsteadily right and left, for it was mounted on a float borne by eight men. Each carried a stave, which he crashed down as he paced forward. A man walked ahead, directing the team, guiding them around corners, exhorting them to greater effort.

As the image came level, Scully noted that great pains had been taken to give a realistic appearance to the painted wooden sculpture. Blood trickled down from the crown of thorns over Christ's agonised waxen features and livid scars marked his back. Dipping and swaying, the image appeared to come to life in the flickering candle-light which sent long shadows racing along the house walls.

"Viva El Nazareno!" shouted a voice from a doorway.

"Viva!" responded participants and onlookers.

Despite himself, Scully experienced a chill chasing along his spine. These were just village people playing games, but the pagan aspect of this ritual, the darkened street and guttering candles, the strangeness of those black-garbed figures, the eyes peering from a secret world, the whole effect, was disturbing.

"The most pleasing is with the women," said a quiet voice at Scully's side and he saw that it was Bruno.

"I didn't think you approved of these old customs, being a Socialist," said Scully.

"It's a spectacle," replied Bruno drily. "The women can be impressive. They come next, with the Virgin."

And then Scully heard the women approaching. As they walked, they sang, in rising and falling cadences, clear, strong voices that echoed and re-echoed along Benamargo's streets. They came on in two files, all in black but with their heads bare, each with a picture of the Virgin hanging from her neck. The soft light from their candles mellowed the worn faces of the older women and leant an attractive aura to those of the young ones.

"What are they singing?" asked Scully.

"It's to the Virgen de los Dolores," said Bruno. "Save me, Virgin Mary. Hear me, I implore you with faith. My heart trusts in you."

Marisa was there. Scully saw her as she was almost up to him. She sang out with youthful fervour and the sweetness of her voice and the glowing, fragile beauty of her face stirred him unexpectedly. Desire and tenderness surged over him and a lump grew in his throat. He could have touched her as she passed by, erect, chin tilted upwards. Then, behind, he saw her mother, swelling with antagonism.

Finally, the Virgin herself appeared. She was enthroned in splendour beneath a canopy. Glass tears ran down her cold, pink cheeks. Her golden crown was studded with gems and her purple robe was embroidered with gold. Flowers were strewn at her feet and about her flamed a hundred candles.

Gasps of wonder rose from the waiting spectators and an

ecstatic voice cried out: "Beautiful, beautiful, beautiful!"

"How beautiful!" echoed the crowd.

In front of the Virgin walked a familiar towering figure. Father Saturnino was wearing his finest vestments and he moved with pride, hands pressed together in prayer. Arrayed in purple from head to toe, the bearers of the Virgin paced along as though without effort.

"Las Animas!" said Bruno. He indicated the first bearer on the left. "See there's Juanito. Behind is Vicente. And the next is your friend Alejandro."

The procession had halted and the priest raised a declamatory hand before the Virgin, presiding in icy grandeur over her subjects.

"How beautiful you are, Our Lady of the Sorrows!" he cried. "Beautiful, beautiful and beautiful! Viva Our Lady! Viva la Virgen!"

An answering roar flew up from the villagers.

"Viva! Viva! Viva!"

The Virgin and her glassy tears moved on. Behind came more hooded figures. At least two trod barefoot on the cold paving. These were the penitents, villagers who had sworn to pay homage in the procession, to give thanks for a favour, to seek her intercession, to ask forgiveness.

Nearer came the resonating drum. Its slow, deliberate beat was accompanied by the solid crash of staffs on the cobbles. Flame and smoke from up-raised torches filled the street.

"Viva las Animas! Viva!"

There were some 40 marchers, distinguished by their disciplined aspect and their conical hoods. They moved in solemn unison, in step and in total silence. Only the eye-holes betrayed a human presence behind those black Inquisition hoods. A taller figure walked between the leaders of the two files, his velvet tunic adorned with a cross and his lofty stave silver-topped. The onlookers pressed back against the walls to give Las Animas free passage and Scully felt the heat of the torches as they drew level.

"No! It can't be!"

Bruno, standing next to Scully, was suddenly rigid. He

stared fixedly down the street.

"What is it, Bruno?"

"Don't you see? Oh my god!" Bruno raised an unsteady finger and pointed. "The cross, for god's sake. They've brought out the cross!"

"The cross! The cross!"

The word rustled from mouth to mouth, from balcony to balcony. A fearful presentiment was borne on the wind that whipped along the street. It was as tangible as cold sweat, as chilling as death itself.

"They've brought out the cross!"

Scully felt the hair rise on his neck. He peered down the street. There, indeed, was the cross. The same one that usually stood above the altar in the church. Now the stained and blemished timber rode, dark and sinister, against the night sky. The crowd fell silent. Only the drum kept up its steady beat as four members of Las Animas bore the cross forward. Then the drum too was silent.

The bearers lowered the cross to the ground so that it rested on its square base and folded their arms, as though waiting for something. With an air of importance, the tall man leading the brotherhood retraced his steps and consulted with the bearers. One turned and nodded an indication. It seemed to Scully that they were looking directly at him. His throat was suddenly dry.

The tall man strode towards him. He could see the glitter of his eyes amid the folds of his hood. But the man did not approach Scully. He halted in front of Bruno and extended his arm.

"You have been warned. The justice of the Lord shall be seen to be done," he declared, in strident tones. "Prepare yourself."

Turning on his heel, he strode away. Scully sensed Bruno sagging, as though about to fall. He put a hand out to support him and discovered that he was trembling.

"Hold up, man."

Bruno shook his head dumbly. Sweat glistened on his forehead.

"You're okay, Bruno. You're okay."

Once again the sullen thud of the drum rang out and the procession moved on, the cross rising and falling in its passage through the night.

"Here, Bruno. Have a cigarette," offered Scully. "Don't tell me you're worried by this play-acting?"

Bruno looked at him wretchedly.

"You don't understand, do you? You've no idea," he said.

The brief spurt of flame from his flint lighter revealed his haggard expression as, with shaking hand, he tried to guide it to his cigarette. He sucked at the pungent fumes as a drowning man sucks air.

"You really have no idea," he repeated, taking another pull from the cigarette. "Enough of this. Come to my house. It's time for a drink."

The drumbeats faded as they threaded their way through the streets. It was clear Bruno lived alone. No feminine tastes had intruded on the spartan decor of the living room. It was almost as sparsely furnished as Bruno's farmhouse. He pulled up a chair for Scully, smoothed out a copy of El Socialista newspaper lying on the table and placed a bottle and two glasses on it.

"I'm sorry," he said, as he poured the wine. "I can only offer you cheese and olives. When my wife was alive, it was different. She was always cooking. But now..." He drained his glass, waited for Scully to finish his, and poured two more. He sat for a moment staring into space, as though Scully was not there.

"What was all that about, Bruno? Tell me, man. You looked as though you had seen a ghost."

Bruno laughed, but with no humour.

"Maybe I had. My own!"

"But what's going on? What did it mean?"

"It means," said Bruno, shaking his head despairingly. "It means that Las Animas are looking for a victim. And they have chosen me."

"But why?"

Bruno shrugged. He looked thinner than usual, vulnerable.

"Because I dare to challenge the priest. Because I'm a Rojo. It's no use explaining to them the difference between a communist and a socialist. They don't want to know. They just want a scapegoat, somebody they can throw to the lions. The people will get the message."

"You don't have to put up with this," said Scully. "You know it's just theatre. We are in the 20th century, after all."

"Are we?" Bruno was scornful. "We're in Benamargo. What do you think I should do? Call the police? They would just laugh. Besides, they are in Cerrogordo. Run away? Where to? This is my village."

Bruno clenched and unclenched his hands. His face was grim, his jaw set.

"They warned me. There was the dog, you remember. If I had been going to leave, then was the time. Too late now."

Scully snorted with exasperation.

"It's beyond me. How can this bunch, Las Animas, how can they have so much power? Is everybody afraid of them?"

Bruno rose and took a picture from the wall. He handed it to Scully.

"You see this. It was taken years ago on an outing to Granada, when we were all kids. That's me, there, making a face. I was always in trouble. And the kid next to me, you see him? That's Felipe. Las Animas killed him, and nobody lifted a finger to stop it."

"Come on, Bruno. Are you serious?" Bruno's face was answer enough. "I don't get it."

"That's because you were not born here. You only see the surface. You can't see underneath, how this place is cursed by its past. You don't know about the guilt. We're suffocated by it. Benamargo is damned."

"But why?"

"Because of our history, because of what we did."

"In the Civil War, you mean? But that was so long ago."

"We've never got over it."

"Terrible things happened everywhere."

"Nothing could be worse than what happened here," insisted Bruno. "Of course, I was too young to know much about it, but afterwards I heard plenty. That was a time when all the old hatreds came out and everybody settled old scores. Everybody was at one another's throat...the communists, the anarchists, the fascists, the landlords, the unions. So many deaths...

"Some people saved themselves by denouncing others. In one village 20 people were put to death on the evidence of one man, and then they found he was crazy, saying anything that came into his head. In Benamargo we were lucky at first. Not much happened. We were so removed from it all. But the politics and the hatred burned us too in the end."

He finished his drink and brooded.

"Either you were with the Republicans or you were with the Falangistas and the big shots. Naturally, Don Ernesto, who owned all the land, and the priest were with the fascists. In those days we hardly had enough to eat here. The children went about barefoot. So you can guess which side the people were on when somebody offered them bread and work. That's what the communists did.

"The truth is that here in the village we hardly knew what a Rojo was. But we had Enrique. He was a violent type. He said he was an anarchist. All I know is that he was a great talker. He promised the people everything. When news came through of another political assassination, Enrique and his cronies decided to take over.

"They kicked out the council and the town hall became the House of the People. Don Ernesto fled and they grabbed his house. You can see the place still, in ruins. Ernesto had land and servants and more children than even his wife knew about. They killed his cattle and roasted them. Everybody enjoyed a big feast, so that made Enrique very popular.

"But the priest was stubborn. He should have run away, but he stayed. He held services, although hardly anybody dared attend them, and he preached against the Rojos. Some said he had balls, but it was inviting trouble, especially as Enrique had a special grudge against him. They reckon it was because, as a young man, Enrique asked Father Salvador to help him with his education and the priest sent him away with a flea in his ear. Who knows? At any rate, Enrique hated the priest, but hated him. He kept telling the people they should kick him out and take over the church for the people. Nobody would go that far, though. They didn't respect Salvador but the church was sacred, you understand. For a while, that is."

Bruno lit another cigarette and sucked in the pungent fumes.

"And then?"

"Then?" Bruno shook his head. "Leading up to the war there had been plenty of trouble, but when the Nationalists rebelled there was real fury against those who supported them. Instead of keeping his mouth shut, the priest spoke out in a sermon, saying God was on Franco's side and the Rojos would be punished. That was too much for Enrique and his gang. They got drunk and broke into the church. It was a black day, I tell you. I mean, Salvador was a rogue, everybody said so, all he cared about was getting his feet under Don Ernesto's table. But that did not excuse what they did."

He paused, as though unwilling to go on.

"What did they do?" asked Scully.

"They smashed in the doors," said Bruno dully. "They destroyed everything, the seats, the images, the windows. They were crazy, like bulls after the picador has goaded them. When they tried to break up the altar, that's when the priest stepped in. Give him his due. He had cojones. He stood up in front of the altar and defied them. He threw their shame in their faces. It almost worked, because, you know, in Spain even the communists are Catholics.

"But then somebody threw a prayer-book or some object and it caught Salvador on the cheek. That was what settled it. Somehow at that point Salvador lost all dignity. He was knocked off his pedestal. He was just a man with a bleeding cheek, a target. They hurled themselves on him." Bruno grimaced. "They beat him unconscious. Then they hoisted him up against the cross behind the altar. They were just a mob. They didn't know what they were doing. One of them had got hold of nails and a hammer. At first, maybe, they thought it a joke. But then it all got out of hand.

"They nailed him to the cross, through the hands and feet, just as they did to Our Lord. Nailed to the cross you saw tonight. You can see the marks where the nails went in, and the bloodstains. Father Salvador's blood."

Scully stared in horror at Bruno.

"My god! And what happened? Did they let him die there, on the cross?"

"Don't ask me." Bruno rubbed his clammy forehead. "Maybe he died from a heart attack, I don't know. Afterwards they set fire to the church. They must have pulled out the cross, but you can see how it's blackened." He sighed. "You see, that's what hate can do, hombre. That's what nobody can forget."

"But Bruno, half a century has passed."

"That's a wink of the eye in the history of this village. It's not so easy to wipe away the sense of guilt. Every time the people go to church they see the cross standing there, as though raised in judgment over them, a reminder of their shame, of the awful thing that some of our own families did. We're all to blame."

"One act at a time of madness...it can be forgiven," suggested Scully.

"Maybe so. But Salvador wasn't the only one to die on that cross," said Bruno.

"He wasn't?"

"No. The following Easter the rightwingers had their revenge. By then, they had kicked out the Reds and they were in control. They used to take people up to the cemetery at dawn to execute them. And that Good Friday they caught one of the anarchists hiding in a farmhouse. They made an example of him. An eye for an eye. The Reds had destroyed the image of Christ so one of them had to suffer in his place."

"God!" breathed Scully. "Madness! Madness!"

"After that, the village never got around to paying for a new figure of Christ. They preferred not to think about it.

They left the cross empty, like a constant reproach." Bruno was unrelenting. He had to finish his story. "What happened to Felipe, you saw him in the picture, well, that was much later, about 10 years ago. He raped a girl, or that's what people said, and Las Animas decided he had to pay for it. You see they regard themselves as the conscience of the village, with a sacred duty to expiate our sins. They seized Felipe and staged a public trial, right outside the church. The whole village was there. And the priest."

"Bruno, don't tell me they crucified him too?"

"Near enough. They might as well have done." Bruno spoke with bitterness. "The trial was a mockery. They found him guilty, naturally. Some of Las Animas began shouting for him to be nailed up. For a moment I thought they would actually do it. You've no idea of the emotion. Nobody was thinking straight. But one or two of us spoke up in the name of reason. In the end they ripped off Felipe's shirt and flogged him. The worst was the humiliation. It was too much for Felipe. A few days later they found him hanging in his barn."

"There was an inquiry? You told the police?"

Bruno spread his hands in helpless appeal.

"The Civil Guards poked around but nothing was done. Many people felt Felipe deserved his fate. He was a rapist, wasn't he? Others were afraid. I tried to speak up, but only made myself unpopular. It was me against Saturnino and Las Animas. And they rule here."

Bruno stood up and began pacing up and down.

"Tonight you saw it. They brought out the cross."

Disquiet tugged at Scully's innards.

"They did. What does it mean?"

Bruno chewed his lip. He halted his pacing and looked at Scully in anguish.

"The last time they brought out the cross was 10 years ago. And they told me, didn't they, there in the street, to be ready. It means only one thing. Another trial."

CHAPTER TWENTY-SIX

As a child, Scully had often experienced nightmares. They had enveloped him at the most unexpected moments, when he had dozed off on the bedroom floor or slipped into a day-dream in the backyard in the sweaty heat of summer. And then the blackness had boiled up, sucking him into a great pit of darkness. He knew that he was not alone in the pit, but no matter how hard he tried he could never actually touch those other presences. They were there. He sensed that they were close. Yet he could never make contact.

Then the droning would begin, a sharp siren that vibrated in his skull, increasing in volume until his whole body was squeezed and battered. Sometimes, at that point, he would awaken, crying in terror, the tears spilling down his infant cheeks. The other times, when the nightmare continued, were worse. The droning soared to a dreadful pitch. When it finally died away, he was left in a lightless void, crouched head between his knees, afraid to move. He felt himself locked in a tomb.

Desperate though he had been to scream for help and beat its sides and smash out of the darkness, he had not done so. Something had told him that, however terrifying his prison was, something worse awaited him outside. The claustrophobia was awful, but out there lurked a greater darkness waiting to crush him, an intangible evil so real that he believed he could hear it breathing.

In manhood, Scully had forgotten those early fears. He thought they had been buried as completely as his work-ing-class accent and his backstreet roots. But, the night of the procession and Bruno's revelations, the nightmare returned. He relived the old tortures, the ghastly noise that tore at his brain, the heavy darkness that turned his limbs into lead, the sensation that he was entombed. Halfway between sleep and wakefulness, he reached out to touch the walls of his tomb and found nothing.

But there was a light. He realised that he was lying in bed and the light was filtering through the heavy shutters. He sat up, then stopped himself. Something told him not to open the shutters. It was that old childhood dread again and cold sweat ran from his pores. He held his breath. The hostile darkness had suddenly become friendly. He wanted to stay hidden in its embrace, anything but find out what lay behind the shutters.

He forced himself to act. Swinging his feet to the floor, he moved to the window, and tugged at the heavy iron bolt holding the green-painted woodwork. The shutters squeaked and complained as he folded them back. Fresh morning air flowed into the room. He leaned out. Nobody was to be seen. Weak sunlight bathed the street and somewhere a mule brayed. It was just another morning in Benamargo. Only spots of melted wax on the cobbles reminded Scully of the previous night. In the cold light of day, Bruno's alarm seemed exaggerated. No doubt bad things had happened in Benamargo, as in the rest of Spain. But that was so long ago. And as for Las Animas, well, if the villagers were prepared to put up with their fancy-dress fanaticism, that was their own silly fault.

Stale tobacco smoke coiled about Sebastián's bar when Scully entered to take his coffee at midday. The landlord was in fine form, leering over the counter and looking as though he had not slept in three weeks. The other customers took little notice of Scully. Some who had greeted him warmly enough in the past now appeared embarrassed to acknowledge his presence. Nothing had been the same since he and Marisa's attempted flight. In one corner, two flush-faced men were murmuring together. Scully paid no particular attention to them, until one raised his voice heatedly, and then he saw they were Juanito and Alejandro, the domino-player. Their eyes were bloodshot and their voices slurred.

"Holy Friday," said Sebastián. "It's the big night. You shouldn't miss it."

"What's so special?" asked Scully. "You had a procession last night. That was impressive enough for me."

"Ha!" Sebastián managed to wink one bleary eye. "You've seen nothing yet. This is something special, unique."

The church bell had begun tolling and Juanito and Alejandro and some of the other men started leaving the bar. Sebastián nodded.

"There they go. Las Animas. They have to get the images ready for tonight."

"I think I've had enough of processions," said Scully. "Tonight all I want is a good sleep."

"What's the matter, hombre?" Sebastián worked at his leer. "Is Carmencita tiring you out?"

The thought of Carmencita was enough to drive Scully to the hills. When would that accursed road be open again? He had asked about alternative ways out of the village, but everybody agreed there was none, unless you counted the old mule trails, which were disused and overgrown.

He took one now. It climbed abruptly out of the village, dropped steeply into a ravine and wandered up the other side. He reached the crest of a ridge and saw it corkscrewing into the distance. It was several days' walk to the next village, if you didn't get lost or the track had not been totally obliterated. He and Marisa would just have to wait for that bus.

At least the weather had improved. The threat of further storms had gone. White cloudbanks mushroomed above the sierras and there was a drying wind. Sustained by a few raisins and almonds, Scully tramped far from Benamargo, listening to the sound of running water and the occasional jingle of goat bells. Out there, amid the beauty of the mountains, Bruno's story, Las Animas, the whole business, seemed ludicrous, the product of incestuous village gossip.

After straying from the track, Scully had to scramble across country to find a new path and he was late returning to the village. He was in no hurry. Yet he felt the pull when, from quite a distance, he heard the church bell ringing out, as it had for centuries, since the mosque constructed by the Moors had been razed and the Christian settlers had erect-ed their place of worship on the same site. The cracked, flat tones drew him like a magnet. By the time he entered the village, the shadows had already rushed up the valley and muffled its streets in darkness. Another power cut seemed to have struck, for there were no lights and he saw nobody as he trudged rather wearily towards Carmencita's.

Passing the bar, he noticed an oil lamp glimmering but the place was deserted. Then he heard a strange sound and paused. He looked inside the door. It came again, a groan. Scully crossed the floor littered with cigarette butts and discarded paper napkins, and peered behind the counter. The barman lay in a welter of broken glass, blood leaking from a smashed nose.

"Sebastián!"

Scully bent over the barman. He was semi-conscious. One eye was closed, in a face that looked as though it had been through a mincing machine. Scully staunched the blood with a damp cloth. He filled a tumbler with brandy and held it to Sebastián's bruised lips. The bar-man rolled his one good eye at Scully and gulped some of the liquor. But he groaned again when Scully tried to prop him upright.

"Careful!" he pleaded. "My ribs! I think they're broken."

"What happened?"

"Give me another drink," breathed Sebastián.

He sank it and let out a stream of obscenities, interspersed with moans of pain.

"Who did it, Sebastián?"

"Who do you think? Francisco, it was Francisco. I shit on the mother who bore him."

"Francisco? What's he got against you?"

Sebastián spat a broken tooth from his mouth.

"Ask him! Ask that son of a whore."

Scully jumped as somebody tapped him on the shoulder. He whirled around, imagining Francisco had come back. One of Las Animas stood before him, with three more of the brotherhood to the rear, all in their ceremonial robes.

"Don Carlos. We've been looking for you," said the brother softly.

"Well, you've found me," said Scully. "What is it?"

"You are to come with us. Now."

Scully gaped in surprise. He recognised the voice, muffled as it was by the hood. It was Juanito.

"Come where?"

"To the church. You are wanted there."

Scully shook his head.

"There's a man hurt here. He needs attention."

"This cannot wait. You must come now," said Juanito, moving closer with his companions. Scully felt a shiver of apprehension.

"Now just hold on a second..."

Before he could say more, they seized him and propelled him towards the door. His protests and fierce struggling made no difference. Their calloused hands held him in a relentless grip. Without a word, they steered him briskly through the streets towards the church. Then, the absence of humanity in the streets was explained. Virtually every inhabitant of Benamargo appeared to be in the church plaza. Flaming torches lodged in wall brackets or held by members of the brotherhood fitfully illuminated the seething mass of people. Scully's escort forced a way through the crowd. They were halfway to the church steps when a powerful baritone voice cut across the crowd's mutterings.

"There we have him — the sinner!"

Father Saturnino stood on the steps, gesturing dramatically in Scully's direction. The crowd responded with an angry roar.

"There he is, the son of a whore!"

Amid a torrent of curses and a blur of faces Scully was swept along and cast down before Saturnino. Awesome in his imperious stance and righteous anger, the priest was waiting for him. To Saturnino's left was the Virgin, coldly surveying the crowd from her candle-lit float.

To his right, Scully saw as he was pushed up the steps, was the fire-seared cross. Dark and implacable, it towered over the excited scene. At its foot stood its guardians, rank upon rank of the brotherhood of Las Animas in their black hoods.

CHAPTER TWENTY-SEVEN

Scully knew all this could not really be happening. It was just an extension of that childish nightmare. If only he had not opened those shutters.

The priest's voice boomed out.

"Is this the man?"

Scully looked down on a restless sea of faces, from which rose a murmur like that of waves dashing against shingle. He had arrived late at this fiesta. The intoxicated villagers had already been stirred up to boiling point. The priest raised a hand to quiet the crowd, then pointed at Scully.

"Is this the man?" he repeated.

"Yes!" responded the crowd.

The priest directed himself to a figure standing with bowed head before the cross.

"I ask you. Is this the man?"

Slowly, unwillingly, the man raised his head and gazed at Scully. His expression betrayed his torment. It was Bruno.

"I say again," declaimed Father Saturnino. "Is it he?"

"Yes," said Bruno. "Yes, it is."

"And what did you see?"

"You know what I saw."

Bruno was unable to meet Scully's eye. He appeared a beaten man, all spirit drained out of him.

"Repeat it now, that the people may know," said the priest. "And remember! Remember that the Lord is your judge. Let he who gives false witness suffer the consequences."

He flung out his arm, pointing at Scully.

"What do you know of this man?"

"I, I saw him...out there, near Piedra Negra."

"What did you see? Speak for all to hear."

Bruno was on the point of collapse. A vein pulsed above

his brow. Watching him, Scully felt mesmerised. None of
this had anything to do with him. He was seeing it all from
a distance, as though watching a film.

"There were two of them." Bruno stumbled over the
words. "I came across them together. Him and the girl."

"What were they doing?"

Breathless, the crowd waited.

"They were...they were making love."

"Love?" demanded the priest, magnificent in his omni-
potent role. "Love, you say?" He thundered at the wilting
Bruno. "You mean they were fornicating? Is that what you
mean?"

Bruno turned his head from side to side as though seeking escape.

"Yes!" he yelled desperately. "Fornicating! That's what
they were doing."

"And the woman?" The cry came from amid Las Animas.
"Who was the woman?"

The crowd took up the demand.

"Yes, who was the woman?"

Bruno pointed a quivering finger.

"There she is, there, so help me."

As though shying away from infection, the crowd parted and pulled back from Marisa so that she was suddenly
isolated. Two of the brothers sprang down and seized her,
bundling her up the steps until she stood next to Scully. In
a state of shock, she gazed speechlessly at him.

"Leave her alone, cowards!" he yelled, anger coursing
through him. "What right do you have to judge her or anybody else!"

He felt hands restraining him even as Father Saturnino
rounded on him fiercely.

"By the right handed down to us by our Lord. In his mercy he forgives, but evil shall be smitten. Thus it is written."
He appealed to the gathering. "Those who flout his word
and break his commandments, do they not deserve to be
punished?"

Clamorous approval greeted this. Scully recognised some
of the faces. Marisa's mother was there, carved from stone,

staring straight ahead. And with a shock he saw Amelia, pale as a ghost in the shifting torchlight. But most of the villagers were not recognisable. A ferment of emotion had transformed their familiar, everyday features and they were no longer the people Scully knew.

"Punish them, yes, punish them!"

"Daughter!" The priest raised his voice above the noise of the mob. "Daughter, is this true? Did this man take you in adultery?"

Marisa trembled and cast an appealing glance at Scully.

"Answer!" insisted Saturnino.

"I love him," sobbed Marisa. "He said we would be married."

"But does not this man already have a wife?"

"I don't know. He said he loved me," cried Marisa.

Nobody was listening to her, least of all Father Saturnino.

"You believed him, this man who brought so much evil to our village, provoking the death of your own brother? The tragedy of innocence! In your youth and female weakness you put your trust in this seducer and let him lead you into temptation."

"Look! Look!"

A woman forced her way up the steps and Scully saw that it was Carmencita, puffed up with exultation and malice.

"See!" she screamed. "See what I have. This I found in his room." She tossed down a bundle. They were Marisa's possessions which Scully had retrieved from the roadmenders' hut. "Those are Marisa's. He was going to steal off with her. And this, see this." Triumphantly, she flung down a book. "It's one of Ramón's books. He stole one of Ramón's books."

"It's his fault Ramón died. He killed him," yelled one of the brothers. Slurred by drink though the voice was, it belonged unmistakably to Alejandro. And it was answered.

"Murderer! Swine! Violator! He killed Ramón!"

Ugly as the crowd's mood had been before, it switched now to something more frightening. A collective madness blotted out human features. Scully saw only age-old fears and prejudices vomited from distorted mouths that salivated with hate. These were no longer individuals but a frenzied animal lusting for blood. It was a rampaging mob. Unreason ruled.

"Murderer! Adulterer! Put him against a wall!"

Sickness dragged at Scully's guts. Life had gone out of his legs. He tried to shout, but nothing came from his clogged throat.

"The cross! The cross!" yelled Alejandro, carried away by his lust for vengeance. Others of the brotherhood took up the cry and it swelled as the hundreds of villagers joined in.

"The cross! Nail him! Nail the sinner to the cross! Nail him!"

Belatedly, Bruno spoke up.

"Madness! Madness! Stop this! In the name of god, stop!" he beseeched his fellow-villagers.

But he was a leaf in a whirlwind. His voice, cracking with strain, was ignored. Alejandro pushed him violently aside and, arms outflung, appealed to the priest.

"This man has committed the worst of sins. He has driven one of the brotherhood to his death. He has defiled a virgin. He has brought the shadow of evil to our community. Let the adulterer atone for his sins. Let him take his place on the cross and we of the brotherhood shall carry him in procession. Thus shall we win redemption, because the Lord will see that we have punished the unworthy."

"And what about the girl?" asked Carmencita. "She must be punished too."

Swollen with grotesque pride at her successful denunciation of the foreigner, she strutted before the crowd.

"Yes, the girl's guilty too," said Alejandro feverishly. "She has shamed her family and our village. She went with her brother's murderer. She is nothing but a Jezebel!"

"Punish them both!" echoed the crowd, pressing closer. Ashen-faced, Marisa swayed on her feet. A clod of earth hurtled past Scully's head. Carmencita danced along the steps, malevolence issuing from every greasy pore.

"Scourge her!" screamd Carmencita. "That's what she deserves. Scourge the whore! Scourge the whore!""

A gaggle of women began chanting the same litany and Scully saw, with stunned surprise, that Amelia was among them. He sensed as a physical blow the bitter antagonism emanating from her, saw the words forming on her lips, "whore, whore, whore..."

"There'll be no scourging."

The priest raised both hands in appeal, trying to regain the initiative.

"This young girl sinned, it is true. But she was an innocent corrupted by the lies and cunning of this servant of Satan. The Lord is merciful. If the girl truly repents, she can be saved. But the man bears the greatest guilt. He must be punished and his wickedness purged."

"Ask the priest why he defends the girl!"

A deep, clear voice rang out from the far corner of the square. Heads turned.

"Ask Saturnino! See if he dare speak the truth!"

The priest tried to ignore the interruption, as the villagers craned to see who was speaking. A dishevelled figure was thrusting through the crowd and a gasp went up.

"Francisco! It's Francisco!"

CHAPTER TWENTY-EIGHT

Francisco's face was bruised and his eyes blazed wildly. He stormed up to the priest.

"Mierda!" he snarled. "Enough of lies and hypocrisy! Do you hear me, priest?"

A terrible rage possessed Father Saturnino.

"Get thee from this place! You have no right here. You do not belong to this pueblo."

Francisco seemed about to strike Saturnino.

"And you? Where do you belong, miserable cleric?" The crowd was hushed. Nobody had ever spoken to the priest in this manner before. "If any sinner is to be punished, then let it be the true sinner, say I. If there be any god up there, let him be the judge of who is guilty." Saturnino's face had turned a purple hue, but Francisco ignored him and addressed the people. "You have been led by the nose too long, you sheep! It's time to open your eyes."

As Saturnino tried to intervene, Francisco stepped between him and the goggling crowd.

"Dolores!" he cried. "Come up here."

His wife stared up at him from the front ranks but remained unmoved, as though welded to the spot.

"Woman! It is your husband who calls. Or have you forgotten who I am?"

Francisco leaped into the crowd and grabbed Dolores by her arm. Amid stricken silence, he hauled her on to the steps, ignoring the priest's remonstrations. The brothers of Las Animas shuffled uncomfortably but made no move. They were as fascinated by the turn of events as the rest of the villagers.

"Now we shall have the truth, priest!" declared Francisco. "I have waited half a lifetime for this."

He confronted Dolores.

"Marisa is your daughter, is she not, woman?"

Dolores nodded dumbly.

"And who is her father?"

Dolores stared at Francisco like a hypnotised rabbit. He glared back at her.

"You," she said in a low voice.

"Bring me a Bible," cried Francisco. "I want to see you swear to that on oath. A Bible!"

Somebody darted into the church to hunt for the book. A hum of conjecture rose from the crowd as the priest tried to exert his authority. At that moment Scully heard a whisper in his ear.

"Don Carlos, please forgive me. I know I'm a coward. But they blackmailed me. What could I do?"

Scully did not turn his head. Bruno was standing directly behind him. He had edged there in the swarm of villagers pressing closer to hear what was going on.

"Enough of this farce!" bawled Saturnino. "You are shaming both yourself and your wife."

But Francisco already had the Bible. He laid the right hand of Dolores upon it.

"Now, priest, the truth will be known," he said. "Dolores, am I the father of Marisa?"

Dolores looked around in panic, all composure gone. She began to weep hysterically.

"Answer, woman!"

"Please, please!"

Francisco did not relent.

"Speak now. On the Bible. Am I the father?"

Dolores was beaten, humiliated.

"No, you're not." Tears coursed down her cheeks. "Have mercy. It was so long ago"

Shock surged through the crowd. They turned to one another with stunned faces. Father Saturnino was shouting.

Dolores swayed on her feet, as though about to swoon. But Francisco was like iron. He gripped her fiercely.

"Then, if I'm not the father, who is? I said, who is? Point him out, woman. Now! Who is Marisa's father?"

Everybody held their breath, gaping at this unexpected

drama. For seconds Dolores stood moaning and shaking her head, then raised her eyes to meet her husband's implacable gaze.

"Speak!" he commanded. "Tell them!"

Dolores was deathly pale. Her lips quivered. Finally, she indicated with her head.

"The father," she murmured. "The father."

The crowd craned forward, not understanding.

"Who?" demanded Francisco.

Then Dolores broke down entirely, screaming and weeping hysterically.

"Father Saturnino! He's the father, I tell you! God help me! Father Saturnino! He's the one!"

A gasp of amazement went up from the crowd, then a roar. The priest's face was crimson. He raised his arms to call for silence, but the villagers ignored him. He tried to browbeat them with his powerful voice, but they no longer listened to his words. Instead, Francisco had their attention.

"You heard! You heard!" he cried. "Now you know the truth. You know what sort of a man you have for a priest. You always knew, didn't you? But you were too proud to admit it, God help you!" Francisco's eyes glowed. He was possessed. "Saturnino! There he is! The man who preached at you to obey the Commandments, lectured you about virtue, and behind your backs he was screwing your wives and daughters. You never had the guts to challenge him, did you? Because you were scared of him, scared of this son of a whore!"

"This is Satan's talk" stormed Father Saturnino, "This is blasphemy!"

"Blasphemy it is!" agreed one of the hooded brotherhood. "These are filthy lies!"

"Lies?" Francisco rounded on Las Animas. "May the Lord above judge! You of all people, Alejandro, know the truth. What happened to your sister? Died in childbirth, did she not? And the postman's daughter, why did she have to go off to Granada? We all know who was responsible. We all know who the fornicator was. But nobody dared speak. Because of you of Las Animas. You have been the curse of this village."

"He's right!" said a villager. "We all know he's right."

"The priest has sinned. He's the real devil in Benamargo!" cried another voice.

"Damn you, Saturnino!" yelled one of the brothers.

The murmuring of the crowd swelled to a crescendo.

"Saturnino is the guilty one! Hypocrite! Fornicator!"

Duped and humiliated, the villagers transferred their fury to the new victim and Father Saturnino withered before their hatred. One of Las Animas pushed his way towards the priest and shook his fist at him.

"You fooled us! We trusted you and you made idiots of us."

He swung his fist. It caught Saturnino on the cheek, sending him staggering. Suddenly, the priest was no longer the imposing figure of authority he had always been, but only a pathetic shell of a man dabbing nervously at his bleeding face. The villagers lost any remaining inhibitions. They were consumed by the lust for revenge. The animal had to be sated.

"He's the one we should punish! Nail him up! That's where priests like him belong!"

Scully was forgotten in the rush to lay hands on Saturnino. He looked for Marisa, but she was lost amid the mob. Members of Las Animas picked up the priest and bore him into the church. Scully saw his cassock bobbing on a wild sea of humanity that swept towards the altar.

"Enough of this madness!" bellowed Father Saturnino. "You are profaning the House of the Lord!"

They paid him no heed and any further protests would have been drowned out in the pandemonium. But the priest made no more protests. Nor did he offer any physical resistance. Instead, he appeared oddly detached, almost resigned, as the inflamed mob surged about him. Even when they lugged in the great stained cross, Saturnino regarded it with surprising composure. It was as though he were being reunited with an old friend, thought Scully, watching in unbelieving horror from the rear of the church.

They brought hammer and nails and spread-eagled Saturnino on the crossed beams. The nails were the crude, hand-made affairs used by the Benamargo carpenter to fix door hinges. Animal fury breathed hotly over the priest as the hammer rose and fell and the iron parted his flesh. One by one, the nails were driven home. But Saturnino did not cry out. He appeared impervious to pain. The church echoed to yells and imprecations. Only the man at the centre of the whirlwind was calm. His eyes were closed and his lips moved, as though he were praying.

The mob struggled to raise the timber and slot it into its position behind the altar. They fumbled and cursed, until at last with a lurch the foot of the cross found its home. Then, suddenly awed by what they had done, they fell silent.

The figure sagged from its bloody pinions on the crossbeam above the high altar. A shudder ran through the priest's body. He opened his eyes and stared into the distance, as though seeing something far beyond the view of those below him.

"Hear my confession, O Lord!"

His words rang out clearly, echoing from the vaulted roof. Scully, trapped in the crowd, felt sick. Next to him a woman collapsed.

"I have sinned. I have betrayed your trust, Lord. I was weak and I have yielded to the temptations of the flesh. But worse than that, I have killed. I am a murderer."

A gasp came from his parishioners. The torches they held aloft threw a fitful light over the bizarre scene. Smoke from the torches coiled about the pews and images of the saints and about the man nailed to the cross. Scully felt a tug at his arm and heard Bruno's voice.

"Get out now! Before it's too late. There's a side door on your left."

The villagers of Benamargo could not take their eyes off their priest.

"All my life," cried Father Saturnino. "I have done penance for my mortal sin, for one moment of madness, the terrible sin of my youth. I bear the guilt for what happened to Father Salvador in this very church. I struck him down.

I killed him! The devil himself guided my hand that day. It was I who threw a fragment of the holy image at Father Salvador."

The tears rolled down Saturnino's cheeks and the crowd fell silent.

"Yes, it was this miserable sinner who threw the arm of our Most Holy Virgin at Salvador. I deserve to be punished, I deserve it. But, O Lord, spare me from Eternal Damnation! Have mercy! Forgive this sinner, I beseech Thee."

A groan escaped Saturnino, then his voice boomed out in a last agonising plea.

"Forgive me, Holy Father," he begged. "Forgive us all!"

Women were weeping. Some of the onlookers crossed themselves. Others jeered. Scully saw the priest's eyes were shining, as though suffused by an inner light. His lips parted once more. Scully could have sworn that Father Saturnino smiled. Then a spasm shook the priest's frame and his head slumped forward.

Amid the tumult, guided by Bruno, Scully slipped through the side door. Behind him he heard a cry go up from the crowd. Was it of triumph, anger, frustration at losing its prey? He sprinted blindly down an alley, along side-streets. At every corner he expected to be confronted by those hooded figures or to hear pursuing footsteps. At the village edge, he paused to gulp air. His heart seemed ready to pound through his chest. A clamour of threatening noise came from the plaza. He had to get away, anywhere.

He ran on, his head bursting with images of shapeless mouths screaming for vengeance and of the smiling figure on the greedy, blood-smeared cross.

EPILOGUE

La muerte viene sola.
La vida hay que buscarla.

Where the track curved past the oppressive bulk of Piedra Negra, Scully paused to rest. Twice he had stumbled and fallen, grazing a forearm and his knees, but it had not slowed him. He had been grateful when a faint waning moon had sailed clear of the clouds and given him some indication of where the path lay, until the thought had struck him that the same light would aid his pursuers.

The soughing of the wind was the only sound up there on the mountainside, although several times he swore he could hear voices somewhere to his rear. Near exhaustion, he stopped and sat on a flat rock, gazing back down the valley.

Only a glimmer of light betrayed the village's position amid the dark backdrop of the sierras. He thought he saw the flame of a torch, blinked hard and stared again. No, there was nothing. There was no indication of the tumult he had left behind. If they were following him, they would expect him to take the road to Cerrogordo. It was the obvious route. That was why he had headed in the opposite direction.

He knew that without help he was lost. He could never find his way through the sierras. If he could get to Celestina, maybe she would give him food and put him on the right track. He did not relish meeting her again, but anything was better than facing that mob down there in Benamargo.

Sheer terror had driven his steps. Now he began to torture himself wondering about Marisa. He had abandoned her to that mob. Panic had sent him scurrying from the village like a frightened rat. He had left behind the only person he cared about, left her to the mercy of Carmencita and her kind, to Amelia screaming the hate of a spinster scorned. It was unforgivable. Yet what could he do? He sought to placate his conscience. What could he do alone against that mass insanity? In their present mood, the villagers were capable of anything, of sacrificing him as they had their priest.

They had come close to doing so. He shuddered and clenched his hands at the thought of the nails being driven into his flesh and the crowd baying for blood...

Suddenly, Scully was on his feet. A stone had tumbled, somewhere down the track. They were after him, those crazies. He lurched into movement, trotting upwards along the twisting path, banging into boulders and gnarled tree roots. But there was no escape. Every time he paused he swore he could hear footsteps, footsteps that steadily gained on him. This was a nightmare that would never end.

In desperation, he increased his pace, slipping and stumbling, sweat pouring into his eyes until he hardly knew or cared where he was going. There was no shaking off his pursuers. They were born amid these crags. They knew every gully, every spring, every short-cut. As agile as mountain goats, they could keep going indefinitely. Already that day he had walked a considerable distance and he felt his stamina ebbing fast. He cursed. He had to keep moving. He had to hide somewhere. It was his only hope. He could hear them, gaining with every stride. He tripped, fell, dragged himself along. Hide, he had to hide.

A dark shadow loomed over Scully. Vicious pain pierced his side. The boot struck again. They had got him then. It was all over. He had tried, but it was no use. Somebody grabbed him by the shirt-collar and pulled roughly. He smelled garlicky breath and sharp body odour. A man's face peered into his.

"Mierda! It's the Inglés!"

The man released his shirt abruptly, so that he fell to the ground.

"I'm not going back," yelled Scully.

He scrambled to his feet.

"There's no way you can make me."

And then the man threw back his head and laughed.

"Go back, idiot? Go back? Are you crazy? Go back to that inferno?"

It was Francisco. Exhausted, Scully wiped the sweat from his eyes. It made no sense.

"What do you want? Why are you following me?"

"Follow you?" Francisco spat. There was scorn in his voice. "Hey, English, have you lost your brain? Or has that accursed priest melted your backbone? You spent too long in Benamargo."

Francisco turned and began striding up the track.

"I've got a date with Celestina," he said over his shoulder. "It's up to you what you do."

After a moment's hesitation, Scully followed him. He did not know what to make of this man, but at least he knew the way to Celestina's and anything was better than returning to the village. Scully dragged himself along mechanically, afraid that he would lose Francisco.

They climbed steeply past limestone outcrops, ghostly under the feeble moon, and traversed the bleak slopes of Piedra Negra. Francisco moved fast but easily, negotiating the difficult zig-zag path with springy confidence, as though he were bounding up a flight of stairs.

An outburst of barking greeted their arrival at Celestina's miserable dwelling. The two mangy dogs barred the approach, growling and cringing.

"Bruja!" yelled Francisco.

"Witch! Call off these damned curs. D'you hear me? Celestina! It's your old friend Paco."

Eventually a match sparked inside the ramshackle shelter and Celestina appeared, lantern in hand, wheezing suspicion. As soon as she caught sight of Francisco, however, her attitude changed. Discoloured fangs were bared in what Scully took to be a smile and she clutched Francisco's arm as though she never wanted to let go.

"Hijo!" she cackled. "It's been a long time."

She caught sight of Scully.

"You've got the Frenchman with you. What's he doing here?"

"I've no time to waste, woman," said Francisco. "I have to make tracks. Give me some food and water and I'll be gone."

"Hmph! You all come to Celestina when you need help," she muttered. Grumbling to herself, she wandered off.

"You wouldn't believe it, but once she was the beauty of the village," said Francisco.

He crouched down on his haunches and lit a cigarette.

"You know a way through the sierras?" asked Scully.

"I should do. I spent three years up here. That was long after the Civil War, when we still thought we could drive Franco and his crew into the sea. Us and a few rusty guns against his army! The Civil Guard was at our heels day and night. Celestina used to tip us off about their movements. She saved us many a time. But then there were the traitors. They would sell you out for a handful of figs, the bastards. I lost many a comrade shot in the back." He smiled without humour. "But I settled one account tonight."

"Sebastián?"

"Yes, Sebastián. That bastard!" Francisco spat the words out. "He cost me eight years in jail, eight years! It was near the end of the rebellion in the sierras. They'd killed most of the comrades. Others had escaped to Africa. We were desperate, hunted like dogs. One night we heard food had been left for us in an old farmhouse. It was a trap. The Civil Guards were waiting, with machine-guns. They finished off two of my group and I was so badly hurt I hardly had a drop of blood left in me. It was Sebastián who tipped them off, the son of a whore."

"Why did he do it?"

"Why?" Francisco was scornful. "Because he has always been a miserable squealer. His bar was always the first place the police visited when they came to the village. And there was something else. He was soft on Dolores. He thought he could have her for himself, if only he could get me out of the way."

"Francisco. About Marisa."

"What about her?"

"I want to marry her."

"And so?" demanded Francisco harshly. "Didn't you hear, English? She's not my goddamned daughter. What she does is of no consequence to me."

"I can't believe it, about Saturnino."

"Then don't. Put your head in the sand, like those idiots down there. All these years, they didn't dare say boo to the swine. Until tonight. And now what?" Francisco crushed the half-smoked cigarette in his hand. "Now the whole fucking world knows that I'm a cuckold. I, Francisco, who fears nothing and nobody. Humiliated! But I couldn't let him get away with it any longer, I couldn't!"

He hurled a stone at one of the yapping dogs.

"When I first learned that the priest had put the horns in for me with Dolores, I was so crazy with rage I was afraid of myself. I wanted to kill the both of them. And I'd have done it, if I'd stayed in the village. But I didn't want to go to jail again, not for the likes of Saturnino. So I took the coward's way out. I left and swore never to return."

Francisco scowled.

"Then I heard my boy had died. I had to come, one more time. And what do I discover? Nothing has changed. After all this time, that son of a whore still rules the roost."

Scully jumped to his feet. He gazed down the valley. A fierce glow had erupted in the darkness.

"See that! Something's burning."

"It's the church," said Francisco indifferently. "They were waving those torches around. They can burn the whole village as far as I'm concerned. Let it all burn."

"But Marisa is down there!"

Francisco shrugged.

"What do you want me to do? I'm not the one who gave her a child."

A wind coursed down the mountain, but it had nothing to do with the chill that struck Scully like a blow.

"What did you say? What the hell do you mean?"

"You mean you don't know?" Francisco looked at him in surprise. "Didn't Marisa tell you she was pregnant?"

"For god's sake, no!" Scully was aghast. "She said nothing."

But she had said something. He recalled her words about having children together. Suddenly he realised why Marisa had changed her mind and been ready to flee the village. And now he had abandoned her.

"I have to go back," he said. "I can't leave Marisa."

Francisco laughed shortly.

"You're even more foolish than I thought. What could you do against that mob? They'll tear you limb from limb."

"But Marisa…"

"Forget her. They found a new target, didn't they? It was Saturnino who cheated them. Well, they got their revenge."

Celestina appeared with half a goat cheese, a can of tuna, some bread, some dried figs and a water bottle.

"Here," she said. "This is all I've got."

"I have to go back," muttered Scully.

Francisco ignored him.

"Bruja, you're more beautiful than the angels," he said, embracing her and passing her his pack of cigarettes.

"Devil!" she said. She looked at him with affection. "You always were a devil! Where are you going?"

Francisco pointed into the darkness.

"Up there. Across the pass of Los Lobos."

"Nobody's been that way in years. There have been rock-falls," said Celestina.

"All the better. The times we went over there in the pitch dark with the Guardia chasing us. In the snow once. This will be like a picnic." Francisco nodded at the red glare from the village. Flames were leaping. "And this time I won't be coming back."

Celestina was prancing about, more grotesque than ever. The distant glow throbbed and swelled.

"Hellfire!" she shrilled. "Judgment day has come, just as I said."

Scully stood uncertainly by, torn by guilt. Francisco slapped him across the shoulders.

"D'you still want to be a martyr, English? Go ahead. But in 24 hours I'll be in Granada."

He turned and strode away, leaving Scully with the old hag. She leered and mocked him. He gazed after Francisco's retreating figure and then back towards the village. The blaze had grown fast. It ripped at the night sky, silhouetting the ragged figure of Celestina. She was rocking to and fro with glee.

Scully paid no more attention to her. He looked up at the stars and took a deep breath. And at that moment it suddenly seemed that the scales finally fell from his eyes. What was he agonising about? It was all so simple. It was up to him to remake his life. Even as he sensed that, the weight lifted from his shoulders. He started walking and the walls of old nightmares crumbled before him. There was nothing to contain him. He was out of the tomb.

For a while, Celestina's cries pursued him along the track.

"Hellfire! Hellfire!"

Soon her voice faded. He did not look back. Ahead the skyline above Benamargo was smeared blood-red. To Scully it looked like the first hint of a new dawn.

———

Buy Maroma Press books
from your local bookseller
or direct from the publishers

For more information, contact:

Maroma Press
Calle Real, 76
29788 Frigiliana
(Málaga)   Spain
http://maromapress.wordpress.com/
email: maroma.press@gmail.com

Maroma Press specialises in books
with Spanish themes,
fiction and non-fiction.

Maroma Press